Sinful BITE

K. N. Gallo

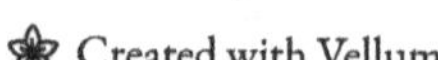 Created with Vellum

Sinful Bite is a dark adult fantasy romance. This story contains sexually explicit scenes, as well as mature and graphic content this is not suitable for all readers.

Reader's discretion is advised.

PLAYLIST

Staring at the Sun - Post Malone
Hopeless - Halsey feat. Cashmere Cat
Shameless - Camilla Cabello
MIDDLE OF THE NIGHT - Loveless
No Promises - Cheat Codes feat. Demi Lovato
Starving - Hailee Steinfeld feat. Zedd
You should be sad - Halsey
Prisoner - Miley Cyrus feat. Dua Lipa
Better Now - Post Malone
We Can Make Love - SoMo

Chapter 1
Anita

"Yes, Mom, I'm walking up to my door now." Wedging my phone between my shoulder and ear while holding my purse and digging for my apartment keys.

"A mother worries about her daughter even when she's twenty-six." She huffs which brings a smile to my face. Her over protectiveness never fails to make me feel her love. "Who knows what creatures you could've come across on your walk home."

"Mom, I'm a nurse that treats all kinds of different beings on a regular basis." Replying with a roll of my eyes while finally fishing out my damn keys. "Besides, this part of town is pretty strictly human. You know they don't like to mix with us when it's avoidable." I say placing my key in the lock and giving it a turn to let myself in.

"Like I said, a mother worries."

I know she worries for me. For my entire life it's only been her and I. My father never wanted to be involved from what she's told me, but she never made me feel like I've been lacking anything. She's a truly strong woman and I hope to be at least half the mom that she is one day.

Sighing, I make my way inside, placing my keys in the little bowl at the entryway table and hanging my purse and coat up on the hooks. "I know you do, and I love you for it. I just got inside so I'll talk to you later okay?"

"Sure honey, I love you too."

I turn after hanging up and placing my phone in my scrub's pocket. I trip and nearly fall over before catching myself. I look down to see boots in the middle of the hallway and my eyes follow down the hall where a trail of socks and pants are littered on the floor.

I take a deep breath and pray for patience as I follow the path, picking up the discarded clothing as I go. Turning the corner I see pretty much what I expected.

My boyfriend, Kevin, on the couch in his boxers showing off his lean but toned muscles with his headset on top of his messy brown hair and gaming controller in hand surrounded by wrappers and empty cans.

His blue eyes flick to meet mine momentarily before focusing back on the game at hand, "Hey babe, didn't hear you come in. How was work?"

"It was fine." I answer automatically, still staring at the disaster left in his wake. "And yours? Get off early today?"

"Only had a half day today in the middle sector. You know their shit doesn't need as much work as ours does. I mean how much construction and maintenance could they really need? Our streets are filled with potholes for days, street lamps that don't work, buildings about to crumble, but all they care about are the middle and upper class creatures, not the lowly humans."

I hum in agreement as I listen to him rant like he does every day when he gets off from work. It really isn't fair that us humans are treated lowest of the low but then again there really isn't anything we can do to change that. The only humans that get any kind of standing have the money to make themselves heard. Even then they care more about keeping a higher status than slumming it with the rest of us or fighting for equal rights.

"I know."

"I'm starving though, what's for dinner?" He asks with his eyes still glued to the screen in front of him.

I look from him to the mess scattered around the room and back. Like every other day I take a deep breath, swallow a string of curses, and smile before responding.

"Let me see what we have."

I turn and move my way to the kitchen of our small apartment, carrying the trash I've collected so far to throw them away, and dumping the clothes against the wall for me to grab on my way to our room.

Everyday is the same. I work my twelve plus hour shifts at the hospital where I have to deal with complete disrespect from higher level creatures because I'm only human. I come home to a mess, Kevin is almost always already home playing his game, despite him being home I am apparently the only one capable of making food and cleaning when all I want to do is take a shower and relax in bed. After three years of being together it's become a routine I can't seem to break. I can never say no to him. I'd rather just do it all to avoid the confrontation.

I quickly work on making us both some taco salad that's fast and easy to make while I'm practically dead on my feet. I bring him his bowl and drink before disappearing into the bathroom for a long overdue hot shower.

Standing under the spray as the hot water works out the knots in my muscles from today's work I let my thoughts run and let them flow down the drain with the water.

Today had been a moderately easy day, just very long and meticulous. I was the on call nurse for the ER today and we were busy as usual. A couple of ogres with work related injuries, a cyclops with a broken leg, two goblins with stab wounds from some domestic confrontation, the rest were just typical vital checks and easy to discharge. I don't get to treat the top tier creatures because of my own race but that doesn't mean I'm not busy enough without the extra work. I'd have to jump through more hoops treating patients like vampires, dragons, and werewolves anyway. Being on my feet all day still leaves me completely exhausted by the time I make it home.

I know Kevin is tired from his construction job out in the heat all day but I'd like to come home to a clean house and dinner made for once too. I work hard even if it's in the air conditioning. It just never feels like a two way street with him.

After getting dried off and dressed I make my way back to the kitchen to get my dinner.

"Hey babe I got your food over here for you with a glass of wine." Kevin calls me.

I turn to see that he's reheated my food and a half full glass of red wine sitting beside it. I look up at him to see that same smile that always used to make me weak in the knees. I don't see that smile as much anymore.

"Thanks, hun." I smile back. I pick up my glass and take a much needed sip of wine. "Mmm, my favorite." I lean over and give him a kiss on his cheek as he stares at the TV.

We sit in silence as we eat and watch TV now that his game is turned off.

I don't know if it's just us or the amount of time that we've been together but it feels as though Kevin and I are in a rut. We don't talk like we used to, don't laugh and smile like we used to, and we aren't even intimate like we used to to the point that I don't even want to do it anymore. At all. At this point, I don't know what I can do to fix us.

"Hey, are you off tomorrow?" I ask, taking another sip of my wine.

"Yeah. I was going to hang out with the guys." Kevin says, taking a sip of his own beer. "Why?"

"I was just going to see if you wanted to cook something tomorrow." I try to inconspicuously say it's his turn to cook dinner.

"Like I said I'm going to be with the guys."

"But I have to work late and it would really hel-"

"*Anita*." He grinds out. "What's the problem, huh? I work hard all week long in the heat, busting my ass. Are you seriously going to get mad at me for wanting to relax with the guys? It's not like I get to do that very often. Not all of us get to work in the A/C."

I hang my head and let out a deep breath.

"It's fine. I'll just pick us up some fast food instead, okay?"

"Of course babe, that's fine with me." He leans in to kiss my cheek, "you're the best."

He stands up to go take his own shower, leaving his bowl and empty bottle for me to pick up and put away.

I don't know why I bother to even ask. I knew what his answer was going to be. It's always the same. It always seems like Kevin's wants and needs are the only ones that matter in this relationship and he couldn't give two shits about mine.

I've been doing it all for so long now I can't imagine it changing any time soon. I take our plates to the sink, rinse and stick them in the dishwasher. I pick up the remaining trash around the living room before pouring my tired body into bed. I lay there slowly drifting off before the bed dips and Kevin crawls in behind me, pulling me to his chest with his arms around my waist.

"I love you, Annie." I feel his lips leave a trail of kisses along my neck.

"I love you too, Kev." I keep my eyes open and stare at the far wall. I know where this is going.

The desire that used to flood my body at his touch is gone now. I'm indifferent to the intimacy with him, numb to it all.

Kevin continues to kiss along my neck as his hands explore my body he knows like his own. He cups my breasts over my shirt before moving down to squeeze them from underneath as he rubs his dick against my ass. His fingers trail along my thigh and over my hip before hooking his thumb in the waistband of my shorts and slowly pulling them down along with my panties while still kissing and nipping at my neck.

I'm still laying here unmoving as he works my shorts down to my knees before licking his hand to apply to my dry entrance to wet it enough for him to enter. He starts to pump his hips immediately, giving me no time to adjust as he chases his release and only his. After about five minutes he pulls out and finishes on his stomach, wipes himself off, rolls over and drifts to sleep without another word.

I pull my panties and shorts back up and I lay here, eyes open staring at the wall in front of me, wondering if this is what a relationship is supposed to be like. Is this what I have to look forward to for the rest of my life? Is this even what I really want anymore? Do I deserve more?

Chapter 2
Sinclair

The sound of my alarm pulls me from my sleep. Blinking the sleep from my eyes as the light from the window shines into the room I groan and reach to silent my phone's alarm. Reaching over I feel a weight on my chest. I look down and remember where I am.

I remove the nymph's arm from around my torso and stand from the bed to search for my clothes from last night. Grabbing my phone and my clothes I make my way to her bathroom to shower last night off of me.

Hanging my head under the hot water I start to remember more and more from the previous night and think ahead to all of the things that I need to get done for the day. I should really stop drinking that damn fairy enchanted blood before I really fuck up.

Stepping out of the shower I wrap a towel around my waist. I reach for my phone to check for any messages and am not at all surprised to see more than ten from my assistant, Mia, three from my mother, and six from my pain in the ass best friend, Maverick.

"Why are you out of bed?"

I pull my gaze from my phone to the voice in the doorway. I let my eyes rake up and down her still very naked figure. Long curly brown hair cascading messily swept to run down one side of her neck grazing her full breasts that compliment her petite body. Her wide hips are leaning up against the door frame with her thick thighs crossed in front of her blocking my eyes from the main reason I'm even in this apartment at all. I raise my eyes back up to see her full lips in a pout before resting on her muted green eyes.

"I'm a busy man Robyn, I have things to do." Rubbing the towel across my body, drying myself off slowly letting her eyes devour me before I start to pull my clothes on ignoring her heated stare at my body.

"Being king is a lot I'm sure." I feel her manicured nails rake across my firm chest as she snakes her arms around my pecs from behind me as I'm trying to button up my shirt. I grunt as I remove her hands from me as I finish getting dressed.

I hear her huff at my dismissal leaving her standing in her bathroom. I make my way to a chair in the corner of the room, getting my shoes on and the rest of my belongings in my pockets before pulling my suit jacket on.

"That's it? You're just going to leave now? I'm your mate!" The irritation in her voice was unmistakable and annoying.

"*Potential* mate, and as you said," I correct, turning back to her as I pull her apartment door open, "being king is a lot. Don't forget what we're doing here, Robyn. This is just a convenient fuck. Now, I have a region to run, people to govern, kingly shit to do." I wave dismissively exiting her apartment.

"Fucking vampires." I hear her grunt as I press the elevator button.

She wasn't complaining while I was ramming into her last night.

I sigh as I pull up Mia's number to call her back first.

"Your Majesty!" She rushes out after picking up on the second ring.

"Mia."

"King Sinclair."

"Mia."

"Mr. Archer..."

"Mia!"

"Sin..." She sighs and I can't help but smile at her reluctance still in calling me by my preferred nickname instead of always being so formal. "You have a meeting in less than an hour!"

"Calm down. I just need to stop by my loft then I'll be there. It'll be fine."

"I see now why you've gone through so many assistants." The wood nymph says with a huff.

I chuckle softly at her. In truth the reason I've gone through so many is because as soon as I go between the girls legs they would become too clingy and I had to let them go. Mia's general disinterest in me sexually is refreshing.

After going over the rest of my schedule today. I dial my mother as I make my way up to my penthouse loft after paying the taxi driver.

"Sinclair Garrett Archer!"

"Hello, mother." I sigh as I quickly strip off my rumpled clothes and pull on a crisp navy blue suit. "Why do you insist on calling me by my full name? You are the only one that does."

"Because you are the king of Minaoz, Sinclair. I will not call you by a shortened version of the name I gave you. You should stand tall and demand respect. You are too easy going on most of these people you surround yourself with."

"Mother, please spare me the lecture." I roll my eyes.

"Fine, for now. So son, why didn't you answer your poor mother's calls?"

"I was preoccupied..."

"I'm sure you were." Her disapproving tone is as apparent as ever. She probably knows exactly what I've been up to.

Even though she isn't the queen anymore after my father passed the crown over to me, she's still active in Minaoz as ever. Because she's my mother it's hard to deny her much until she pisses me off. I'm going to have to start treating her like everyone else if she doesn't stay out of my business. She seems to think that because I don't have a queen at my side she needs to continue doing that for me.

Fuck no, thank you.

"What was it that you needed to tell me? I am on my way to a breakfast meeting." I sigh, taking a look down at my watch to see that I still have thirty minutes before my first meeting at nine o'clock. My locks automatically engage as I make my way down my private elevator to my personal car garage.

"Your father and I need you to be here for dinner this weekend. We are having guests."

"You're not trying to push more potential mates at me are you?"

"Honey, you're a grown man and a great king needs a strong queen at his side. I just hate seeing you alone."

I start the ignition on my Aston Martin and rest my head on the steering wheel.

This isn't the first time I've had this conversation with her. I'm one hundred and thirty years old and in an immortal lifetime that's hardly long enough to think about settling down with a mate. I'm enjoying my bachelor life away from the responsibilities of being the Northern Vampire King, adding a mate nagging at me is not appealing in the slightest.

She doesn't even want me to pick a queen because she's worried that I'll live a lonely life. She wants a woman that she can mold the way she sees fit. The last thing I need is a woman she can pull the strings on. I need a woman that won't be swayed by my mother or anyone for that matter.

"This would all be so much easier if you lived at the palace like a king should."

"I don't want to live in that place until I absolutely have to. It's too big for me. It's cold and empty. Being in my loft gives me some space from all the politics that constantly go on inside those walls. You know this."

"Your father and I are here. Are we not good enough company for you?"

I don't answer because I'm choosing to ignore her attempt at guilt tripping me and I know she won't like my answer. She's already too far into my personal life. I can only imagine how bad it would be with us under the same roof. I suppose I could move her to a house that's not in the main building, but still that's too close.

"So we'll see you this weekend, yes?" She presses.

Knowing she won't stop shoving these women down my throat until I do finally pick one and it's easier to indulge her than argue. She doesn't have to know I don't plan to actually pick one for a while.

"I'll see you for dinner."

I end the call and make my way across town and pull into my favorite café.

Making my way inside my phone starts to ring, I glance to see Mavericks' name briefly before I accept the call and stand at the counter.

"Hel-"

"Why in the hell am I even your best friend?" He grumbles cutting me off.

"Well good morning to you too, Ricky."

"Don't fucking call me that! You know I hate that stupid ass nickname."

I chuckle as I meet the eyes of the barista.

"Hello, Your Highness, what can I get for you today?" The little sprite flushes as she looks at me before lowering her eyes.

"Well I'll have a large black coffee with O negative please, sweetheart." I flash my smile at her and her blush deepens before she scurries away.

"Do you have to do that everywhere you go?" Maverick asks.

"Do what?" Focusing back on the phone.

"Try to get in every woman's pants."

"I was simply being polite and smiled. Am I not allowed to smile now?" I ask.

"You know very well what you're doing. Anyway, where did you go last night? I turned around and your ginger ass disappeared."

"I went to Robyn's."

"That chick seems batshit crazy, dude."

"She's a good fuck none the less."

I hear him sigh over the phone and can imagine him shaking his head disapprovingly. The conversation ends soon after and I'm getting my coffee when it's ready and making my way to my city office for my meeting.

The rest of the day runs by quickly after meeting with some werewolf business owners for projects to get approved. The soon to be alpha of the Huntley pack is already starting to implement new ideas and take his pack into a new direction. I respect Aiden Huntley and when he officially takes over from his father I'm sure we'll be working together more.

Aiden presents his ideas and we work out the nitty gritty details before I sign off on everything. By this time next year his new multi-facet company will be up and running.

In the afternoon I had mid level fairies wanting rights to expand their territory. Fairies are on the smaller end of the creatures here in Minaoz and have a strong bond to nature. I can understand their need to be away from the city. The area of the surrounding woodlands is unclaimed. After going over the paperwork, fees, and taxes. We have finished the details and they'll start building their new extension next month.

While I didn't have much of a choice about being the king, I do enjoy it. The rush of power that comes with knowing you get final say on just about anything that happens in everyone's lives here in Minaoz is addicting. Luckily I have people like Maverick to keep me grounded. That doesn't mean I don't have to rule heavy handed when it's needed.

I feel like I can finally breathe without the weight of who I am threatening to crush me as I step into the VIP section of my club, *Sins*. The place I can always count on to provide the distractions I need.

I immediately see a bombshell at the end of the bar that looks like just what I need for the night.

I catch the little siren's bedroom eyes and smirk. My eyes trail up and down her curvy body from my place at the bar. She has the kind of curves that wet dreams are made of and I can't wait to make every one of those dreams a reality.

I make my way to her knowing tonight is going to be a long one as I use her body to relieve the stress in mine while bringing her blinding pleasure. It's a win for us both, and with the way her eyes darken with lust as I close the distance between us I know she's ready for whatever I'm going to give her. This is going to be fun.

Chapter 3
Anita

Sending a sharp knock on the door to room 403 alerting those inside of my presence before turning the handle and entering the room. My eyes connect with young cyclops looking around in a daze.

"Perry Williams?" I ask.

His one large eye focuses on me as I make my way further into the room. I stand at the foot of his bed and scan over his medical chart.

"How are you feeling?" I smile, meeting his gaze again. He hesitates for a moment before admitting that he's experiencing dizziness. "That's normal. Do you know what day it is, what happened, or where you are?" I ask.

"It's Wednesday. I'm pretty sure I fell off my bike..." He trails off a pensive look over taking his features as he searches his memory for more information.

"That's right. You were with some of your friends as far as we know and you were trying to be quite the Daredevil and this is Minaoz Central Hospital."

"I was trying to make that big jump. I remember now."

"I'm just going to check your vitals and then the doctor

will come see you about when you can be discharged, okay?" I giggle at his toothy grin at his failed jump attempt with his mother's scolding glare trained on him and make my way to his side checking his blood pressure, pulse rate, temperature and other vitals before leaving the room and placing Perry's chart outside his room for the on-call doctor.

The lower level of the hospital is having a relatively slow day so far. Only an hour left in my shift and I pray it stays this way.

"Hey Anita." Turning to the sound of my name to see my fairy coworker with a straight face.

"Hey Sarah. How's it going?" I ask hesitantly.

Sarah is beautiful with a petite body, blonde hair and flawless skin. She's always turning heads and she's become a good friend to me here at work. She takes a deep breath before letting it out heavily letting me know I'm about to hear a rant.

"Don't even get me started!" She huffs.

"That bad, huh?" I giggle.

"It was going fine until about an hour ago and this male goblin comes in being as difficult as freaking possible! Like dude, it's not my fault you decided to be adventurous with your partner and got something stuck up your ass that should never be there!" She whisper-yells at me clearly getting worked up again over the situation as she retells the story.

"Do I even want to know what it was?" Holding my hand over my mouth, trying to hold my laughter in.

"A toy car."

I pause, not sure exactly what to say or think about that.

"I didn't know a little car could be sexual..." I trail off. It's not like I have variety in my own sex life to really know. Kevin and I haven't done more that lay on our sides, he gets off and then we go to sleep. I'm not sure I even want to spice things up with him anymore. I know for sure I wouldn't want a children's toy anywhere near me while trying to be intimate though.

"It's not." Sarah deadpans.

I can't help but laugh now that she quickly joins in.

"Oh good I was starting to worry."

"Girl, I don't care if it was the newest and sexiest thing to do in the bedroom. I would not let someone shove a little car up my ass."

We laugh even harder at that as we make our way to the lower level nursing station. I have to wipe my eyes to make sure I don't have tears running down my face as I sit in front of one of the monitors and enter in Perry's information from his chart I copied on my personal tablet.

"When do you have to go back to the mid level station?" I ask, putting Perry's physical copy of his patient chart in the filing cabinet. Sarah being the type of creature that she is gets her placed in the mid level section of the hospital automatically. It wouldn't be hard for her to work her way to the upper level section either. For me though, it would take a miracle.

"I'm going to head that way in just a minute. I just wanted to rant for a moment to my favorite human." She smirks and we laugh again.

"What are you both so giggly about?"

I turn and give Aaron, the handsome fairy nurse, a smile pointing at Sarah as she takes a deep breath getting ready to retell the story again to him. I shake my head and finish my notes in the computer system before spinning in my chair to face them and check my watch to see if I can head to clock out now.

"You always get the interesting patients." Aaron pouts. His dark green eyes stand out against his dark complexion and chocolate colored hair. He's truly breathtaking. He's probably prettier than me. I sigh at the thought.

"Next time, you can have them." Sarah tells him.

"All I got today was a grumpy old ogre refusing to cooperate with anything I asked him to do. Those are the worst. Having to fight with them with a smile on your face like you're not murdering them repeatedly in your mind." He says.

"I'm sorry. Why are you a nurse?" I raise a brow and ask.

"Don't start with me, human woman. I didn't get any sleep last night because my neighbors were going at it like rabbits and the walls are like cardboard." He grunts.

"Bet you jacked off to it though." Sarah smirks, taking a sip of her coffee, keeping her eyes zeroed in on him.

Aaron's cheek tint pink as he huffs again before standing up to leave, "Got to get something out of their constant fucking." He grumbles walking away.

We hunch over and laugh until tears come to our eyes as he turns the corner.

"Alright, I'll see you tomorrow Sarah."

She's already starting her way back to the mid level nurses station as she waves me off and smiles at me over her shoulder.

Just as I'm about to clock out another nurse stops me to see a last minute patient. I sigh but turn and make my way to the patient's room, grabbing the chart on my way. I'm always the one they push all the unwanted work on to. There isn't anything I can do about it either. I'm considered the lowest of the low here and they take full advantage of the fact that I'm human and can't fight back.

I stop short of opening the door when I read over the details on the patient. I know why they made me come back for this now.

I give a soft knock on the door before making my way inside. I look at the older man sitting down silently as he looks in the direction of the door with a soft but scared smile on his face. My heart clenches at the man that looks like life's been far too hard on.

"Hello." I say softly. "My name is Anita and I'm going to

be your nurse while you're here. Can you tell me what the problem is that you're having?" I stay a few feet away from him while I wait for his response.

"Honestly, I'm not sure. I collided with someone and they told me I should be in a hospital so here I am." He chuckles and looks slightly over my left shoulder. "I told him I probably should get my eyes checked."

I can't help but giggle with him as his milky eyes seem to shimmer with humor.

"I'm glad you are in good spirits at least." I say.

"Being human is hard enough in this world but being a blind human is something else entirely."

I admire and worry for this man all at the same time. I know how hard it is to be a human in a world surrounded by creatures that want to keep you at the bottom feeling less than. I couldn't imagine being blind in a world of monsters.

"I understand what you mean." I check his vitals and everything seems to be in order. "I don't see any reason for you to be here any longer. I'll have someone come in with your discharge papers and you'll be free to go."

"Thank you." He smiles sweetly in my direction as I make my way out the door.

After handing another nurse the chart and telling them that he's free to go I make my way to the employee exit for the hospital. I wave at a few of the other humans working here that greet me as I pass them. Most of the other creatures that work at the hospital don't bother to talk to humans unless it's necessary. Luckily it's mostly just humans that work the lower level, though I'm the only nurse, unless we get some others that are getting punished for one reason or another. I get an occasional visit from the two fairies that don't seem to mind humans like the rest. Sarah and Aaron have really been a blessing as far as work friends go.

Hundreds of years of all creatures and humans coexisting

and almost all of them still have a superiority complex leaving us humans at the bottom of the social hierarchy. The social status never really bothered me much. I've always wanted to be a nurse to help people and I'm doing that. I may have had to work five times as hard as everyone else. I took as many internships as I could to learn everything within my field so when the time came they could only overlook my resume because I was human. My experience didn't give them the luxury of dismissing me. I don't care if humans can only work on the lower level and treat the lower level creatures, I'm still helping others.

OPENING THE DOOR TO MY APARTMENT I HEAR SOME shouts coming from the living room.

I set my things down at the entry table and make my way to the commotion. Kevin and a couple of his friends are all sprawled out on our furniture with game controllers in their hands shouting back and forth while they play what looks like a shooting type game.

"Hey boys…" I say.

"Hey babe, I didn't hear you come in." Kevin says without taking his eyes off of the TV screen.

I don't say anything else as I turn to leave the room. I need a long shower and some wine if I'm going to have to deal with them the rest of the night.

I don't know what's been going on with Kevin and I lately. As the years go by its like we're completely different people. I know that people can change but our entire dynamic has morphed into something I'm not sure I can live with forever.

We used to be so in love.

Kevin would never be able to keep his hands off me. The sex was amazing because he was always so attentive, making sure I was always taken care of. We would cook together, cuddle on the couch watching our favorite movies and shows, and cling to each other at night wanting to be as close as possible.

The past year I can tell something's shifted, and I'm not sure if it's me that's changed and he's changing because I am. Now we feel more like fuck buddies that live together and that's using the term *fucking* very loosely.

I don't want this kind of relationship for the rest of my life but I don't know what to do. I do still love Kevin but I'm not sure if I'm still *in love* with him. I also don't want to just walk away from three years of giving everything I have to him. Kevin and I have had our ups and downs but I know that when it all comes down to it I can count on him to be in my corner when I really need him and he knows that I will do the same.

Feeling the hot water beat against my back, working out the tension from the day at the hospital, I let the thoughts continue to circle around in my head.

I can't help but feel like it's my fault that we are the way we are now.

I know that I've pulled away from him physically and emotionally the past few months. I don't touch him and initiate any intimacy like I used to. I don't try to sit and spend time with him anymore. I don't wrap my arms around him in bed anymore.

Maybe I highered my expectations of him unjustly. He hasn't done anything wrong to deserve the cold shoulder from me. How can I really get upset over him doing the exact same thing to me? How can I be mad at his lack of effort when I don't put in any effort of my own?

Sighing, I step out of the shower to towel off and get dressed.

As I step back into the living room I see an empty room. I look around wondering where they could've gone in the now eerily quiet apartment. I walk to the door and pull my phone out of my purse to see no messages so I decide to give him a call.

"Hello?" Kevin answers.

"Hey babe. Where'd you guys go?" I ask.

"Oh, we decided to go get some take out and hit the bar."

"Oh. Alright." I guess I'm on my own tonight then.

"Is that okay?" He asks as if me having a problem with it would change anything at this point.

"Yeah, that's fine. Have fun babe. I'm just going to eat something and get some sleep."

"Alright. I love you."

"I love you too."

I hang up and look up the closest Chinese food restaurant and order some delivery.

After eating alone while scrolling through social media on my phone I drag myself to bed and read the book I've been trying to finish for a few months now. I can never read at night when Kevin is here because he complains that I don't spend enough time with him...while he's playing his game.

One night of peace and quiet losing myself in the romance novel that only makes my current situation with my relationship with Kevin seem all the more unfulfilling. I finally drift off wanting more out of life, out of love, and just...*more*.

Chapter 4
Sinclair

Checking my watch I see it is about time for lunch and hit the intercom to buzz Mia.

"Mia?"

"Yes sir?" She responds right away.

"What have I told you about being so formal?"

"What do you want, Sin?"

"See that's so much better." I laugh. "Was that my last contract to go over you sent?" I ask.

"Yes and by some miracle you don't have any meetings scheduled for today. You do have some kingly duties to attend to though."

"Of course I do." I sigh, rubbing the back of my neck trying to ease the tension there. "What is it that the king of Minaoz has to do today?"

"You only have to sign off on some creature transfers for people wanting to move into this territory, nothing major."

"Looks like it's my lucky day then. Just send me those and if you finish what needs to be done for the day you can clock out as soon as you're done. I'll call if I need anything, I'm going to head out to get some food as soon as I'm done." I say.

After Mia sends the files I look them over meticulously because I have to be careful of who I approve to live in Minaoz. There's always going to be crime and corruption but if I can weed them out in any way I will.

Looks like there's only a handful of cases ranging from job opportunities, connecting with family, and or simply wanting a fresh start as the reasons for the transfers. Transfers from other regions don't happen a lot. I comb through their reasons and background checks before finding that I can approve them all. I'll come back and check on their cases in a few months to make sure they aren't trying to trick their way in.

Once I finish the last signature and email them back I collect the paper work on my desk to file away and gather my things to leave.

I pull out my phone as I step onto the elevator and call Maverick.

"Hello?"

"Hey, best friend." I say.

"What do you need, Sin?" He asks.

"I'm heading to a late lunch. Do you want to meet up at our usual place?"

There's a pause on the other end and I can hear papers shuffling in the background.

"Yeah, I'll meet you there." He says ending the call.

"Well goodbye to you too then." I grumble putting my phone back in my suit pocket walking to the parking garage to slide into my car and make my way to the restaurant.

When I walk inside I'm only sitting for a few minutes before Maverick slips into the seat across from me.

"I don't know why they keep giving us menu's when we order the same thing every time we're here." He says but still picks up the menu looking it over as if he could possibly change his mind today.

I smile and shake my head. I glance over the vampire

section of the menu before letting my eyes drift to the other creatures having their lunches.

This particular place is middle level so there are a lot of sirens, nymphs, and fairies flitting about with the few upper level creatures like us mixed in as well. It's not uncommon for upper level creatures to drift into the middle level establishments but never the other way around. The hierarchy makes it difficult for the lower levels to move up in this world.

My place as the Northern King gives me the freedom to move between them as I wish but even I can't change the social structure that's been in place for centuries. I try to make it the best place I can to live in but there will always be problems.

A little sprite makes his way to our table.

"Hello, my name is Danny and I'll be your waiter. What can I get for you both today?" He asks politely, making eye contact, and trying to keep the slight shake out of his voice. Being a vampire I can sense the fear slowly rolling off of him as my deep red eyes study him.

"Hello. I'll have an Iced Tea and we're ready to order if that's alright." Maverick cuts in.

"O-of course. What would you like to eat today, sir?" Danny trains his eyes on Maverick now.

"I'll have the steak medium rare but more on the rare side, with a loaded baked potato and sweet potato fries." He says, handing his menu over.

Typical dragon.

"I'll have a glass of O Negative and the pasta with your best blood sauce." I say handing my menu over to the now trembling sprite as well.

"Of course, Your Majesty."

I send Maverick a questioning look before looking back to the waiter as he scurries away.

"Always making everyone uncomfortable."

"I didn't do anything you asshole." I grumble. "Seriously Rick, what was that guy's problem? It looked like he was about to piss himself every time I looked at him."

"You know a lot of people get jumpy around upper levels like us and you being the king of this region probably wasn't helping." He smirks. "You don't really see a lot of vampires out during the day either, you know that."

I forgot about the time of day it was. Being from the royal family gives me more advantages than just the political and social power. All vampires tied to the royal family along with some chosen high standing families were all given a special mark. It looks more like a brand to me. The mark of a day-walker. A crescent moon, the top half of a star, two circles, and a lightning bolt through it. I couldn't tell you where the symbol came from or what it truly represents but I do know that I've had it as long as I can remember and that with it I can go out in the sun.

"That doesn't usually happen." I say trying to think if people really reacted to me that way regularly. I absentmind-edly rub my shoulder where the day-walker mark lies. Not many have seen it and if they do they just assume it's a tattoo.

"That's because you're used to women waiting on you and they can't see past their lust to be afraid and you just eat that shit up." He chuckles.

I smirk. I can't argue with that. I don't want my people afraid of me though. I'll have to figure out a way to ease the lower level creatures so they don't shake in fear when all I want is to order my lunch. Being the king of Minaoz causes me to be fearless, cold, and ruthless at times when dealing with business and politics. There are too many people who think they could possibly overthrow the Archer family in ruling this region. I have to keep up certain appearances to make sure everyone knows their place and the consequences there would be if such action was ever taken against the crown. More often than not though I am the complete opposite as a person. I never really wanted to rule Minaoz but places of power have been handed down through high ranking families for centuries. At least I have a conscience and heart though they might not know it. I do have the people's best interest at heart, no matter their species.

"Sin."

I snap out of my thoughts and focus back on Maverick looking at me with a sad expression.

"I know, I know." I try to wave him off.

"You'll figure out the right balance. The people deserve to know who you really are. I mean you're one of the very few who even like humans."

This is true. I've never had a problem with humans. I think it's unfortunate they have the shit end of the stick at the bottom of the food chain but they literally can't do anything about it. I've tried for years to subtly give them more rights but when it comes down to it they just can't defend themselves and it's better for them where they are at the moment for their safety. At least until I can figure out a better way to integrate them.

"So I see you're eating your veggies again." I smirk, switching the subject away from me.

"Yes, well, apparently they're important...occasionally." He pouts.

"Nana's on your ass again, isn't she?" I smirk, Nana Sophie is particularly hard on Maverick which I find hilarious. "She just wants her grandbaby to grow into a big bad dragon someday." I coo at him.

"I am a grown ass big bad dragon thank you very much."

Not long after our food is brought out by a still overly jittery sprite comes back with our orders and scurries away with his eyes down and a slight bow. I let out a heavy breath and we ate our meals in relative silence with light conversation carrying us through our lunch.

THE WEEKEND ROLLS AROUND AND I PULL UP TO THE palace where my parents still live in just enough time to be considered early for this dinner with our family's *guests*.

As soon as I step through the fourier I know that this dinner is going to be torture.

There sitting across from my mother and next to the only empty seat at the already full table is Xari Belmont.

She's a gorgeous woman that I've known is one of my potential mates for a while now. While I can understand why she would be someone I'm partially pulled towards to have as my queen and why my mother invited her family to dinner so she can play matchmaker, we just aren't that compatible.

Xari is a strong and independent woman from a powerful dragon family. She runs her family's corporation on her own and has the respect of many upper and middle level influential families. She is beautiful and smart but she also has a very domineering personality. While that's very admirable, I feel that we would only butt heads over who wears the pants in the relationship. While I always see women as equals there are times that I want a submissive partner.

Particularly in the bedroom.

I give them all a polite smile though it's forced and make my way to my seat.

"Nice of you to join us, son." My mother says with a tight smile but I ignore her little jab because I didn't really want to come to this dinner before and I really don't want to be here now that I know she's trying to set me up with Xari.

She may be my mother but I'm still the king.

"How was business today?" Xari asks.

I look at her, "It was like every other day." I say. This is all she ever mentions when I'm around her is business and status. Both are things I could live without honestly. I suddenly remember why Maverick always avoids her like the plague when the dragon council gets together. She's always gunning for more power and Maverick's family is at the top in her way so they naturally are at odds.

"He is doing amazing things with Archer Enterprises. He's taken our family business to a new height as well as being the best king Minaoz has ever seen." My mother gushes.

I look at my father and he only shrugs while taking a hefty swig of his brandy. I signal for a server to bring me my own glass of scotch, following his lead with the liquor. If I'm going to get through this dinner without blowing a fuse I'm going to need it.

My mother, Xari and her mother are going round and round in conversation over various topics I stopped listening to. My father and I talk a little about business and things going on with the kingdom with Xari's father commenting here and there but it's clear that us men would rather be anywhere else.

The dinner finally comes to an end and we all stand at the entrance while saying our goodbyes.

"Seraphina, Dryden, thank you so much for having us over for dinner and Sinclair it's always nice to see you." Xari's mother Xena says as Tony nods along with his wife while shaking my fathers hand then my own.

"Sinclair, a pleasure as always." Xari bats her eyelashes at me while raising her hand for me to take which I do reluctantly then press a kiss to her knuckles after I see my mothers glare.

"Of course." I smile.

Once they're finally gone I give my parents a quick

goodbye without allowing my mother a moment to either scold me or hype Xari up as a mate.

I'm in desperate need of a drink and sex at this point, something that I can always count on to get my mind off of all my responsibilities and expectations as king. Maverick decides to stay home tonight but promises to come out with me another night this week. As soon as I step into the VIP section of my club my eyes immediately hone in on a sexy little busty dragon on the other side of the bar. I lick my lips and smirk when she catches my stare. Her smile is confident as she stands from her seat and sways her hips as she makes her way over to me and slides onto my lap without prompt seeing the desire and invitation clear on my face. She runs her manicured nails lightly down my chest.

"Does the king need some company?" She asks boldly.

As I expected she only sees me as a conquest because I'm the king, but tonight I don't care. I do find it ironic though that it's a dragon that's currently rubbing her greedy pussy on my ever growing cock in my slacks, considering I just ignored the attention of Xari earlier.

I don't respond, just smirk, take a fistful of her hair and slam my lips to hers. She moans in my mouth, the little dragon likes it a little rough then.

Good.

I've got my scotch in one hand while the other holds this woman as close to me as possible. Just what I need for the night.

Chapter 5
Anita

RINGING WAKES ME UP AND I ROLL OVER CHECKING the time seeing it's past ten in the morning. Checking the caller ID I smile as I answer.

"Hey..." I start only to be cut off.

"Hey, girl. Get your ass up and meet me for some coffee." Diana demands.

"Why yes best friend I'm doing okay this morning thank you for asking. How are you on this fine morning?"

"You're still with the douche canoe, we know your morning is not okay. It could be though if you had a fine ass man instead of what ever the fuck he is." She scoffs, going off on another one of her rants about Kevin that I'm sure I'll hear more of later.

"D, don't start please. I'm not awake enough for this conversation to take place for the umpteenth time." I sigh.

"Fine, fine. So...coffee?" She chirps.

"Yea, the usual place in half an hour?" I ask.

"Yes ma'am. Love you. Okay, byyyyyyeeeee." Then the line goes dead.

I just giggle and get out of bed and head to the bathroom

to get myself ready for my crazy best friend. No matter what is ever going on I know I can count on Diana to lighten the mood and make me have a good time.

Walking out of the bedroom to head out I look around for Kevin but don't see him in the apartment. I know he was out with the guys last night so he must have had too much to drink and crashed at one of their houses. I check my phone but don't see any messages so I send him a quick text checking in on him but don't wait for a response and head out to meet with Diana, desperately in need of caffeine.

The bell over the door sounds as I step through the door and spot my redheaded friend in the back corner in our usual spot. She seems invested in what she's looking at on her phone because she jumps when I sit across from her with her hand on her chest.

"Jesus. You scared the shit out of me." She breathes out. Her light green eyes are wide with surprise. Diana has always been beautiful with flawless pale skin covered in freckles and her long red hair.

"What are you looking at that has you spacing out?" I ask.

"This guy I fucked won't stop blowing my shit up so I had to go all Satan on him." She huffs then smiles sweetly at me trying to feign innocence as she sets her phone to the side.

"Mhm....did you already order for us?"

"Of course, bestie."

I look at her, not sure I trust her current demeanor. Overly sweet Diana usually leads to trouble or me doing something I really don't want to do. I choose to ignore it for now, I better enjoy my peace while I can before she lays it on me.

"So when did this man go from a fun night to the devil's target?" I ask.

"Two nights ago I think?" She furrows her brow thinking hard then nodding as if agreeing with her answer.

I shake my head and laugh silently. She's crazy but I love

her and her antics are at the very least entertainment for my boring life. Diana has always been a free spirit with a little rebellion thrown in there. She does what she wants, when she wants, and with who she wants without remorse. Most of the time I envy her.

"So how's the leech?" She asks.

I sigh, "Come on D..."

"I'm just asking a simple question."

"Kevin is fine."

She nods unconvinced and uncaring but luckily doesn't say anything more on the subject.

We sit and enjoy our coffees just catching up on what's been going on in our lives lately, all light subjects and enjoying each other's company. Diana and I could always talk for hours about anything and everything, our conversations always flowed through various subjects that we would usually cover almost every topic imaginable.

"Any cool stories from work?" She asks.

I think for a moment before I remember. "Yes, actually. There was a blind man that came in recently."

"A blind human?" I nod my head. "That must suck like a mother fucker."

I bark out a laugh, "Why do you say that?"

"Think about it. Being human already sucks balls most of the time but can you imagine not being able to see either? How does he work? It'd be hard for him to find a decent job even with his sight let alone without it? Not a chance."

"I guess you're right." I sigh thinking about the man and feeling sad all over again.

"I bet he runs into shit constantly too or people just trip him." Diana adds as she sips her drink.

I shake my head at her dark humor but let it go for now or I'll spend the rest of the day worrying over a man I'll probably never see again.

She invites me back to her loft in the upper mid sector of the city where very few humans go because of the overwhelming creature population and even fewer actually live there. The creatures that rule over us in the hierarchy of our world have always seemed to thrive on the segregation of species. Being that humans have nothing special to really offer we are obviously at the bottom of the food chain.

Diana's parents are influential and wealthy even by moderate standards in Minaoz. They both came from wealthy families and both of her parents have starred in hit movies, modeled for name brands, and her mom even started her own clothing line that does well enough that even the other species buy her products.

Given her upbringing it isn't a surprise that her loft screams wealth and she's beyond gorgeous. My crazy best friend is a bit of a rebel though.

"So what is it that you've been plotting? I'm surprised you haven't busted at the seams waiting to tell me yet." I eye her suspiciously as she too casually strolls around her loft to her room and straight to her closet as I follow behind her.

"Whatever do you mean?" She asks, one brow raised. I give her a droll stare and just wait. "Fine. We're going clubbing tonight at *Sins* and I have the perfect dress for you."

"Nope."

"Yup."

"No."

"Yes."

"No, D." I place my hands on my hips.

"Yes, A." She mimics my movement.

"Why." I whine out. I don't want to go out to a club, that's more Diana's scene than mine anyway.

"Because you're my best friend, you love me, and you need time out to have fun away from that asshat." She reasons, turning from me and putting her full attention back on her wardrobe to continue picking out dresses for tonight.

I've learned to just ignore her attitude toward Kevin by now.

"You know I don't like clubs." I huff.

"No, you used to love clubs before you got with that shithead and he made you feel like trash every time until you just stopped going to avoid an argument."

I gape at her. That is not even close to the truth. Sure when we were twenty-one we'd go out and have fun like everyone else but me stopping doesn't have anything to do with Kevin.

I mean I work a lot of hard hours at the hospital and I don't want to jeopardize my chances there because it was a miracle they let a human work alongside the other creatures and not just clean up after them. I can't show up hung the fuck over, they barely need a reason to fire me now but I work so hard they have no reason to and I want to keep it that way.

"Don't even try to deny it." She adds.

"I mean sure Kevin doesn't like me getting drunk and guys flirting with me but that's normal boyfriend stuff, nothing to freak out over." I reason.

"Girl, I love you, but that shitstick goes out with his boys all the time or has them over and they get hammered every damn time, probably doing more than just drinking but I digress. Whens the last time we were able to hang out at your place or go out without him having a fucking cow?"

I think about what she's asking and unfortunately she's right and by the look on her smug face she knows it and pulls out our outfits for tonight.

"I'm going to shower first and then you can after *then* we're getting sexy as fuck and having fun tonight, capice?" She smiles at me and disappears into the bathroom.

I blow out a breath and check my phone for any messages, finding one from Kevin.

Hey babe I got overtime for this night shift so I won't be home till tomorrow. Love you, behave.

I roll my eyes at the behavior part like I've given him a reason to doubt me but I am with Diana so there's no telling how this nights going to go. She can get a little wild.

He won't be home anyway so I guess spending time with Diana is better than sitting at home alone even if she's dragging me to a club.

Once Diana is done and we're both showered. I look down at the dress she picked for me and only one thought comes to mind.

Lord, help me.

I START TO GET ANXIOUS WALKING BESIDE DIANA IN these heels trying not to stumble like a dumbass and the fact that we are walking by the long line of creatures waiting to get in. There are only a handful of other humans in sight and they sure as hell are waiting in line like everyone else while Diana drags me with her toward the entrance like she owns the place. Just as I am about to stop her and ask her what the hell she's doing, the bouncer at the entrance looks up at her and nods his head toward us and we immediately get let in.

"How in the f..."

"My parents being who they are comes in handy every now and then. It's the very least they can do since they only do the very least." She says.

I let it go knowing the subject of her relationship with her parents is a touchy subject. Diana may seem slightly out of control at times and rebellious but there's always a method to her madness. They hated that she's friends with such an *unworthy* human but her friendship is priceless to me.

"Alright Annie, shots then cocktails to sip. Let's go!" She shouts, attracting attention to us before dragging me to the bar. She eyes the handsome siren bartender before giving him a smirk. "Two wet pussies, two lemon drops, a sex on the beach and a rum and coke, please."

He smirks right back at her before getting our drinks and shots ready. "There you are ladies, anything else I can do for you?" He asks, looking Diana up and down slowly.

"If I do I'll be sure to find you when I do." She bites her lip while I roll my eyes. She's on the hunt tonight apparently.

"Anything you need, I'll be happy to deliver, babe. Just ask for Arden." He winks at her before going to wait on his next customer.

"Mmmmm, sirens always get me going girl. I just want to ruffle his feathers, so much better than the ones with the scales and shit." She says still eyeing the man. I'm sure that's why most bartenders are sirens anyway, they captivate people just the way they need to. I laugh a little at her usual antics and bump my shoulder with her while dividing up our shots. "To a kickass night!" We clink our glasses together taking both shots back to back before picking up our drink and heading to the dance floor.

This is going to be a hell of a night.

Our bodies move to the beat, grinding against each other. I try to stick close to her to keep unwanted hands off me as much as possible. I have to move carefully so I don't flash everyone within sight. The dress Diana picked out for me is short, just passed my ass with a slit up both sides to my hip in a dark forest green color, plunging neckline, halter top and backless. It's like she's trying to get me laid instead of herself, her dress has straps everywhere mainly only covering the goods up top and down below. It fits her body and personality perfectly unlike mine.

I'm not sure how long we've been dancing and drinking but the buzz I feel has me feeling freer than I've felt in a long time and I'm soaking it up for as long as I can. I turn my back to Diana and start to rub my ass against her front. I lift my head and lock my gaze on the most gorgeous man I've ever seen.

Dark red hair, pale skin, and mesmerizing deep red eyes looking straight back at me.

Chapter 6
Sinclair

Maverick and I sit in the lounge of the VIP section of *Sins* sipping on our whiskey eyeing those around us. Over where we are we can still see almost all areas of the club. Though when I had this place renovated I could've put the lounge on an upper deck but already being king and held on a pedestal made me want to be on level ground with everyone else. Here I wanted to feel like a regular vampire, not only be seen as Sinclair Archer, Northern Vampire King of Minaoz.

"I swear to whoever the fuck I have to that if that sprite bitch doesn't leave me the hell alone tonight I'm going to burn her to ash. I mean it Sin, keep her the hell away from me." Maverick grumbles out, fist tight around his glass, glaring daggers across the lounge to the girls by the bar.

I follow his gaze and groan. Robyn and Krista, of course they're here tonight. "I didn't invite them, Ricky."

He scowls at the nickname. "You didn't have to. Your current flavor of the week is about to turn into a stage five clinger if you don't put her in her place and end that shit. Unless of course you want to mate with her."

"I am not mating with Robyn." My face screws up at the

mere thought of being attached to her permanently for the rest of my life. No, thank you. "And what the hell is a stage five clinger?"

"It's an expression for someone that goes beyond the limits of normal clinginess. You're the king, you're supposed to know shit Clair."

"Do not call me Clair, you know how I hate it. I do know things, Ricky, just not whatever nonsense you're spewing. By the way, please keep the fire out of my club will you? Go find a girl to have on your arm tonight and I'm sure Krista will get the hint, I may actually do the same."

That sounds like a better idea the more I think about it. Having someone else around would be a nice change of pace and maybe get Robyn to back the hell up. I know we're potential mates and everything but she's not my True Mate. I don't want to be fully mated to anyone right now. I know I will have to eventually but for now I'll enjoy everything about being unmated that I can.

Robyn has been more high maintenance lately. I've probably been seeing her too much. That conversation with her is going to be a headache. She's a great fuck, but she's not the kind of mate I want to have to deal with for eternity. She's shallow and demeaning to other species as if she's above them all, that's enough to know I don't want anything more from her than I have now.

"I'm not a man whore like you, I don't want someone just to get my dick wet."

"I'm not a man whore." I argue, but he just stares at me blankly. "Well, not all the time. And there isn't anything wrong with you finding a girl to keep you company and have a conversation with. I didn't tell you to go bang her in the bathroom."

He just huffs and says he's going to get another round. I watch amused as he moves to the farthest spot at the bar as he can from the girls. I smile and turn to survey the club, watching all of the different species having a good time all intermingled is why I wanted to open this place. I may be king, but everyone should be treated with the same respect at the very least. I wish I could be treated like every other vampire but that's something I could only dream of happening.

I go to turn back around when the most mouth watering scent reaches my nose. Vanilla and citrus. Saliva pools in my mouth and I feel my fangs start to ache with need to come out, as well as Sin Jr. My eyes close as I take a deep breath trying to savor the smell and commit it to memory. I open my eyes and scan the crowd in a mild frenzy until they lock on to their target.

Big, bright hazel eyes are staring right back at me. As soon as our eyes lock I know immediately what's happening.

My True Mate. The pull I feel for her is unlike anything I've ever felt but have heard of.

Though a sliver of fear pulses through my veins, the need to get closer to her, to know her, overwhelms me completely. My eyes trail from her shoulder length brown hair, past those captivating eyes again, to her cute little nose, those plump lips I want to nibble on, the column of the neck I want to dig my fangs into, and her perky breasts barely contained in that dress.

That dress, *Dear God*, the material is clinging to her like a second skin, covering just enough to tease but still be tasteful and make me ache for more. Her waist is slim and her hips are begging me to grip them tight in my palms as I ram into her. I don't think I've ever been this turned on with a glance in my life. My semi hard on is now at full attention. Especially when my eyes get to her creamy thighs I really want to bury my face in between right now. I readjust myself in my pants while keeping my eyes trained on her.

Fuck. I need to get laid. Preferably by that little vixen.

"Here you go, man." I snap out of my thoughts as

Maverick all but shoves the drink in my hand. "What were you spacing out for?" He asks, taking a sip of his own whiskey, raising a brow at me.

"I think I found my mate. My True Mate." I whisper absentmindedly. No, I knew she was my True Mate. The problem was that I hadn't actually meant to tell him that and I don't know if I'm ready for a mate.

"What!" He spews his drink out, thankfully not on me. "Where?!" He whips his head around like he would be able to magically tell which of the women in this club is my mate without me having to point her out. Idiot.

"Doesn't matter." I shrug, finding my whiskey swirling in my glass very interesting as I follow the ice with my eyes.

"What the fuck do you mean it doesn't matter? Of course, it fucking matters Sin!" He rages.

"Keep your damn voice down." I hiss.

"Sin, you can't possibly still be thinking about what I think you are. You cannot let that shit ruin your chance at happiness with your True Mate, man!" He whispers aggressively at me, leaning in my direction.

"This isn't about Freya, this is about the fact that I haven't wanted a mate." Blocking out the thoughts of the hybrid that broke my heart.

"I would kill to find my mate..."

"Fuck, Rick, I know you would. I'm just a little frazzled right now." I sigh.

"Can you just point her out to me, I won't tell anyone." He pleads, poking his bottom lip out.

"A dragon giving me the puppy dog face, what is the world coming to?" I shake my head and bite my lip to keep my laughter in. I raise my eyes to see him trying to stick his lip out even further and that's when a full belly laugh escapes before I can keep it in. "Alright, alright."

Still chuckling I turn back around to where she was before

but I don't see her now. Slight panic grips my heart that I may have lost the chance to even talk to her. I take a deep breath and catch her delicious scent and my eyes finally zero in on her at the bar for the regular patrons. "Right there, a dark green backless dress at the bar." I nod my head subtly to him and he whips his head around to see.

A low whistle leaves his lips. "Damn, dude. Good for you." He smiles and nudges my shoulder. Then whispers, "anything is better than Robyn regardless." Smirking at me before taking another sip of his drink.

He wasn't wrong, but something told me it didn't matter who my mate was compared to. She was going to be the most extraordinary of them all.

"Are you going to go talk to her?" He asks.

I'm ready to say no when I see Robyn across the way making a beeline toward us with Krista in tow. "Oh fuck, nymph and sprite incoming." I say heatedly.

He pales and looks over his shoulder and then cringes. "Save yourself, go talk to your little mate and I'll make up an excuse for you but you'll owe me." He says pointing a finger at me then shooing me along.

Not wasting a moment, I walk as fast I can without running over to the bar where my little brunette is sitting on a stool waiting for the bartender to get to her. The closer I get the more powerful her scent gets and I have to actively swallow to keep from drooling. When I get close to her I come to two revelations.

She obviously can't feel the mate pull or any type of bond because she hasn't noticed my presence yet.

She's a human.

Not many humans come to my club. All species are welcome to come here but that doesn't mean that everyone makes them feel welcome. There is a lot of prejudice between the races, most of all toward the humans. I never really understood what the issue was but you can never please everyone. Everyone is going to have their own opinions and more than likely nothing even I say or do is going to change that.

Club Sin is usually where more of the elite come to unwind. Though I can't stop the way everyone treats others, even as king, I do my best to stop what I can when it's in my control and within my knowledge.

My True Mate is a human. How in God's name did that happen? I may not really care about the fact that she's a human, the absolute bottom of our hierarchy, but I am painfully aware of the backlash that would come of this. No one would accept a human queen. The council could try to force me to mate with a daughter of an elite family. So many scenarios run through my head as I close the distance between us but once I'm almost right behind her, all those thoughts stop. I'm overwhelmed by her vanilla and citrus scent and it's causing my brain to short circuit.

Problems for another day, right now I just want to meet my little mate.

Taking a deep breath I sit down next to her, swiveling my body slightly to get a look at her profile. Even though her body is mostly turned from me I can tell she is stunning. Perfect, she's perfect. Her shoulder length golden brown hair is swept over her shoulder giving me the perfect view of the creamy column of her next. My fangs throb at the desire to drop and sink into her vein and see if she tastes as amazing as she smells. I bet she tastes incredible, fuck, now my dicks throbbing too.

I readjust my pants and clear my throat. "Hello." Seriously, hello? What am I fucking hormonal teenager who forgot how to give a proper greeting? She doesn't move an inch, maybe she didn't hear me. I guess I can attempt to redeem myself and buy her a drink at least. Owning the club comes with some perks. "What are you drinking, beautiful?" I ask.

She finally turns to me and my breath gets caught in my

throat. She is beyond gorgeous. The most beautiful woman I've ever seen. Her hazel green eyes meet mine and her breath hitches and a small blush coats her cheeks. Adorable.

"You were talking to me?" She asks in the sweetest little voice while pointing to herself as if to make sure it's her I'm referring to.

"Of course." I flash her a smile and her blush takes on a darker hue and that blood is singing to me and tempting my self control not to lean in and have a taste.

"Oh..." She looks around her before meeting my eyes again. "What was the question?" She asks with a little giggle that made my smile grow and my heart melt. I want to hear that sound more.

"I asked what you're drinking, beautiful." I look at her watching her clew on her bottom lip that I really want to be biting too while she looks at me as if debating something then she sighs and gives me a smile that makes butterflies erupt in my stomach. The fucking vampire king getting butterflies from his little human mate. I'm a goner.

"Rum and coke."

I give her a little smirk before looking at the bartender, raising my hand to get his attention. Once he sees it's me his eyes get large for a second before hastily making his way over.

"Your usual, Boss?" He asks fidgeting slightly. He's a newer siren bartender but I've heard only good things about him and having sirens run the bar gets more tips for them and business for me, they are hard to resist.

"Yes, and a rum and coke for this gorgeous lady." I say resting my arm around the back of her stool. My comment makes her lower her head, having her hair like a curtain around her but not before I see her cheeks blaze red which only makes my smirk grow. I love making her blush already.

"Of course." He smiles, his eyes darting between us but

says nothing. He gets our drinks ready fast before bringing them back over. "Here you go."

"Arden, can you add this to mine and my friend's tab." My little mate says catching him before he can walk off. I don't really like that they're on a first name basis.

"It's on me, let Axel know." I say leaving no room for argument. Though he just nods and smiles, my little mate's eyes furrow when she looks back at me.

"You didn't have to do that." She says.

"I wanted to, beautiful." I smirk and take a sip of my whiskey.

"I have a name, you know you don't have to call me that."

"I am only calling you what you are but if you tell me your name then I will know what it is." I smirk, rest my elbow on the table and lean my chin on my fist with my body tilted in her direction.

"Oh! I'm sorry!" She rests her cheek on her palm, flustered yet again and I'm loving every second of it. "I'm Anita." She introduces and gives her hand out for me to shake.

I take her hand and my skin buzzes. I turn her hand in mine so I can place a kiss on her knuckles. "Anita, I am Sinclair, but you can call me Sin."

She smiles and brings her cheek to her shoulder for a moment. Adorable. When she has her eyes back holding mine she furrows her brows, flicks her eyes between my eyes and her hand still being held by mine. "Sin..." God, I love the way my name sounds coming out of her mouth. "Like the club." She adds, looking around the room.

"Yes, this is my club." I smirk and give her hand a little squeeze. This makes her snap her gaze back to me and search my eyes, for what I'm not sure.

"Well it seems you're doing well for yourself." She giggles then takes a long sip of her drink and gives my hand a gentle squeeze back before pulling her hand from mine and I immediately miss the feeling of her skin on mine.

I don't think she knows who I am. I don't think she knows I'm the king. That thought intrigues and excites me at the same time. It's rare that I can go anywhere without everyone knowing who I am, wanting to be around me, treating me to a higher standard, or wanting something for me. I like that she sees me as normal. It's what I've always longed for.

"It does pretty well." I say and let my eyes scan the club. I put a lot of work into it and I'm proud that it's as successful as it is. "So what do you do my beautiful Anita?"

She blushes again, "I'm a nurse at the central hospital." She says.

"Impressive." It really is. Not many humans would get an opportunity to work at the central hospital unless they were extraordinary. My little mate must be very dedicated and smart to have achieved such a goal and I couldn't be prouder for her.

"It was a lot of hard work but I love being able to help everyone and make even a little bit of difference." She says with passion.

"I don't think I've seen you in here before, I would have remembered a beautiful face like yours." I smirk.

"Oh, no." she giggles, making my stomach knot with need. "My best friend dragged me in here with her to-"

"Hey babe, I've been looking for you. Why are you over at this bar instead of the VIP one we always use?" The annoying voice of Robyn rings out then she kisses my cheek. My body freezes as her arms curl around me and press her breasts against me like an animal marking its territory. It both pisses me off and scares me shitless because of the mixture of emotions flickering through Anita's eyes. Hurt, sadness, guilt, and the worst of all defeat.

"Thank you for the drink, Sinclair. I have to find my

friend. You both have a great night." She smiles and waves but the smile doesn't reach her eyes like it was moments before.

"Oh, we will." Robyn's smug attitude grates on my nerves but for some reason I'm stuck, stone still, watching my little mate disappear in the crowd leaving me with this clingy nymph.

"What the fuck was that, Robyn?" I sneer and finally remove myself from her hold. A little too late for that now.

"What do you mean, baby?"

"I'm not your baby. I'm not your mate. We are nothing." I tell her and head back to where Maverick is so we can get the hell out of here. I scan the crowd on my way but don't see Anita anywhere and her scent is already starting to fade. She must have left already.

"What are you talking about? Of course we're mates!" She screeches after me trying to keep up with my long strides as we break through the VIP area, gathering attention as we go because she can't help but cause a scene.

"No we aren't." I say, coming up next to Maverick telling him with my eyes that it's time to go the fuck home. "You may have been a potential mate for me but we were never going to be long term. You were never going to be my queen. We had our fun in bed, Robyn, but that time is over now." I say before walking past her stunned face and making my way out the back of the club where I parked my car.

"I take it didn't go well with your mate?" Maverick asks once we're both seated in the car and pulling onto the road.

"It went amazing with my little mate before Robyn showed up trying to claim me in front of her and I was frozen like an idiot." I grumble. "I don't even think she knows I'm the king." I add.

"Damn, what kind of rock is she living under to not know who you are?" He asks, shocked.

"Don't know. Maybe because she's human?"

"I mean maybe but damn she must not give two shits about politics or something." He says not caring at all that I just said my True Mate is a human.

I let the thought roll around in my head the rest of the drive to my penthouse. Maybe she really just doesn't follow what's going on with the people that run this sector or maybe she's so busy with her work that she doesn't have time to worry about that sort of thing. Everything about her keep swirling around in my head, telling me I'm a fucking idiot for letting her go. I can still fix this if I want to. Sure she's human but she's my True Mate so that has to count for something. Am I ready to let go of the past pain and let her in though?

A smile comes to my face as I remember a little project I have coming up.

I'll be seeing you soon, Anita.

Chapter 7
Anita

After dragging Diana out of *Sins*, I dodged her questions until we were back inside her loft. I gave her the run down of meeting the sexy vampire and having a nice conversation before his nymph girlfriend showed up. While she understood me wanting to leave the club that didn't mean she was going to let me finish drinking. So, we got trashed and watched movies until we passed out.

I shouldn't be upset about what happened with Sinclair anyway. I have a boyfriend I've been with for years, I can't be thinking about other men in any way shape or form. We both have a relationship and he was probably just trying to have a conversation with one of the customers in his club. I mean he was the sexiest man or creature I've ever seen and him calling me attractive shouldn't have affected me the way it did because you make money at a bar by buttering up your customers. I just wasn't used to being approached by a man like him and took it to heart when I shouldn't have.

Nothing could've happened. I still have Kevin at home waiting for me and we still love each other. Sure, things aren't as they once were but that doesn't mean we can't get back there. It's not unfixable.

I can't forget the fact that Sinclair is a vampire either. Vampires are at the top of the food chain. They're the ones that run the world, govern our societies, and sit at the top of our hierarchy. Why would a normal vampire, let alone one as gorgeous as Sinclair, ever look twice at someone like me seriously. I mean I have nothing to offer someone like him unless it's my body or blood. I don't plan on being anyone's fuck buddy or blood bag any time soon.

I've got to stop reading so many romance books that make me think any kind of fantasy like that could ever happen. It's best to forget the whole thing and get back to my regular life.

THE PAST FEW WEEKS HAVE BEEN FLYING BY. I KEEP myself busy with work, try to find that spark with Kevin again to snuff out the one that won't die for Sinclair, and I spend as much time with Diana as I can without going back to that club.

I step through the doors of the emergency room for my morning shift and make my way to the nurses station. When I get there, there are a lot more females hovering around than normal unless I wasn't aware we're having a meeting.

I catch Sarah's eyes and she waves me over to where she's standing with Aaron.

"We have a meeting I'm not aware of?" I ask, gesturing around to the abundance of nurses crowding our station.

"No." Aaron laughs.

"The king is here opening a new wing in the hospital with his associate and is making the rounds so everyone is going a little crazy."

"I've never seen the king before." I say.

"Man are you in for a treat, that man is *fine*." Sarah fans herself with her clipboard.

Aaron rolls his eyes at her while I giggle. I am curious to see what the man looks like. I've heard girls gush about the insanely handsome King Asher but haven't had the pleasure myself. I turn from the crowd and pull my hair up into a ponytail while making my way to my station to see what's on the agenda so far for today when the squeals start. I shake my head at their unprofessional behavior but can't blame them either. It's not very often any of us regular workers would get to meet any of the royal families. I resist the urge to turn and get a peak at King Asher until I hear that familiar voice.

"Hello, ladies."

I whip my head around fast right as he raises his eyes and locks onto mine. No. It can't be him. Sinclair is the Vampire King of Minaoz? Oh my god, I probably sounded so stupid to him at his club. Damn, whatever sliver of hope I had that a man like him would be interested in me is now completely blown out of the water. King Sinclair Archer.

"Anita." Sin nods his head in acknowledgment with that sexy smirk on his face. I have to press my thighs together discreetly and desire pools between my legs at his husky voice saying my name with that heated look in his eyes. *Fuck*. I shouldn't be feeling like this for this man while I'm in a relationship. He's so far out of my league we're in different solar systems.

"Sin." I breathe out, my heart is beating violently in my chest and I can't seem to catch my breath. I didn't think he'd remember me and the fact that he's talking to me now is going to bring so much unwanted attention from the others around us but I can't find it in me to care when despite everything I crave his attention.

All of the desires that I've suppressed since meeting him

back full force now that he's standing in front of me. The thought of having those strong hands undress me the same way his eyes are right now. I want to know what his hands feel like on my skin and his tongue on my-

"It's good to see you again." He says waking me from my thoughts with a deadly smile like he knows the dirty thoughts going on in my head. He walks toward where I'm frozen in place, completely ignoring the slack jaws, glares and stares our way. "How are you doing, beautiful?" He asks in a hushed voice.

"I'm doing fine, Your Majesty." I say.

He frowns at the use of his title. "You're never one I want to hear calling me that, beautiful."

"Why is that?" A mirrored frown now on my face. Why wouldn't I have to call him by his title? He is the king and I'm one of his human subjects.

He doesn't answer, just smiles secretively.

"Anita." I break my eyes away from Sinclair and look at Dr. Stevenson. "I need your assistance with something." He then cuts his eyes to Sinclair before locking back on me.

"Of course." I look back at the handsome vampire in front of me and smile. "It was good to see you, Sinclair."

I turn away from him and make my way over to Dr. Stevenson reluctantly when his voice stops me.

"Sin." I look over my shoulder at him and give him a questioning look. "Please, call me Sin."

I give him a small smile and a nod before closing the rest of the distance and following Dr. Stevenson around the corner and into an exam room. I look around to see it's empty before facing the doctor.

"What did you need help with Max?" I ask.

"You know the king?" He asks instead.

I cross my arms across my chest. "Not really. I met him a

couple weeks ago but I didn't know he was the king. Just chatted a bit. Why?"

He just shakes his head, "Just be careful around men like him, Annie."

"Men like him?" What the hell is that supposed to mean?

"He's a player, Annie. A very powerful and influential playboy. You've worked hard to be where you are and I'd hate for all that to be destroyed because of what could happen if you get involved with him."

Though I know Max's intentions are in the right place I can't help the anger building inside of me. It's none of his business what I do outside of work as long as it doesn't affect my ability to do my job. We're work friends but he doesn't know shit about me and my life. I have a boyfriend so cheating isn't on my list of to do's. Does he think just because a powerful man shows me attention I'm just going to jump into his bed to climb the social ladder. Is that what he thinks of me?

"Thank you for your concern but that is not something that's going to happen. I have a boyfriend and I didn't plan on jumping into the king's bed so if that's all you needed me for I'm going back to my station to do my rounds."

I don't give him time to respond and make my way back to the nurses station. The commotion and crowd are gone which means Sinclair is gone. Aaron and Sarah give me the look of wanting to ask what the hell is going on but they must have seen the, *don't even start,* look on my face because they didn't ask and for that I'm grateful.

The rest of the day goes by as normal and I'm able to avoid the subject of the king for the most part besides simple questions I was able to answer quickly. I couldn't really give anyone any juicy information anyway. We met at his club, had a very short conversation, then didn't see each other until today.

There isn't much to tell and when they realized this they moved on to the next topic of gossip.

I finished my work as I always do but today that red headed vampire king was constantly on my mind. I don't know what it is about the man I can't seem to let go of. Sure, he's sexy as hell but it's more than that. It's the fact that a man of his stature treated me as an equal. He made me feel like the most beautiful woman in the world. He made me feel important because he seemed interested in what I had to say no matter what it was about. He made me *feel*. Not even Kevin's made me feel anything as close to what Sinclair has and that's dangerous. Being around a man like Sinclair Archer is dangerous for my heart.

THE LAST WEEK HAS BEEN THE SAME ROUTINE OF ME going through the same motions at work and at home with Kevin except now I have a certain vampire invading my thoughts constantly. I haven't seen him but his presence is with me.

Getting off of my graveyard shift, I walk toward my favorite coffee shop nearby for some caffeine to get me home because I'm practically dead on my feet right now. We had people in and out constantly with no time to rest all night long. I don't understand what some of these people are thinking when they do these things that get them sent to the emergency room, no matter how funny some of those accidents are.

I see the shop up ahead and smile, I can almost taste that coffee already. I pass the window to get to the door and freeze. There sitting in the corner right at the window with a beautiful woman practically hanging on his arm is Sinclair Archer.

The Vampire King of Minaoz. The sexy redheaded bachelor playboy of our sector. The man that's been plaguing my mind for over a week now.

I'm an idiot.

As I'm scolding myself for the stupid tears threatening to fall from my eyes over a man that I couldn't have had even if I wanted and it wasn't until that moment that I realized I had wanted Sinclair even though I'm still with Kevin. That revelation slams into me and guilt grips my heart. I finally break out of my thoughts the moment those deep red eyes catch mine. I shake my head and walk as fast as I can all the way, not looking back once.

I know I should've known better than to let that hope plant its seed in my heart but it did. It's a good thing seeing him like that with that woman though. Even though it hurt to see, I needed to see it. Now I can wipe my hands of the king and focus on what I do have. I have a relationship with a man I've loved for years that needs to get back on track.

Kevin and I used to have the kind of relationship everyone strived to have. I don't know when or why things changed but that doesn't mean that we can't get it back. Instead of getting lost in a fantasy I need to focus on what I have in my reach.

A vampire king would never be with a lowly human anyway, best to stay at my own level than reaching for something that I was never going to be able to grab onto anyway.

Chapter 8
Sinclair

SEEING ANITA THAT DAY IN THE HOSPITAL, EVEN though I knew I'd probably see her, completely fucked with my self control. There was no amount of preparation I could do once I was physically in front of her, seeing her looking sexy in her nurse scrubs, beautiful face free from makeup but looking flawless, and her mouth watering scent that sent my instincts into a frenzy. My little mate doesn't know it but she has me by the balls and I'm doing everything I can to keep that to myself.

I have to put aside the fact that every nerve ending in my body is craving her. Unfortunately for me, I'm not afforded the regular luxuries that come with finding one's True Mate. I have a sector to run. I am the King of Minaoz and sometimes king's have to make sacrifices. I have a feeling Anita is going to be something I'm asked to sacrifice.

There is a lot to being king that most people wouldn't be able to handle. Sure, I get liberties and freedoms some others may not but everything comes with a price. The job is stressful and that's what it is, a job. I have the lives of so many depending on me to keep the peace and balance so that we function the most effectively. Some situations are easier to solve than others.

The royal court is a completely different matter. Each species has a small group of leaders that help bring the issues and needs to the head council, keeping their race's needs heard. On the head council sits a head representative of each species that gets to make input and suggestions for Minaoz but I have final say. These are the wolves in sheep's clothing. These representatives act like they have their species best interest at heart while some are only looking to better their own situation. There's so much narcissism and manipulation that takes place in court you have to keep your cards close to your chest and eyes in the back of your head. Each of them would probably tear down whoever they needed to to get what they want.

I'm not sure my little mate could handle what it takes to handle these stuffy men and stuck up women in court. I don't want to doubt a woman I barely know anything about but the worry is there regardless. Not many can handle the weight of the crown. I didn't have a choice, but Anita does and I'm not sure I should put that kind of pressure on her. She's human so she doesn't feel the mate pull as I do, if at all. If I can just keep my distance from her she'd be better off without me and all the smoke and mirrors running the sector comes with. She deserves peace and royals don't get that luxury.

I don't even want to think of the snark I'd get from the other kings if they found out about my human mate. It'd be too easy for anyone to assassinate my queen if I wasn't around to protect her. I can't handle losing her like that. I'd rather her live her life with another man, no matter how much the thought makes me rage, than have her death on my hands that way.

I can't deny a part of me wants Anita more than anything but there's still that small seed of fear rooted in my heart. Freya stole my heart then stabbed it repeatedly with the way she betrayed me. That experience never left me and even now with my True Mate in reach I still can't let go of the fear of letting someone have that kind of power and control over my heart again. I'm not sure I would survive a second time.

Freya changed what I believed about love and relationships for so long before I met Anita. It made the thought of commitment laughable to me. Why risk the pain when I can get what I want out of it without being tied down? It's worked for me so far over the years but one conversation with Anita has my thoughts in chaos battling with what I've thought for years and what I want now. She makes me want more than someone to warm my bed, I just don't know if I can follow through.

That leads me to having a lunch date with Xari Belmont at my mother's insistence. She is an attractive dragon sure, but she constantly talks about being the CEO of her family's company that renovates other businesses around Minaoz. Our families work together on many projects so it's natural that we would cross paths on occasion. In an attempt to free my mind from Anita I agreed to a lunch date with her. We have business to discuss anyway as we're working together on our newest project for the Central Hospital of Minaoz. Of course that just makes me think of my little mate again. Fuck me.

"I'm so glad we were able to do this, Sin." Xari says with a smile as we take our seats.

"So am I. It's been a while since we were able to do this alone with us both being so busy." I say as I push her chair in for her before making my way to my own seat.

"Doesn't always have to be for business though." She says just as the waitress comes to our table. I don't know how to respond to that anyway. I know what she's trying to hint at and even though this is technically considered a date I don't see myself wanting to *actually* date Xari.

"What drinks would you both like to start with?" The human waitress asks shyly while sneaking glances at me waiting for our order.

"He'll have a glass of sparkling B Negative with a vampire special club sandwich and I'll have lemon water with mint and the house salad with the dressing and fixing on the side." She orders for us both while looking down her nose at the waitress before she shoos her away.

"You did not need to order for me, Xari." I say trying to not show my irritation at her actions. I'm a man. I can order my own damn food, and I didn't even want what she ordered and she sent the waitress off before I could even change it. Now it would cause more of a problem than it's worth since the food is probably already being made.

"I already know what you like so there's no trouble." She says looking at me sweetly.

I would have to say that the blood she ordered for me is probably my least favorite and this cafe has the best soup I was craving today which is why I picked this place. Maybe I can sneak a togo order before I leave. Regardless I can't let her continue to test my patience with her.

"That's where you're wrong." I grind out. "I don't like either of the things you ordered for me. If we ever do this again you need to remember your place, Xari. I don't need anyone to dominate my life. Remember who I am the next time you want to push boundaries that have consequences."

I don't like having to show this side of myself or force my status as an advantage but sometimes it's necessary. If I give everyone an inch they take ten miles and I can't let my ability to lead Minaoz come into question.

"So how do you think the project is going for the hospital?" I ask her, changing the subject before I say something else about her attempt to emasculate me like between us she would be the one in charge and wearing the pants. Not going to happen.

"It's going as well as expected. Some of the hospital staff could be improved but that's not my job. The renovations are ahead of schedule so we should be ready to open the new wing in just over a month." She responds, ignoring my previous comment.

"That is great news. What do you mean about the staff?" I have to ask because it is within my power to fix personnel issues if I'm aware and I'm not asking just to see a certain little human. Nope.

She waves her hands dismissively while the waitress places our drinks down. "Oh, you know Sinclair, the fact that they have humans working amongst us creatures on a semi level playing field. It's laughable really. Dr. Stevenson really needs to get his head together and put them in jobs they'd be more suited for. His family is close with mine so I may need to have a word with him." She says like she didn't just insult the women with a now clenched jaw walking back to the kitchen to probably spit in her food.

The Belmont's are among the creatures that feel entitled to their standing in the food chain. They work closely with my family and believe they're better than everyone else. I really hate those kinds of people which is why I know now that there will be no second date after this lunch is over. Yea, I'm gonna get that waitress to put an order for some soup to go and give her a big tip for Xari's bigotry.

"Dr. Stevenson?" I ask because that name sounds very familiar.

"Yes. He is the head dragon Doctor for the Central Hospital of Minaoz and works mainly in the emergency room. He has a little human nurse working with him all the time. It's sickening that he gives her those lovesick eyes even though he knows his race is *so* above hers. I've tried to talk to him but he's all for the equality of the races and all that nonsense." She sneers.

Yea, I think this lunch is over. I can't sit here and hear her talk about the other races like that when I am also on the side with *equality and all that nonsense*. It's disappointing that such an influential family could be so hateful to others but then again I'm not surprised because there are many more like them.

I don't even want to think about what she said about the doctor because I'm positive the human he's pining after is my little mate and that makes me want to find him and snap his neck. I don't like the thought of him trying to get with *my* Anita even if she isn't mine to be jealous over.

Yet.

"I think this lunch is over." I say and push my chair back to stand.

"Wait!" She leans over, wrapping her hand around my arm, leaning over the table that puts her tits on full display. "What do you mean? Where are you going?" She asks.

"Look, I just-" My words get caught in my throat as I look out the window and see the sullen face of my beautiful little mate staring right at me before she turns and disappears out of view.

Fuck.

"I need to go. I forgot I have an important meeting to prepare for." I don't give her time to say anything else as I make my way to the counter where our waitress is waiting for our food. "Excuse me miss." She turns fast and stills as I stand in front of her. "I'm cutting my lunch short and was hoping I could get my order to go and possibly your blood soup special also. I'll pay extra for your trouble." I smile.

She gives me a small smile and relaxes her shoulders. "It's no problem, my king. It will only take a moment." She turns and goes in the kitchen and comes out moments later with my order and hands me my receipt. I give her a hefty tip, apologizing for the treatment she received. I make my way out, ignoring Xari's calls after me. As soon as I step outside I look around for Anita even though I know she isn't there anymore.

My throat clogs with emotion I wasn't sure I could feel anymore. The fear of losing my mate is overwhelming, even when in the beginning I wasn't sure I truly wanted her. Now I would weather any storm to have her by my side. I know how this must have looked to her, me alone with a woman. I know I'd be extremely pissed off if I had seen her with another man after the connection we shared at the club no matter how little time we actually spent together. I want her.

I shoot Mia a text to reschedule all of my appointments to tomorrow and race back to my city penthouse. Barging through the door I head straight to the mini bar and power my phone off. I pour a heavy glass of scotch and down it all in one go before pouring another glass. I pace the floor and head to the large window with the view of my city below.

I think back to Anita. While a part of me is happy that she felt enough for me to even be upset of me being with another woman, I'm still surprised because I wasn't sure if she could feel the connection of the bond that we have as True Mates. There are pros and cons of me pursuing a relationship with Anita.

On one hand she's the most gorgeous woman I've ever seen. She's sweet and has an innocence about her that I want to drown in and corrupt slowly in the most sinful ways possible. She's smart and driven in her work life at the least. I don't know much about her on a personal level yet. I feel that she'll be my perfect balance to rule this kingdom.

On the other hand she's human. While I may not mind that fact and have always seen all creatures as equal, unfortunately that's not the most popular opinion especially with the higher classes. Anita would be picked apart, tested, and mocked relentlessly without me by her side that I'm not sure she could handle that kind of pressure. If she couldn't handle that then how could she handle the weight of the crown? The issues of her not knowing as much about our world and not coming from an influential family both stem from her being human. If she would have been born as a werewolf, dragon, or vampire there would be no problems with her being my queen other than a few that only want to have the title more than me.

Maybe it's a good thing she saw what she did today, now she can live her life without mine turning hers into chaos. Even thinking those lies to myself makes my chest ache.

Practically being brought to my knees by a human woman. I swore I wouldn't let another woman close enough to my heart to destroy me as I have been before, but my little mate wormed her way inside in an instant and there's nothing I can do to stop it but denial. Fighting a True Mate bond is almost impossible and I'm not sure if I want to anymore.

Chapter 9
Anita

LAST NIGHT KEVIN WAS OUT AGAIN WITH HIS friends so I had plenty of time to get my emotions and priorities together. I need to focus on what I have, not on what I don't. I have a boyfriend I've been in a relationship with for years, even if we haven't been doing as good as we have in the past doesn't change the fact that I will always be faithful to him, and I'm human. Though I hate to admit it, being human is a disadvantage. I have to work twice as hard for a job I'm overqualified for, deal with the judgment from the higher creature races, and the likelihood of me ever crawling my way out of the bottom of the food chain is unlikely.

I've had the day off today so I've been cleaning the apartment, making it as spotless as possible to keep myself busy. I'm now in the kitchen cooking Kevin's favorite dinner when I hear the front door open then close.

"Hey, baby!" I call out when I hear him put his keys in the bowl near the entrance. I turn the burner on low and turn just in time to see him coming around the corner to peek in the kitchen.

"Hey, I didn't know you were going to be home." He says.

"Yea, I go back for a double tomorrow. How was work?" I ask.

He looks at me for a moment before he replies. "It was fine, hot as fuck outside, and some dick head vampire was bitching at us for while because our job fixing the damn road was interrupting whatever the hell he was doing." He huffs and trudges off to sink into the couch. I flinch slightly when he says vampire thinking of Sinclair immediately.

I push the thought back and look down to see he's tracked mud in on the carpet because he didn't take his work boots off at the door like he's supposed to. I just cleaned and now it was for nothing. I don't say anything though, I just smile sympathetically at him.

"I'm sorry you had such a hard day, but I made your favorite for dinner." I gesture toward the kitchen where dinner is just about finished.

"Oh, well, I'm going out to eat with the guys. Josh is going to be here any minute to pick me up. Like I said I didn't know you were going to be here so I made plans already." He says as he makes his way to the room, leaving a trail of dirty clothes in his wake. He comes back out in fresh clothes moments later over his still dirty body since he apparently doesn't see the need to shower before leaving the house again.

He looks around the apartment before looking back at me. Maybe he finally noticed I cleaned everything before he dirtied it up again. "You should have really cleaned or something since you've been here all day. I don't know what the hell you were doing but I work hard all day in the sun and would like to come home to a clean house." He wrinkles his nose in distaste at the state of our home, thinking I was lacking when it was all his doing. "I'll be home sometime later. Don't wait up." He kisses my cheek as he walks by me and right out the door.

I stare ahead of me for a moment not knowing what to

think about what just happened. Has he always been this big of an asshole?

Thinking back he probably was but it's not like I have a lot of eligible guys knocking on my door with a better option. I don't let the redhead vampire last more than a flicker in my mind. Sure Kevin is a little rough around the edges but he's a good man at his core. I can just re-clean the apartment and put his share of dinner in the refrigerator for him to heat up either tonight or tomorrow if he wants.

Determined to work as hard as I can to make this relationship work on my end to help ease my guilt for even entertaining the idea of Sinclair and I.

I GO INTO A SORT OF AUTOPILOT FOR THE NEXT FEW weeks. I got to work, clean the apartment, make home cooked meals when I'm home and able, doing whatever I can to make Kevin feel loved and wanted, and even try to initiate sex more than he does. Everything seems to be going better than expected.

Kevin seems to be easier on me with his expectations and in return I feel like I'm finally erasing the spot the vampire king had in my thoughts. Not completely but it's a start. Kevin's definitely loving the extra attention and seeing his attitude and mood take a turn for the better makes me feel wanted and useful.

I've been keeping my head down as best I could at work. I've been ignoring any looks, comments, or questions about Sinclair as best as I can because in truth there isn't anything to tell and really there never was.

My bosses are happy with my work ethic because I've been the model obedient little human. Today is no different, I'm walking back to the nurses station after helping one of the doctors with setting a fracture in place for a cast. I'm looking down at my chart to see if I have any other patients that are priority before I take my break.

"Do you work here?"

I turn to the sound of the woman's voice and almost choke. In front of me is the woman that was with Sinclair at the cafe weeks ago. She's standing confident in a pencil skirt and blazer combo with her stilettos clicking against the floor as she closes the distance between us while keeping her eyes trained on me with a smirk on her lips.

"Yes, ma'am. Do you need help with something?" I ask politely, forcing what I hope is a convincing smile on my face because I really don't want to talk to her even if she doesn't know who I am.

"I've heard about you." She says with a condescending smile on her face. I freeze at her words, wondering how she could've heard of me. My first guess is Sinclair but I'm not sure why he would and that makes me all the more fidgety. "Max is a very good family friend and for some reason he says you are one his best nurses, I don't really see it but to each his own." She flips her curled hair over her shoulder before looking down her nose at me again.

Oh, so she's one of those. I already didn't want to speak with her but now I'd rather get hit by a bus than deal with her snarky, demeaning comments because I'm human.

"He is a great boss." I say with a forced smile.

"I'm sure he is." Her tone is suggestive but I choose to ignore that for now.

"Did you need help with anything, Miss..." I pause not knowing her name.

"Xari Belmont. I'm one of the elite donating to this hospital and constructing the new wing with *my* Sin."

Her Sin.

"Of course. If that's all then I need to complete my rounds." I say trying to side step her and end this torture. Hearing her reference ownership to Sinclair makes my stomach roll.

"You know Max told me an interesting story the other day." She continues and blocks my escape. "He said you seemed to know my Sin." Her perfectly sculpted brow raises.

"I wouldn't say I know him, I've only had two conversations with him in passing." I say downplaying how I felt about our interactions but not really lying either.

"Let's keep it that way, human." She sneers. "I'm the future queen of Minaoz. You should stick to your class of filth in the slums and leave the higher classes alone. He is so far out of your reach it's pathetic if you thought you'd get anywhere with him." She continues and with every word it feels as though another stab goes straight for my heart over and over.

"I'm under no illusion. I know my place. Now I need to get back to work, please excuse me Miss Belmont." I rush out and speed away as fast as I can without running.

I wish her words didn't affect me as much as they do. I'm fighting to keep the tears in my eyes from falling. I knew I'd never truly be with Sinclair even if Kevin wasn't in the picture. I knew I'd never be the queen standing by his side. Despite knowing all this, that small spec of hope was snuffed out by Xari's words. I know they're true but it doesn't make it hurt any less.

I quickly place my chart in its rightful place at the nurse station and head straight for the emergency exit. Once the fresh hair hits my face I feel the tears finally start to fall and stream down my face. I lean back against the brick wall and slowly slide down to the ground and hug my knees to my chest.

I let the guilt consume me from being so upset over a man that isn't my boyfriend, the pain of knowing that Sinclair already has a queen to stand by his side and I never had a chance, and the sorrow of knowing that I'll only ever be a lowly human stuck working harder than everyone else and I'll die here at the bottom of the hierarchy not remembered by anyone other than those few close to me.

Chapter 10
Sinclair

I HAVEN'T STOPPED THINKING OF THAT DAY OR THE look on Anita's face for weeks now. No matter what I do it is seared into my mind. I know I shouldn't feel guilty but I can't help the fact that I feel as though I've betrayed our bond by even being out with Xari.

Xari.

The way she spoke of those she sees beneath her still rubs me the wrong way. I'm the king and no one is above me other than the King of all Vampire Kings and I still would never put down the other races the way she does. The fact that her way of thinking isn't an unpopular opinion puts the equality I've always wanted for Minaoz as an uphill battle. I can enforce as many laws as I want but I can't change the way people think of themselves and others.

The things she said about Anita not knowing she's my True Mate have also been circulating in my mind. I always knew the fact that she's human would be a hindrance in one way or another no matter if it bothered me personally or not. She'd be tested and pushed around by the other species that feel she is inferior and unfit to rule beside me.

The last thing I'd want is other's pushing Anita too hard and changing the sweet woman I've started to know into someone cold and hard to survive at my side.

These last few weeks have me really thinking about what I want to do. I don't want to live my entire life alone and I would've wanted it to be with my True Mate but maybe this is for the best. I've tried to look for her with no luck so maybe this is a sign and I should let her go. The pressure as a human queen ruling next to a vampire king would probably be too much for her to bear anyway. By letting her go I'm really setting her to live a stress free life with the other humans. No one knows she's my True Mate besides Maverick, so there's still time for her to live a happy life. The thought of her with another man has rage rushing through my veins but it's for the best. I have to tell myself that or I will surely lose my sanity.

This also will relieve a lot of weight off my shoulders as well. Freya Summers ruined me for any relationship anyway after what she did.

That sprite/human hybrid became everything to me in a short amount of time. I don't remember ever feeling more loved than I did from her, but it was all an illusion. She spewed sweet and loving words that had me wrapped around her little finger so tightly that I didn't see the deceit in her eyes. It wasn't until I came home early from a council meeting I was sitting in on as the prince that I walked in on her trying to seduce my very uncomfortable father. While she tried to spin a sob story to turn me against my father it was useless on her part. I know my father, he couldn't seduce a prostitute if his life depended on it. He has zero game, I have no idea how he even got my mother.

Most people that are around me on a regular basis only know me as Vampire King Sinclair Archer of Minaoz not as Sin the man. They look at me as their ticket to a better life if they get on my good side. That's what Freya tried to do because of her difficult life as a hybrid. She tried to get the highest available status she could by trying to get to my father, stepping on my heart in the process. It is very hard to find genuine people in life when you're in a position of power. That is why I value my friendship with Maverick so much. He's a man of status as well but we have been friends since we were kids and he knows me better than anyone.

I look around the room to the men in front of me, talking over each other, trying to argue their cases. I've been sitting in the throne room for over an hour now. Twice a week I meet citizens of all status if need be to see what I can do to help them. Most of the ones that come in are mid to upper lever species and families but I've had some lower level's come in as well.

I started this not long after I took over as king from my father. I wanted a better way to communicate with all of the races and make the crown seem like we do actually give a shit, because I do.

Their aggravated voices keep getting louder before I sigh then slam my hand on the arm of my chair and silence follows.

Finally.

"Let me see if I understand what's going on." I say rubbing a hand over my stubbled jaw and fixing them with an irritated look. "You are here for me to help you settle a lawsuit?" They nod mutely with wide eyes. "Because your lawyers wouldn't take the case?" I ask.

"No they wouldn't." The well dressed older siren says. It's commendable that he has his own successful business but I'm also surprised he's still in business if he has idiots like this working for him.

"Then why are you here?" I ask.

"Because I demand to be accommodated for wrongful termination due to racial discrimination." The little male sprite fumes with red cheeks then looks down immediately when he realizes how he just spoke to me.

"Watch your tone." I grit out. "Your lawyer didn't take the case because there isn't a case." I raise my hand, cutting off the still fuming sprite when he opens his mouth to respond. "You're claiming that you were fired because they have been storing all of your personal information on you then hacking into your personal devices to use against you to terminate your employment because of your race." I start, looking down at the file in front of me. "However, your side of the case holds no weight because you were the idiot that logged into all of your personal accounts on your company laptop. Who watches porn on their work devices?" I ask with a raised brow.

Idiots, I swear.

The embarrassed little sprite huffs out a heavy breath before bowing to me sharply before exiting the room.

"I'm sorry to have wasted your time." The siren said before bowing and also leaving me in the throne room alone.

I lean my head back and groan. Sometimes I hate everyone.

I LOOK OVER AT MY FRIEND SITTING NEXT TO ME once again in my club at the VIP bar.

"Okay, what the hell happened? You look like someone died." He says, taking a sip of his scotch while eyeing me.

I look down into my own scotch glass and contemplate what I want to tell him and after a moment go with the truth because if I can't tell him the truth then who can I tell?

"Might as well. I played judge today in the throne room and the version of myself that ends up with my True Mate has died." I say with a shrug of my shoulders and take a sip.

"Your day of kingly duties doesn't surprise me but what

do you mean? Did something happen to your mate?" He asks with panic building in his eyes.

"No. Anita is fine I'm sure. We just don't have a future."

"Why do you think that?"

"I don't think, I know we don't."

"That's bullshit."

"No. It isn't. She's human. She'd never be accepted by higher society let alone be able to handle the pressure of ruling beside me." I say glaring into my glass. "I never really wanted a mate anyway." I add in a whisper.

"You have got to be shitting me." He rolls his eyes when I look at him. "You're just making excuses, Sin. Self sabotage."

I ignore him, order another double and make eye contact with a sexy water nymph a few chairs down. I give her the best bedroom smile as I can while I choke down the bile and guilt. It's a physical struggle to keep the image of my little mate in the back of my mind as I try to forget about her the only way I can.

"So what, you're just going to drown in alcohol and easy women like you always do and just ignore the fact that you're running away from your true happiness?" He asks heatedly.

I avoid his eyes because he's right and I know how much he's been wanting to find his mate. Maverick is a true romantic at heart and I know the fact that I'm fighting to ignore my mate bond is pissing him off.

He huffs, slams the rest of his drink and stands. "Ruin your life, but I'm not going to sit here and watch you throw away that kind of love for easy pussy. Call me when there isn't alcohol or sex on your mind unless you're with your mate." Then he's gone and I'm alone.

I look back into my glass for a moment before I catch movement in my peripheral vision of the nymph coming my way and sliding into the chair that Maverick just left.

"Hello, my king." She purrs while leaning closer while also pushing her breasts up.

A few weeks ago, I'd jump at the opportunity to fuck her. Now, it's physically painful to make myself act like I truly want her. I still give her my best smile, run my fingertips across her collar bone and over the top of her breasts. "Hello, beautiful. You want to come back and have some fun with me?" I ask in a husky whisper in her ear.

She nods and I lead her back to my private room in the back of my club.

As I pull her through the door and turn the lock I give her a longer look up and down her body. She's fairly tall with curly long blonde hair with streaks of light blue throughout. She has large full breasts, a tiny waist, large ass to grab onto and thick thighs. She has plenty of curves I'd usually love to grab onto while I pound into her. I look back up to her aqua eyes and realize that the only thing I like about her now is that she looks nothing like the woman I really want.

I can do this. I can forget the one I want with women that are so different I could never compare them. I can forget this bond trying to make me want something I've never wanted before. Why would I want one woman when I can have as many as I want?

If I say that lie enough I'll believe it, right?

I don't let her say a word before I turn her and slam her back to the door and crash my lips to hers. I devour her mouth, making her moan and start removing her skin tight dress. It pools at her feet and her hands paw at my own trying to remove mine as well. I lock both of her wrists in one of my hands and hold them above her head and trail my lips down her neck giving little bites along the way.

"Keep your arms here and don't move them." I whisper in her ear before letting go of her arms. I trail my fingertips along the skin of her wrist and her arm slowly before trailing them along the swell of her breasts, the side of her waist, then settle on the curves of her hips. I admire her tanner skin and can't help the flickering image of it being creamy skin instead.

I shake my head slightly and pull her away from the door and push her onto the arm of the couch face down.

"Are you ready for me, beautiful?" I ask while undoing the buckle of my belt before letting my pants and boxers fall to the floor before stepping out of them and up behind her. I press my hard cock against her round ass and rock my hips slightly.

"Oh, yes, Your Majesty. I'm ready for that big cock." The nymph moans out.

I smirk and take a hold of her hip with one hand while the other takes a hold of my hard member as I guide it into her warm core. I close my eyes at the feeling of her pussy clenching around my dick as I slide into the hilt.

I give her no time to adjust before I start to move in and out. I piston my hips into her, increasing my speed and force, causing her body to shoot forward with every thrust. The only sounds in the room are the slapping of our flesh, moans, and groans.

I don't know why but all of the sudden the image of Anita pops into my mind. The thought that she's the one underneath me right now. That she's the one moaning at the pleasure I'm giving her. That her body is the one pushing back into mine, meeting each of my trusts as if begging for more. That it's her creamy hips I'm gripping onto as I keep her in place while my force gets rougher and more demanding.

The thought of my little mate screaming out my name as she comes around my cock, her sweet pussy squeezing the life out of my member as if she never wants it to leave her warm cavern, is enough to have me pulling out and shooting my load all over her back as I let out a loud groan while throwing my head back and my eyes roll to the back of my head.

That was one of the most intense orgasms I've had in a

while. It had nothing to do with the nymph currently covered in my come but the mere thought of her being my little mate instead.

This is all so fucked up.

"Do you need any help cleaning yourself up before we leave this room?" I ask while looking out of my private room's window down to the club as I finish buttoning my pants back. The floor to ceiling windows are double paned, tinted, and one way. I can keep an eye on my club while they can only see seemingly black glass.

"No, Your Majesty. Thanks for the fuck though." She says coming up behind me. I feel her trail her hand along my shoulder blades as she makes her way around me and to the door. "It was everything I thought it would be and more from the vampire king." She winks as she makes her way out of the room as if she just complimented me.

That is exactly why I don't do relationships or romance. She only saw me as the vampire king she wanted to be able to brag to her friends to that she fucked. I'm an accomplishment to them. A challenge to complete. I hate it. I hate being seen as only a small part of who I actually am. But no one really cares about Sin, only Vampire King Sinclair Archer.

I straighten my clothes and make my way out the back exit to my car before speeding home.

Walking through the front door I head straight to the back staircase that leads down to my personal gym. Even after that session at the club I'm still wired with thoughts of Anita, mates, the throne, Minaoz, expectations and pressure on my shoulders.

I take off my jacket, make my way to the small bar I keep in here and grab a bottle of my expensive scotch. I take a long gulp from the bottle as I make my way over to the punching bag. I set the bottle down and remove my shirt then take swing after swing with all my strength into the bag. The vampire enforced material makes it a true challenge to move it. It is like hitting solid concrete or metal for a human I'd assume.

With each punch I hit harder and harder. My breath is getting more erratic and I feel my mind get hazy. The thoughts swirl around in my head until they are all blended together and I just keep hitting the bag letting out my frustration, heartbreak, anger, guilt, and helplessness.

I'm not sure how long I spend taking everything out on the punching bag but when I let my arms fall to my sides I'm heaving breaths into my lungs greedily, my arms are shaking slightly, and I can feel pain in my hands. I look down confused, I don't usually get injuries of any kind. It takes a lot to truly hurt me. I look down at my knuckles and see that they are torn open and dripping blood down on the mat at my feet. I keep my eyes on my wounds and watch as the skin slowly stitches itself back together until there is no sign that they were ever open to begin with.

I fall to the floor and reach over for the bottle of scotch and again take large gulps of the liquid before placing it back down. I lay back on the mat and close my eyes and pray silently for a dreamless sleep not even caring enough to make it to my bedroom. The last thing running through my head though, was a pair of the most beautiful hazel eyes staring back into my own.

Chapter 11
Kevin

Things have been going really well for me lately. Anita is finally reaching her full potential. She's taking less shifts at the Hospital to spend more time at home with me or just to get the things done that she's been neglecting. She's cooking us dinner every night whether I make it home to eat or not so I at least can eat it when I get home if I want to. The house is kept clean. She finally keeps my clothes washed for work and keeps my house spotless. I don't like living in a pigsty. I work all day out in the heat. It's the very least she can do honestly.

And the sex.

An involuntary groan is pulled from me. I don't know what's gotten into her but the sex has been amazing. She has so much more energy. She seems so much more eager than I've ever seen her. The way she's been riding me and using that mouth of hers is making me hard just thinking about it.

"So how's Anita been?" Josh asks, breaking me out of my dirty thoughts.

When I turn my head to him, he has that usual glint in his eyes when we talk about *my* Anita. I know he has a thing for her. I know he'd fuck her if he could. I don't usually like to share but if the circumstances were right I might. Anita does anything I ask so... "Yea, she's been good." I take another sip of my beer.

Me and the guys came out to the local bar we always come to after work, The Docks. Most of the people here are regulars but there are a few newcomers every now and then. It's right by the river in the lower sector so most of the working class like us come in after their shifts end to unwind.

"Didn't you say she was acting weird?" He asks.

"Yea..." She has been acting strange the last few weeks. If I didn't know any better I would've thought she was either leaving me or having an affair but it's like she's done a one-eighty the last couple of weeks since then. "But she's the Anita I know and love." I say with a smirk.

He returns my smirk because he knows all the little bits of work I've done over the years to make her exactly how I want her. I tamed her fiery spirit and made her the perfect woman for a man like me. I needed her beauty and personality to match my tastes. And now they do.

"I couldn't help but overhear your conversation." I hear a woman's voice say behind me and I see Josh's eyes go wide.

I turn my body and my breath catches in my throat. Behind me is the most beautiful woman, nymph, I've ever seen. She's tall, tan, and thin with sexy as sin curves. A full head of curly brown hair, full kissable lips, and the most capti-vating green eyes that are holding me in a trance. Every part of my body is coming to life in a way it hasn't done in a long time, maybe ever.

"Hello..." I say.

"Robyn." She smiles at me and my heart beats violently in my chest. "I couldn't help but overhear your conversation." She repeats. "Were you talking about Anita Carras?" She asks.

"How do you know Anita?" Josh cuts in because I'm still

being held captive by Robyn's overwhelming allure, you'd think she was siren and the fact that she knew my long time girlfriend could not be good for the certain part of my anatomy that is really wanting to make all my decisions for me right now.

"She's a nurse right?" She asks. I nod my head yes as a reply. "She was trying to steal my mate from me." She suddenly sneers and flips her curls over her shoulder.

"Your mate?" I ask, for some reason, the fact that she has a mate hurting more than the fact that Anita may be cheating or trying to cheat on me.

"Yes, he just hasn't come to terms with it completely yet but he is my mate." She insists. I mean if he doesn't want to be her mate I'd gladly take her in a heartbeat. "How do you two know Anita?"

"She's his long-time girlfriend." Josh says then takes a sip of his beer like he didn't just cock block the fuck out me.

Robyn turns her green eyes on me, assessing me up and down before meeting my eyes again. I can't tell what she's thinking but I hope she likes what she sees.

"So, she had a boyfriend the whole time. What a slut." She says with an apologetic smile and I return it. She takes the seat next to me and places her hand on my thigh making my muscles jump. "I'm sorry."

I swallow hard before answering. "It's alright. We haven't been in the best place for a long time." I say, mentally erasing the fact that Anita has been trying extremely hard to make this work. "That would explain why she's been putting in so much effort lately." I think out loud.

I see Josh and Robyn both nod their heads in agreement.

The more I think about it the more the anger inside me grows. I've done everything for her. I work hard to bring money into our home and pay all of our bills and she has the nerve to try to get a man on the side? I don't fucking think so.

"Who the fuck does she think she is? Who the hell does she think she's messing with?" I ask no one in particular.

There's a moment of silence before the phrase that has a sadistic smile spread on my face and plans start to form in my mind.

Robyn smirks.

"Why don't we show her then?"

Chapter 12
Anita

THESE WEEKS HAVE ONLY ACCOMPLISHED A FEW things for me.

One - that this time I've spent working my ass off to get this relationship back to a place it once was with Kevin is starting to seem pointless. He doesn't appreciate anything I've ever done, how hard I always work, and how lost he truly would be without me in his life.

Two - the time that's been passing away from the vampire king hasn't stopped the hurting or kept him from crossing my mind but it is easier to breathe now when I do allow myself a moment to think of him and the small moments we did have. I have learned to treasure the good times we did have because after meeting him I look at my life with Kevin in a way I may never have if not for him. The way he made me feel in an instant is something I can have if I find an available man this time and get out of this draining relationshit with Kevin.

Three - I am still a massive pushover.

Though I know all of this I'm still here with Kevin in our home. I have the night off and decided to cook a romantic dinner as an attempt to get our sparks flying again. No matter how he treats me, Kevin and I have a lot of years of great memories and love. It's hard to let it go even when you feel you should. He's my comfort zone.

I hear the door open and close. I look back to the table set with our dinner and candles lit to give a romantic feeling in the air. If this doesn't do it then I'm not sure what will.

"What's all this?"

I turn to see Kevin stopped mid step on his way past the dining table with his eyes locked on the dinner I've made. "I made dinner for us." I say simply with the sweetest smile I can form.

"What's the occasion?" He asks, squinting his eyes slightly at me before looking back at the spread I've prepared of all his favorites.

"Do I need an occasion to make a nice dinner for my boyfriend on my night off?" I ask cocking my head to the side. I don't know why he's asking so many questions about dinner. Have I really been that off the ball for this to seem like an unusual thing to do?

"Right..." He says trailing off before he moves again to take his seat slowly while keeping his eyes on me. "How has work been?" He asks.

His question surprises me because I can't remember the last time he's asked me about work. I smile nonetheless. "It's been really good actually, they're opening up a new wing." I say while making his plate and setting it in front of him before making my own.

"Who did they send this time to open it?" He asks while looking down at this plate.

I pause for a moment as images of how the king looked in his suit that day at the hospital runs through my mind. I shake the thoughts away before answering. "Xari Belmont." I say, not sure why I only tell half the truth.

"The influential dragon family Belmont's?" He clarifies. Looking at me briefly before his focus goes back to his plate.

"The same."

"I heard the vampire king was there." He says casually.

My breath catches. "I didn't see him if he was there." I lie and deflect defensively for no reason. It's not like Kevin can know about the two times we've spoken and those two conversations weren't inappropriate anyway.

He hums in response then we finish dinner in relative silence.

Kevin leans against the door frame as he watches me wash the dishes.

"You've been doing more around the house lately." He says.

I feel my brows pull together. "I'm not sure what you mean. I always clean the house, Kevin." I say.

"Yeah, but you've been doing it all without even nagging at me." My eye twitches at his take on my *nagging*. "Just seems out of character for you."

"You have something you want to say?" I ask him directly, not liking the fact that he's beating around the bush.

"You've just been different, Annie. That's all I'm saying." He says before pushing off the wall and disappearing into the bathroom. My heart aches slightly at the use of my nickname I haven't heard him use in so long let alone in a remotely fond manner.

Later that night in bed we each lay on our backs, staring at the ceiling. The tension is thickening by the second. I close my eyes and take a deep breath before I swing my body around and straddle his lap and place my hands on his chest.

"I'm sorry, Kev. It's been hard at work lately and I saw someone lose someone that meant so much to them and I don't want to feel that. I guess seeing that made me appreciate what I have that much more." I say.

It's not really a lie. It's just me that lost the connections I could've had with...Sinclair. There isn't a way I can explain it without sounding insane, but we connected. I thought we did anyway. It just wasn't meant to be though. I have Kevin and though we don't always see eye to eye I'm glad I've had him by my side through the years when I really needed him.

"I love you, Kevin." I say.

"Me too." He then slams his lips to mine and rolls me on my back. I let him take control and try to get lost in the sensation his body is giving mine without dark red eyes eclipsing my mind.

Chapter 13
Sinclair

I step out of my Audi and walk up to my favorite coffee shop in the mid sector before my business meeting with Virac Co. I need a good dose of caffeine in my system after the idiotic week long bender I went on, drowning my ridiculous sorrows over a woman I don't even really know.

Some fearsome vampire king I am.

As every time I come in here one of the baristas thinks that they can try their luck with me and catch my attention like most of the women of the Minaoz population but unlike most days, today I am not in the mood to even indulge these women wanting to throw themselves at me. I only have room for one thing on my mind today and I'm trying to keep it to the marketing meeting I have in half an hour. It's hard enough trying to keep the woman haunting me out of my thoughts as it is without adding anything else on.

After grabbing my black coffee with a splash of A negative I head out and decide to walk to try to clear my head and get myself in the right mindset for this important meeting.

A sudden rush of heat grows and grows until I register that I've been burned by none other than my own coffee that I just bought. I look up furious at whoever decided to not look where they're going to bump into me and I'm met with an equally furious redhead glaring holes at me.

"You!" She yells and points her manicured finger at me.

"Yes, me. The one you just ran into and spilt coffee on. Yes, I'm that vampire king." I droll sarcastically. My patience has apparently decided to stay home today.

"This is all your fault!" She spits.

"Look. I didn't run into myself. You ran into me and now I'm covered in coffee and I have a meeting in fifteen minutes." I grunt, trying to keep from strangling this human in front of me.

"I don't give a shit about your meeting or that you're the king of Minaoz. I don't care about your coffee or your stupid suit. What I do care about is the fact that it's your fault my best friend is turning back into a fucking pushover for her piece of shit boyfriend and won't return my calls because she knows I'm going to rip her a new one!" The crazy redhead screams as she huffs with angry breaths.

"I have no idea what you're talking about, Miss. I do have to get going though." I try to scoot around the deranged woman and continue on my way. I don't even care about the coffee anymore, I just want to be as far away from this psychotic human.

"Oh but Sinclair." She says sweetly with a glint in her eyes I don't like one bit. "You don't remember my best friend?" She asks. I shake my head, afraid to answer verbally to this human for unknown reasons besides the fact that I get the feeling that she would gut me like a fish if I truly crossed her. "Anita Carras."

As the name leaves her lips so does the breath from my lungs.

Anita Carras.

My Anita.

My little mate.

My True Mate.

Though her name sounds beautiful, finally knowing her full name brings back a pain I thought was starting to dull but just the mention of her has me hurting all over again. It must have been written all over my face because a confused look overcame the woman's face in front of me. I squeeze my eyes shut and turn my head away from her. I'm not ashamed of showing others my pain, it's that a king isn't supposed to show his subjects any weakness and my mate is my one and only true weakness. Even if she has no idea at all.

"What the hell is that face for?" She asks.

"I'm sorry..."

"Diana Montgomery."

"Miss Montgomery. I didn't know she was with someone but regardless we've only barely spoken twice and if she has a boyfriend then nothing about me should have affected her anyway. I'm..." I look down at my watch, "late for a very important meeting so if you'll excuse me." I push my way around her and take long strides down the street.

I don't listen for a response if she gives one. Once I'm a block away from Diana I speed my way to the office getting there in seconds. I sent a text to Mia letting her know of my arrival, that I need a new suit in my office before I can attend the meeting, and that I need someone to retrieve my car from the coffee shop.

I take my private elevator up to my floor that goes straight to my office. As I walk in I see my suit and immediately grab it and head to the ensuite to change.

While changing I think back on the encounter I had. Diana was convinced I'm to blame for something going on with Anita. At least she's alive, I was almost convinced she was hurt from the fact that I haven't been able to find any information on her or any movement at the hospital about her. I try not to think too much but I physically can't help myself.

Boyfriend.

This stops me in my tracks as I try to fasten my cufflinks. Diana said something about Anita and her boyfriend. Trying to fix things with her shitty boyfriend is what she said.

Anita has a boyfriend?

Volcanic rage fills my veins thinking of another man's hands on my mate, his lips on my little mate, his dick in…

No. I cant even let the thought finish unless I want to go murderous.

I thought we had a connection. I *know* we have a connection. She's my True Mate, she's meant to be with me for the rest of our lives. We're made to be together. Why would she want to fix things with her boyfriend when she has me?

Does she have me though?

I said that I've looked for her and threw a pity party but did I really put the resources I have at my disposal as king to find my one and only True Mate? No. I didn't.

She still shouldn't have flirted with me as a taken woman. I know she doesn't owe me anything, only having two conversations with me but I can't help that the green monster is taking over. I've been torturing myself for weeks over her and she's just been living her happy life with her boyfriend like I never even crossed her mind while she has been constantly haunting me.

I finish the meeting with Mr. Virac and the rest of the day in a blur. I stand at the window in my office and look down at the number on my phone and debate on making the call or not. Every scenario plays over and over in my mind before I take a deep breath and make the call.

"Hello?" I hear her quiet voice over the line.

"Hello, it's Sinclair. Are you free for dinner tonight?"

There's a pause on the line before she answers.

"Sure, Sin. I'd like that."

"I'll send a car to pick you up at six. I'll see you soon, Norah."

I end the call and stare out over my city. Mr. Virac is a sensible man and I decided to take his not so subtle hints about his daughter being my potential mate and a good match for me and put them to action. I hope I'm doing the right thing.

Chapter 14
Sinclair

I'M STANDING OUTSIDE OF THE RESTAURANT, DRAGO Centro, waiting for Norah to arrive. I feel my hands clam up for various reasons. I'm not a typical dating man. I don't take women out to dinners or dates, I usually just bring them home and fuck their brains out but I don't do romance. I've only done romance once and that was a disaster, then there's my little mate.

I shake the thought of her out of mind, I can't think of her especially right now. My attention is pulled to the familiar sleek black car coming to a stop in front of me. I stride to the door and pull it open and hold my hand out to assist the werewolf out of the car.

Norah is truly a beautiful werewolf with light brown hair and her golden eyes locked on me. She has lean muscles under the skin tight floor length evening dress she has on. She's the kind of woman that any man would drool over, and I still find myself thinking of hazel green eyes and creamy skin.

"Norah." I kiss the back of her hand once she's fully standing next to me and I shut the car door before steering her toward the restaurant.

"Sin. You're being so formal tonight." She jokes while nudging me with her elbow.

This is what I love about Norah from the night we met. We've known each other since college. Even though I've never seen her as a romantic partner for life, I like her company and light conversation. She has a way of calming me and helping me get out of my head which is most of the reason I've asked her to join me tonight instead of someone else.

"What do you mean, Miss Virac?"

"You know exactly what I mean, Mr. Archer." She smirks and I return the gesture.

"I just need a light night to get my mind off something and I feel like you're the best person to make me feel like myself again."

I smile at her. Norah and I get along but we wouldn't be truly happy together, though I'm sure she would make an amazing queen.

"Your father's hints during our meeting have nothing to do with it though." I wink.

She groans, "of course he did."

We both laugh as we make our way to the entrance.

"Anyway, I also needed a light night. That's the exact reason I said yes, just for selfish reasons."

I look at her again and I can see the tiredness and stress in her eyes. It seems I'm not the only one going through the wringer lately. Norah's a confident and elegant woman, it's hard to imagine her looking anything less than perfect.

"Anything I can help with?" I offer the sight of her in distress tugs at my heart. Damn potential mate pull.

"Possibly, but I can handle my own problems, Sin. Thank you for the offer though." She smiles a fake smile but a smile nonetheless.

I place my hand on her lower back and lead her inside where the hostess recognizes me immediately and leads us to my reserved VIP secluded table. I pull Norah's chair out for her and push it forward before taking my own seat. I study the menu briefly before settling on the grilled chicken with their famous creamy blood sauce with grilled vegetables then bringing my eyes back to the woman across from me.

I gaze at her as she looks down at her own menu. She truly is exquisite. She has this air about her that screams confidence, elegance, and down to earth. Despite being from one of the top influential families she comes across as nice as can be which is a hard characteristic to have in the world we live in. Many egos tend to inflate at an alarming rate when they get the taste of power or privilege. From one of our previous dinners with our parents, though she seemed in the same boat as me about wanting to be there in general, she gave off the impression that she still wanted to pursue being mates.

Though I never really wanted to commit to one woman as my mate and queen, I have a feeling Norah would be an amazing partner to rule this Kingdom with if we decided to do that.

I never felt that I needed a woman by my side to rule my Kingdom to the best of my ability. My mother disagrees. I know that in theory there are some things that only a woman could have a different point of view on, but I never felt that I needed to go out of my way to tie myself down to one woman.

That is until the hazel eyed woman entered my life and started haunting all of my conscious thoughts and unconscious dreams.

I shake my head. No. I can't think about her right now. She's probably underneath her bo-

No.

"Are you alright, Sin?"

I snap myself out of my thoughts and focus back on the woman in front of me. "Yes, of course. I'm sorry my mind got away from me for a moment." I smile apologetically.

"It's alright." She giggles and sets her menu down. "I'm sure you always have things going round and round in your mind being the king and a successful business owner as well." She smiles.

I go to respond but the waitress comes to a stop in front of our table.

"What can I get for you today, Your Majesty?" She asks making fuck me eyes and completely disregarding the fact that a beautiful woman is with me as my date.

"My date and I will take a bottle of the Uvel Doux Blanc and Syrah. Thank you." I say without taking my eyes off Norah. I think we're both going to need the extra boost these wines have with the enchanted blood for me and wolfsbane for her to get a little buzz.

She blushes before shaking her head with a silent laugh. I find myself smiling as well at her modest behavior because I am far from it.

"Of course, I'll get that for you right away." With that the waitress walks away.

"So I am curious, what made you want to have this dinner?" She asks.

"You're a beautiful woman, why wouldn't I want to take my gorgeous potential mate out for dinner and see if the sparks fly?" I ask, laying it on thick with my flirty smile.

"There's that charm I've heard so much about." She giggles again and I'm finding that I don't mind the sound as much as I thought I would.

"What do you mean?" I ask.

"You do have the reputation of being quite the ladies man." She says so politely it almost hurts. I can tell that she wants to say something more crude I'm sure. I know the reputation surrounding my name and the women that have been in my life as Maverick as so candidly explained to me. I've never really cared what people have said about me because I know who I am and I'm the King of Minaoz so there isn't too much out there to hurt my position regardless of what happens around me.

"That's a very nice way of saying it." I laugh. "I know my reputation, but I like to think that I'm just being nice and charming and I have gotten that label unjustly." I smirk. I know that's a flat out lie.

She laughs knowingly. She knows I'm lying too. She hums as our bottles and glasses come back. "I'm ready to order when you are." She says as she reaches for her glass.

I grab it from her hand gently and open her bottle before pouring her a glass to drink. "You go first, Nor." I say before grabbing my own glass and bottle to pour myself a drink, then place our bottle back in the bucket of ice.

"I'll have the grilled chicken pasta please." She smiles and hands the waitress the menu.

"And I'll have the chicken with the creamy blood sauce and grilled vegetables" I say, handing my menu over as well.

"If you need anything else at all, don't hesitate to ask me." She gives me a flirty smile before walking away. I roll my eyes before looking back at Norah who has her hand over her mouth trying not to laugh.

"Does that happen often?" She asks, still giggling.

"More than I care to admit." I say.

"You never did say the real reason why you wanted to come to this dinner." She asks.

I sigh, "I am being...pressured for a lack of better words to find myself a queen. You are one of my potentials so I wanted to have a more one on one outing to see how things go." I say honestly.

She nods her head and takes a sip of her wine. "I can honestly say that I also came out with you to appease my parents a bit. The other reason is a secret." She winks, peaking my interest.

"Care to share?" I ask sipping from my own glass.

She studies me for a moment. "Let me ask you a question first and you have to be completely honest before I continue. Deal?" Unable to help myself I nod my head in agreement. "Have you met your True Mate?"

I choke on my air as the words leave her lips and images of my little mate flash in front of my eyes. I clench my eyes closed trying to keep the images of her from continuing to bring the ache in my heart along with them.

"You have." She states with a sad tone and when I meet her eyes her face is sympathetic to match her tone. I want to shake my head and deny the truth but I can't. I don't want to deny Anita anymore than I'm already having to. It's killing me but I have no other choice right now. Despite the fact that I don't know a way to save her while having her as my human mate, she is still in a relationship. "Why are you not with her?" She asks.

I take a deep breath and push the pain down. "There are too many things against us so I felt that it was easier to let her live her life as she knows it without dragging her into my world." I say.

Norah leans forward and places her hand over mine and whispers, "She's a lower creature too isn't she."

I snap my eyes to her and open my mouth to answer her before the words she said register in my mind. "Too?" I ask. Her eyes grow wide as she realizes her mistake. "You've met your True Mate and he's a lower level creature?" I ask her in return.

"He is an ogre." She says softly but I can hear the smile in her voice. I can't imagine such a powerful and beautiful woman with an ogre but the heart is an amazing thing. You can't help who you love.

Love?

Do I love Anita? The mate pull must be confusing me.

There's no way I could love a woman I've had two conversations with. That would be insane.

"Is that the problem for you? That he's a lower level creature and your family would not approve?" I ask and she nods her head.

"He also doesn't want to make my life harder despite how we feel about each other. That's Colt for you." She gives a sad laugh.

"Colt? Colt Shavers?" I ask, leaning forward.

"Yes. Do you know him?" She asks with an unreadable emotion in her eyes.

"He's a good friend and bouncer at my club." I say and lean back thinking back. I was deep down in my own shit so I didn't notice at first but Colt has been a little more down than I've ever seen him before but I would've never guessed this was the reason. He's slowly been working his way up with me, gaining my loyalty and respect as time passes.

"Why aren't you with your mate?" She asks me.

I look at her and debate on telling her the biggest secret I have at the moment and one that could put Anita in danger if it's discussed so openly. I look around as discreetly as I can. "She's human and she doesn't know we *are* mates." I whisper quickly while my eyes keep shifting around the area trying to see if anyone overheard our conversation and avoiding Norah's eyes.

"So you're here to get over her?" She asks incredulously after a moment of silence.

"Not entirely. I do still need a queen and she has a boyfriend anyway. She wouldn't survive the court or the pressure of the crown." I say.

"How are you *so* sure the one meant for you wouldn't be able to handle the same burdens as you. She was made for you for a reason, Sinclair."

I can tell she's serious now because for the first time of the night she's said my full name.

I wish I could believe that, believe that my little mate could stand strong and fearless against the world's most fearsome creatures, but I can't allow her to get hurt if I'm wrong. At this point I would rather her live a life without me than being forced to live life knowing she is no longer breathing. Her safety comes first.

We avoid the topic of mates for the rest of the evening and we have a really nice time. I can see our friendship growing in the future but I can't see it ever becoming romantic, especially now that we know that we both have met our True Mates.

After sending Norah home, I have her words playing around in my head. Anita was made to be my one true love and why would she be mated to me if she couldn't rise to the challenge that is being the queen of Minaoz.

I wonder if I'll ever get the chance to see if she can.

Chapter 15
Anita

THINGS HAVE BEEN GOING AS WELL AS THEY CAN.
Kevin and I have been finding our new rhythm and routine.

He works, I work, I come home and cook, I clean up then shower, he comes home and showers, we eat dinner together, then we fuck and go to sleep. Repeat.

I'm sure I could be happier but I'm happy with the way things are. He's putting in more effort. He makes me feel beautiful everyday and like I'm irreplaceable in his life. That's what I really need, to be needed.

I know that sometimes I don't do everything the exact way he may want but I do the best I can and I do truly love him. Kevin has been by my side through a dark time in my life with my family and I can't just ignore all that he's done because things aren't perfect. No life is perfect, we just have to find the right amount of bullshit we can deal with and the right amount of selfless love we need as a minimum to be the happiest we can be.

Tonight, Kevin's taking me out for the first time in forever. We're going to a lower midtown bar that usually will have a good mix of creatures but is a place where humans are more welcome. I'm wearing a dress that stops just past my knees. It's a navy blue color that's tighter around the bust and stomach and flows from the waist down. This dress accentuates my body without showing too much which is how Kevin likes it. He always used to want arm candy but not to the point that he had to worry about other men. It's been a long time since he's taken me anywhere like this, so I'm excited to spend some time with him away from home.

As we come out of our building I start to make my way to the bus station but Kevin's hand on my arm stops me.

"Josh is going to pick us up and he should be here any minute." Kevin says and pulls me back to his side.

So much for having some us time.

Josh arrives about five minutes later. Kevin jumps in shotgun leaving me to let myself slide into the back seat then we're off to Redbird Bar. The boys jump out and start to make their way around the car and the parking lot as I hurry to get out and catch up. As I reach them I grab Kevin's hand and walk by his side. He squeezes my hand and looks down at me with a sweet smile that has me smiling back.

There's no line for a place like this but on the inside it's crowded with shoulder to shoulder standing room only. There's a local goblin band playing smooth music in the background. They sound amazing so I can see why it's so busy.

"I'm going to get us some drinks from the bar. Requests?" Josh yells over the music.

I go to speak but Kevin beats me to it.

"Just get us all some shots and mixers." Kevin grins and Josh winks at me before disappearing into the crowd.

I turn to Kevin to tell him that I really just wanted to stick to something light like beer but I don't get the chance. He shakes his arm around my waist and pulls me tight against his chest, the front of our bodies touching everywhere, and he starts to sway our bodies slowly while grinding his lower half against mine.

I try to get into it as much as I can. In reality I let him lead this grinding dance because I don't usually like to use such explicit moves in public and I need alcohol in my system to really relax. Even around my boyfriend.

It's not long before Josh comes back barely balancing our shots and drinks. We each grab our own and I watch them down theirs like it's water before they turn their eyes to me and I look down, take a deep breath, then throw the liquid back and swallow forcefully while praying the nasty liquor stays down. I've never been much of an alcohol shooter. I always preferred to sip my drinks and enjoy myself while being completely aware of what's going on around me. Diana is the only one I ever take shots with.

I guess if I'm here with Kevin that I can let loose a little. He'd never let anything happen to me.

The boys cheer and we all laugh. I sip on my fruity drink that Josh brought back for me, wishing it was rum and coke instead. The last time I went out that's what I was drinking, even though it's my preferred drink, I can't help but think of the king when I drink it now. I take a deeper pull of the alcohol in my hand trying to chase the images of him out of my mind. I'm out with my boyfriend and his best friend tonight, I can't be thinking of the redheaded vampire king.

I'm pulled out of my thoughts by a tug on my elbow leading me to the bar. Kevin is pulling me along as he trails behind Josh. As we cut through the crowd I sip my drink and let my eyes scan the crowd and fall on a pair of deep red ones burning through me.

No.

I take a deep breath and close my eyes trying to calm my body's reaction to him and open my eyes again and sure enough he's still pinning me with his stare. The way my body reacts to just his attention even from a distance is unreal. My body wants to move closer to him like a planet being pulled to the sun. I unconsciously take a step in his direction before I reach the end of the space I can without pulling from Kevin's hold as a body bumps into mine on their way past me.

"Sin!" The feminine voice shouts.

I flinch at the sound of his name but mainly because it's coming from this woman's mouth. I thought I saw his expression flinch and falter for a second but he composes his face so expertly in seconds I can't be sure. Seconds pass as he returns his gaze on me before a mess of curls block my view and I think I was projecting the pain I feel inside in his eyes. There's no reason for him to look pained seeing me at a bar with my boyfriend while he meets women.

If I keep repeating that in my head enough times I'm sure it'll start to stick and I'll believe it.

"Shots!"

My attention snaps back to Kevin and Josh as they shout and laugh as they order more shots to take. I was going to be the responsible one like always but I want to drown in alcohol now after seeing Sinclair. They chat as they wait for the bartender to work their way to us so we can order and I keep my eyes forward, resisting the urge to turn around and keep my eyes on the handsome man that I can feel has his sights on me again like a caress along my skin.

I lift my eyes away from the boys engaged in a heated conversation that I can't hear and to the mirror in front of me. The back of the bar has a line of liquor along the bottom but with plenty of room above them for me to lock my gaze with the deep red ones. The eyes that sear my skin and spark my blood that's singing for him to come closer and have a taste like I've dreamed about. The heat in his gaze grows like he can read my mind and I have to fight the blush that's threatening to bloom on my cheeks. The smirk that's growing on his lips tells me that the blush is very much there and that thought has it growing further down my neck and disappearing beneath my shirt.

Sinclair's eyes follow the blush and stops on my breast that are most likely red as well but hidden and his eyes turn almost black as he meets my eyes again. Though I want to deny it I know that's desire in his eyes as he absentmindedly nods to whatever the woman next to him is saying as we are locked in a silent tug of war of want and desire.

I've never wanted to throw caution to the wind as much as I do now. To turn away from Kevin and make my way across the room with those captivating red eyes tracking my every move as I make my way to him. Walking slowly with a sway to my hips that comes naturally when walking in heels that has the fire in his eyes stoked and raging. Smiling as I close the distance, the woman is nearly forgotten and she gets upset and storms off once she sees that Sinclair's attention is mine and mine alone. The sexy smirk I love that has my panties wet on his lips and I run my eyes down his frame and see his large cock straining in his jeans has my mouth watering. I've never wanted a man like I want him. I pull my eyes back to him and once I'm in his reach, he lifts his hand to touch me and as his finger tips touch my skin...

"Anita! Come on, we have the shots!" Josh shouts.

I blink and shake my head as I move my eyes away from Sinclair as the fantasy fades out. As I look away from him the entirety of his eyes looks black as night and that can only mean one of three things with a vampire. Rage, hunger, and lust.

I give a sheepish smile to the boys and grab the shot Josh holds out to me with a smile. I turn to Kevin seeing that he already has his shot in his hand but has a calculating look in his eyes as he watches me. I have a sliver of panic shoot through my veins but keep my face neutral. He probably watched me eye fuck our vampire king through a bar mirror.

As the thought starts to shake me more he smiles and clinks his glass with ours.

"To an unforgettable night!" He yells and slams his shot followed by Josh and me.

After that I'm dragged to the dance floor by Kevin as he pulls my front flush with his and the way he's holding me I can only see him before I feel a body come in behind me.

"Room for one more?" Josh rasps in my ear as he grabs my hips with his hands.

Unease shocks my system as the words hold more meaning and I try to move but I'm only pushed tighter between them.

"Of course, man!" Kevin shouts over the music and starts to grind his growing dick on my front and Josh mimics his movements into my ass.

I give Kevin a pleading glance but he ignores me with a fire of desire in his eyes as he bounces his sight between me and his best friend. Bile comes up in my throat at the thought that they could possibly take this further than dancing but shake the thought away. Kevin wouldn't do that to me, he's never made any indication that he would ever want to add someone to our sex life and I would hope he'd know that that isn't something that I'd be comfortable with.

"I'm going to run to the ladies room!" I yell, trying to move from between them. After a few moments of struggling they let me go with a groan and I rush through the crowd of sweaty dancing bodies. I keep my head down until I'm behind a stall door. I lean against the locked door and try to control my breathing and get it back under control. After an undetermined amount of time I go to the sink and splash some cold water on my face and pat my face dry to keep as much of my makeup intact as I can.

Looking at myself now in the mirror for a moment my surroundings tilt slightly. I guess that shot hit me harder than I thought it would. I shake my head to clear my thoughts before heading back out to find the boys with my head held high and the determination to not drink any more alcohol so I can be as clear headed as possible.

On my way back through the crowd I scan the bodies around me trying to find Kevin but my eyes stop and lock with the pair of dark red ones that have been haunting me constantly for weeks.

Sinclair holds my stare with a mixture of emotions running through them but masks them all before I can pin one down. I let my eyes fall down to the beautiful woman currently grinding her ass on his crotch with her eyes closed and head thrown back on his shoulder and one arm wrapped around his neck. I can see his hands on her waist and they flex under my scrutiny. My heart pangs violently in my chest. I rub the area to ease the pressure I have no right to feel. I raise my eyes back to him and give him a sad smile that has his expression softening before I turn away from him to look for Kevin and Josh at the bar.

Everything about the vampire king shakes my foundation. I'm never sure what I should be feeling when I'm around him or even when the thought of him crosses my mind. The guilt of my unfounded desire for the vampire while I'm here with my boyfriend rocks my sanity. Kevin may be a lot of things but he doesn't deserve me entertaining the thought of another man.

As I suspected I find Kevin and Josh laughing and throwing back a shot as I close in on them. I place my hand on Kevin's arm and smile at him. He hands me a drink and I go to protest.

"It's just coke, baby. I thought you'd want to go easy tonight since you have work tomorrow." He smiles and hands me the beverage.

My heart cracks at his sweet and thoughtful gesture. The guilt piles on higher.

"Thank you, that's just what I need." I smile and take a sip. There's a slight bitter taste to it but most creature based establishments have their own variations of soda type drinks and it's hard to pinpoint exactly what you'll get when you go somewhere unless you only ever drink water. It doesn't taste bad, just off so I continue to drink hoping if I finish it quickly I can just go without one for a while as I sober up and then I can only pray by then they're ready to head home. With the way they're throwing the shots back I wouldn't be surprised if I have to try to carry them both out.

I keep my eyes and focus on them as they laugh and joke about a variety of things and try to ignore the weight of the stare that I've felt on me from the moment I came out of the bathroom. He should focus on the woman he's with and not me. I'm nothing but a human anyway. I don't know why we are constantly gravitating around each other like a planet to the sun when we're in a vicinity to each other.

I'm not sure how much time passes but the room steadily spins more and more rather than slowing down. Before I can say anything to Kevin about it he and Josh pull me back to the dance floor and I find myself stumbling over my feet but following them the best I can.

This time I let them hold me without fighting as I try my best to just stay on my feet. I know both of their hands are on various parts of my body but I couldn't tell you whose hands they are and where they are exactly. My vision blurs and I try to lift my head to tell Kevin that I feel off and want to go home, but I can't find the strength to lift my head let only open my mouth. They squeeze me tighter between them and I feel a mouth on my neck and though I want to feel panicked I find myself drooping down, exhausted.

"Let's head home and have some fun, babe."

I don't respond and they start half leading, half carrying me toward the exit. I roll my head to the side just enough to catch Sinclair's eyes before we disappear behind the door. And even in my state I can see the rage burning in his eyes as he starts to make his way towards us. Then the door closes.

There's a cab waiting for us at the curb as we exit and Kevin slides in first before they both help me in with Josh following behind and we're off pulling into traffic. My head pulls to the side and time escapes me then the next thing I know I'm being carried through my front door, down the hall, and laid on my bed.

I sigh, so ready for sleep and to wake up tomorrow and leave this night behind me.

As I'm just drifting off I feel my clothes being pulled on.

"Kevin, I'll just sleep like this." I mumble trying to bat him away so I can sleep.

"I thought we were going to play." I hear a deep voice say.

That's not Kevin. I pry my eyes open to look back as Josh is the one undressing me. A chill rushes over my skin. And I look around for Kevin and see him coming out of the bathroom in only his boxers with a mischievous smile on his lips.

"Let's play." He claps his hands together with a laugh and nods to Josh as he makes his way toward us at the bed.

"Kevin what the hell!" I try to hell at him but my voice comes out in a whisper.

"Come on, babe. You've been dancing on us both all night, now we're going to finish what you started at the bar." Josh says.

I shake my head no and try to scoot away from them but they each grab one of my ankles and pull me toward them. Panic flashes through me like lightning and I use all the strength I can muster to kick out at them as hard as I can. I hear them groan and I roll off the bed and see Josh holding his balls while Kevin is holding his nose while blood pours out.

"You bitch!"

I don't look back as I run barefooted out of the apartment

with only my clutch from tonight. Adrenaline pumping through my veins pushes me faster as I rush out the door and down the stairs onto the street and just run as fast as I can for as long as I can. I don't know how much time passes but the sun is starting to peak over the horizon as I come up to Diana's complex. I ring her buzzer relentlessly until I hear her groan over the microphone.

"Who in the fuck is here so God damn early?"

"It's me." I choke out.

The door immediately clicks open and I continue my previous pace up to her door where she's waiting for me more alert than she seemed a moment ago. The sight of her has me bursting in tears and collapsing in her arms.

"Who in the fuck do I have to murder?" She growls out.

Chapter 16
Sinclair

THERE'S NOTHING I HATE MORE THAN BEING FORCED to do something I really don't want to do, and that seems to be a revolving concept happening to me lately. You'd think that being king would prevent me from having to suffer through anything like that or that it'd keep people from believing I'd do anything they say. I'm the vampire king, I rule Minaoz, and yet here I am. If I wanted to go out and drink I would go to my own club where I don't have to pay for my drinks and keep to my own space without groups of people bumping into me on purpose with flirty smiles hoping to get lucky. Men and women alike.

The night I had with Norah ended with me frustrated and ending up in bed with the last woman I should've because she's already getting clingy but I needed to forget and release and I knew she would be easy and always ready for me. That's how I've now ended up at Redbird Bar being dragged around beside Robyn as she shows me off like I'm some show pony she's using to elevate her status and make her friends jealous. I don't give a flying fuck as long I keep the alcohol coming and can get my dick wet at the end of the night fantasizing it's my little mate.

Yes. My little mate.

I've gotten to the point that I know that I'll never be able to rid her from my mind so I do the next best and most toxic thing possible. Have sex with women and pretend it's my Anita and that it's even close to as amazing as it would be if I were making love to my True Mate.

I'm not sure if it's the strain on the bond, the constant state of alcoholism, stress from work and my mother on my ass, or a combination of them all but I'm even starting to see her everywhere.

I keep my eyes on the hallucination version of Anita in front of me being pulled through the crowd to the bar. My heart stutters in my chest and my mouth waters as I can actually smell her sweet scent of vanilla and citrus. My mind is really going above and beyond tonight. The navy blue dress that's hugging her breasts has my cock straining in my slacks and I shift my weight to relieve some of the pressure. I lick my lips imagining what I would do if it were really her in front of me now.

Those thoughts stop before they can even begin because when she raises her eyes in my direction and we lock gazes I nearly choke on my spit.

It really is my little mate.

Anita.

My eyes train on her like lasers and I can't break my gaze from her even if I wanted to but I could drown in the sight of her for eternity. I see the blush start to work its way from her cheeks to the column of her neck. What I would give to bury my face in her neck and just take one little bite...

"Sin!"

My fantasy once again implodes because of Robyn. She

knocks into my mate on her way to me in the most ostentatious way possible that has a flash of anger pulse through my veins. That's when I look back to see that my little mate is being pulled by a human male by her elbow toward the bar that Robyn just came back from with our drinks.

He's average height with short brown hair, seems to have some muscle but looks like a twig compared to me. His tight grip on Anita's arm has rage building in me for handling her in such a way but he must be the boyfriend. This is who she loves? This little toothpick? While my ego is simultaneously boosted and shattered at the sight of him my attention is taken when Robyn practically throws herself into my arms.

"Sorry, baby. The line was so busy and the bartender obviously didn't know who she was getting the drinks for or the slut would have gotten mine first." She rolls her eyes as she hands me my drink. I grit my teeth to keep my comment to myself on her nasty words. I don't feel like having a fight with her tonight.

I nod my head as she chats away not even noticing that I'm not listening and my eyes go back to Anita. After a few minutes of admiring her delicious ass she catches my eyes in the mirror as her group settles back at the bar. She must be able to see the heat and lust in my eyes judging by the crimson blush that's traveling down her creamy skin. I follow it's travel all the way down to her breasts where it disappears behind her neckline. I lick my lips at the thought of following it all the way down with my tongue until her blush either stops or covers her entire body. I want to run my tongue over every inch of her creamy skin and nip at the flesh right above her beating heart and taste that sweet blood that will be my own personal aphrodisiac and exclusive blood source.

When vampires meet their True Mate and drink from them that becomes the only blood they can stomach. Almost all creatures mate for life, especially vampires. Imagining tasting Anita's sweet blood for the rest of eternity has my fangs aching for a taste right now.

I raise my eyes back up and see her pupils blown wide with only a sliver of hazel to be seen as she holds my gaze. Nothing else needed for us to know our desires are going wild for each other right now. What I wouldn't give to go and whisk her away now and have my way with her.

She whips her head to the side, cutting off our connection because one of the boys she's with called her and she doesn't look back. I try to simmer down the lust and rage I have raging inside my body at her and the guys that she's with. I want her all to myself. That's all I've truly wanted since meeting her, whether I wanted to admit it at the time or not. I keep my eyes on her but they connect with a pair of angry blue ones as if he's trying to murder me with his eyes.

It's cute really that this human thinks he can intimidate me or that I couldn't have her if I wanted to at this very moment.

I rip my eyes from Anita when I feel a tug on my arm. I look down at Robyn's scowl and cringe inwardly.

"Done eye fucking that human slut?" She props her hand on her waist and cocks her hip out with a brow raised in question. I have to swallow down the retort I want to say back down for no other reason than the fact that I don't feel like fighting with her right now. I also don't want to give anyone any hints that Anita is actually my True Mate.

I give her a cocky smile to mask my true emotions. "For now." I wink and she just rolls her eyes and turns her body back around and backs her ass up against my hard cock that still hasn't deflated from the sight of my little mate.

"Looks like I'm the one making you hard though, babe." She purrs and throws an arm around my neck and continues to grind her ass on me.

I place my hands on her waist, about to stop her movements before she realizes that my dick is starting to deflate at her movements but I raise my head and lock my gaze once again on those beautiful hazel ones that have been in my mind constantly chasing away any thought I've had about anything other than her.

The emotions running through me relentlessly hit me like a tidal wave as I see her wide and red teary eyes. The need to sweep her in my arms and kill whoever made her cry is overwhelming. I school my face immediately to keep suspicion away but the rage building again has my hands gripping tight.

I hear Robyn's moan at my movement and she presses into me further that has me releasing her immediately not remembering that she was the one my hands were on. Anita follows my hand movement before she meets my eyes again and gives me the fakest smile I've ever seen that has my heart squeezing painfully in my chest. She drags her gaze from mine and continues through the crowd.

I'm not sure how long I stare after her but Robyn's hands on each side of my face bring me back to the present and I look into her green eyes that are close but not close enough to the ones I want to be staring into. Her calculating stare would raise alarm if I wasn't who I am. Regardless I smile at her seductively and wrap my arms around her, pulling tight to my chest. She runs her hands from my face and down my neck to my chest, dragging her nails on the way. A move that always made my cock jump in the past but now I have to imagine it's someone else to get a reaction. I always have to picture Anita now to get it up.

The joys of the mate bond.

She'll never know that the one pulling the reaction out of me has nothing to do with her. Robyn has always only looked out for herself and what she can get from people so I doubt she'll notice. That's what always made her my go to fuck buddy because I don't ever feel bad about using her the same way she uses me.

"I can't wait to feel that giant dick stretching my wet pussy out as you fuck me." She moans in my ear.

I close my eyes battling with myself on if this is what I should be doing. I don't know what I'm doing anymore and seeing Anita tonight isn't making the decisions any easier.

"Let's have one more drink and we can get out of here." I whisper in her ear and she gives me a wide smile, nods her head, and skips away to get our drinks.

At least she's always a good fuck so the torture I'm putting myself through isn't all for nothing.

"To us." Robyn says as she comes back holding up our drinks. I take mine from her and we clink our glasses together before each taking a large gulp out. I down mine in one more swallow before setting it down on a nearby table. She gives me a playful smile as she takes another pull from her straw. I try to smile back and look around the bar once more, wanting one more look at my little mate before I do what I need to do to get off and I'll drown in guilt later.

I sweep my eyes across the bodies grinding on the dance floor and start to think maybe she's left already but I stiffen and pale at the sight of her going through the rear exit door. She has a panicked look in her eyes as she's practically being carried out by the two guys she's with, barely being able to stand on her own feet. I take two steps in her direction on instinct before the door slams and cuts off our connection and my own wave of panic rockets through my veins.

I had planned to just keep an eye on her from afar to keep up the pretense that I don't know her or that she means nothing to me but my basic instincts are propelling me forward to protect our mate from danger.

"Sin, where are you going!" I hear Robyn yell after me as I

pick up my pace to get out the door and to my little mate. Something doesn't feel right, something's wrong.

I burst through the door and look up and down the street but she's nowhere to be seen. My heart beats violently in my chest, adrenaline running wild. I scramble to get my phone out of my pocket and dial the only person I trust to help me.

"Clair, why are you calling me at this late hour when you're supposed to be getting your dick wet in that psycho's gaping cunt?" Maverick jokes as he answers.

"Somethings wrong with her." I rush out and keep looking around praying I get a glimpse of her.

"Uh, yeah. There's a shit ton wrong with that crazy nymph."

Nymph?

"No! I'm talking about Anita. I saw her here tonight and something's wrong."

"Your mate?"

"Yes, Mav. I need your help. She was being carried out by the two guys she was with but she seemed fine maybe an hour before and then she was barely conscious. I'm starting to freak out."

"Alright, alright. Calm down for me, dude. Where are you?"

"I'm at Redbird." I say and sway on my feet as my surroundings start to duplicate.

"Ok. I'm on my way and we'll figure it out ok?"

"Y-yeaaaaah." I stumble and lean my back on the wall behind me and brace myself with my free hand not holding my phone and try to stay on my feet. "Ugh, my head."

"Dude how much did you drink, damn." He tuts at me.

"Two. Only two...." What in the hell is happening to me? My throat feels like it's closing in and I struggle to get oxygen to my lungs. "What the f-fuck is going..." I start but black spots cover my vision and the phone slips from my hand. I try to reach to catch it but lose my balance and fall towards the pavement. On my way down I think I hear Maverick yell something but everything goes black before I even hit the pavement.

Chapter 17
Anita

MY EYES FLUTTER OPEN SLOWLY, STILL SWOLLEN from all of the crying I did the night before. I look around and see that I'm lying in the middle of Diana's queen sized bed alone. I prop myself up on my arms shakily, my body lacking the energy to do anything. I push myself up and out of the bed anyway and make my way to her bathroom. Inside I turn on the light but keep my eyes down as I make my way in front of the mirror and do my business but when I'm washing my hands the temptation is too much and I raise my eyes and get the full view of my red and splotchy face, swollen eyes, and tear stains still marking my cheeks.

I don't remember much of last night after I fell into Diana's comforting arms and then telling her how my night went that followed with me holding her back from actually committing murder. She always has my back when I need her.

Thoughts of my best friend have me abandoning my reflection and moving through her high rise apartment to find her.

I turn the corner and see her walking away from her coffee

machine with two mugs in her hand and she jumps slightly at the sight of me.

"Damn, woman! You about gave me a heart attack." She breathes out and meets me halfway to hand me the mug she filled for me.

"Always so dramatic." I mumble and take a sip of heaven in my mug.

"Lies." Is all she says as she walks past me to the nook that overlooks the city from her floor to ceiling window with a small little two person table that we always sit at for our coffee chats. It's been a while since we've had one.

"How are you this morning?" She asks softly.

I shrug, "I'm fine. I promise."

"Don't do that."

"Do what?"

"Don't just brush off what happened like it's no big deal. Those assholes almost took advantage of you, Annie."

I take a deep breath and look into my mug but don't say anything. She's right but if I dwell on it then I will never not think about it and I need to think about something else.

"I know. I just need a little more time. It's too fresh to think about right now." I sigh.

I can tell by her expression that she doesn't want to let this go but does for now. I need to feel normal right now, not that I was almost assaulted by my long-time boyfriend and his friend. As if reading my mind, she changes the subject.

"I saw our blood sucking leader recently, spilt hot coffee on him, chewed him out, then went on about my business." She says so nonchalantly as if telling me she just got some more ice cream from the grocery store.

"I'm sorry, what!?" I choke out.

"You heard me." Her lip twitches as she fights to smile and continues to sip her coffee while looking out over the city as if she didn't just tell me she assaulted our king and the man that's been on my mind constantly.

"Why would you do that? Do you know what Sinclair could do to you for that?"

"He won't do shit." She laughs.

"How can you be so sure?"

"I'm your best friend duh." She rolls her eyes like I should already know this.

"And you being my best friend matters because...?"

She just shakes her head and takes a sip of her coffee and I sigh knowing I'm not going to get anything else out of her.

"Do you mind if I stay with you for a while?" I ask after a few minutes of silence.

"Well yeah. You sure as fuck aren't going back to live with tweedle dick." She grumbles and I fight a laugh at the new nickname. "You are going to end this relationshit now aren't you?" She asks.

"I don't see how I can stay with him after what happened."

"Not like you were super happy with baby dick anyway."

I shake my head at her with a smile. I can always count on Diana to put a smile on my face even when it's the last thing I feel like doing.

"I know. I can't force a feeling that just isn't there anymore." I agree with her and it's like a weight immediately lifts off my shoulders just saying the words.

"You work today?" She asks.

"Yeah, not till tonight so there's plenty of time for me to get myself together before I have to be around other people."

"Luckily for you I still have some of your spare scrubs and such here and we can go get your shit from your place later and pray Kevvy is there so I can kick him in the balls."

"Why." I laugh.

"He'll know why." Is all she says with a smile.

Diana and I spend the next few hours catching up on everything that's been going on in our lives, which was really her just telling me about her latest conquests and shit she's been giving her parents. The *Montgomery Rebel Child* is what the tabloids have been calling her. With her parents being in the spotlight more now due to them being well known human actors, Diana's been more difficult lately it seems but seeing the huge smile on her face right now as she tells me of all her shenanigans I can't help but laugh and love her all the more for it.

"Do you know where my phone is?" I ask after realizing I haven't seen it since waking up this morning.

"Yea I plugged it in in the kitchen." She says as she points toward the kitchen.

I stand and make my way over to my phone. Picking it up I see that it's dead which is probably a good thing. I hold the power button to bring it back to like and set it back down. As I suspected it starts dinging and vibrating non stop as notification after notification comes in back to back. After a few minutes when it finally stops I pick it up and see the damage. There's about one hundred texts, calls, and emails combined from Kevin alone, Josh has some thrown in there too. I skip over those for now, not ready to see what could possibly be in them and move to the rest. A few from Mom, and Diana I hadn't seen from earlier in the night, and two more from Mom this morning. I quickly message her back and tell her that I'll call back later.

The last message is followed by a missed call and voicemail from the Hospital. I quickly read over the message that only says to call as soon as possible and the voicemail saying the same. I quickly dial the front desk.

"Minaoz Central Hospital, how can I help you."

"Hey, this is Anita Carras. I'm an emergency room nurse and I have a message to call as soon as possible." I say.

"Oh! Yes, yes. They've been waiting so let me patch you through immediately ma'am." I hear the background music start as I wait for the line to reconnect to the nurses station in my section of the hospital.

"Anita!"

I pull the phone from my ear as Sarah screams through the phone.

"Damn Sarah, my human ear drums are sensitive." I grumble.

"You need to get here as soon as possible! A very powerful patient is here and is refusing to let anyone in the room to see him, even his parents and the doctors. He says he'll only let you into the room."

"What the hell?" I say. "Who is it?"

And just like that the breath is stolen from my lungs and I'm rushing to get to the hospital as fast as possible.

"It's King Archer and he's been poisoned."

Chapter 18
Sinclair

Beep.

Beep.

Beep.

Beep.

The sound of constant beeping is what wakes me up. I try to roll over to hit my alarm and groan at my stiff muscles. My entire body aches. What in the hell did I do last night? I need to lay off the booze.

I reach my arm out but it gets snagged on something. I open my eyes to see that it's not snagged but a needle in my arm with an IV attached to it. I look around more to see that I'm in a hospital room. What the fuck happened last night?

"Oh, honey you're awake I'll get the doctor!" I turn at the sound of my mothers voice just as she speeds out of the room and closes it behind her.

I'm in the hospital. I'm a patient at Minaoz Central Hospital. Anita works here. I wonder if my little mate is here.

Wait.

The bar, Redbird.

I was with Robyn and saw Anita there with those guys

and they ended up carrying her out when she was practically passed out. My breath comes in short pants as the adrenaline and panic I was feeling in the moment comes back full force. I need to know what happened to her.

Now.

"Hello, Mr. Arch-"

"Get Anita Carras in here now." I cut off the same fucking doctor that pulled Anita away from the conversation we were having that day I visited the hospital.

"I'm sorry, sir. Nurse Carras is not on duty today, I have another nurse that is here to help you." Dr. Stevenson says motioning for the female fairy nurse in her too tight scrubs walking through the door and I lose it.

"Get out." I say through gritted teeth trying to rein in my anger.

"Mr. Archer..."

"I said get out!" I shout. "If the next person that walks through this door is *not* Anita Carras, I will drain them where they stand." I sneer at them and when they're stunned forms don't immediately move I reach for the pitcher of water on the bedside table and launch it against the wall next to them. That seems to work as they scurry out of the room as fast as they can.

How dare they? They think they can tell their king what to do? Like my demands shouldn't be met? If I want a specific nurse then that's what I get. Not some sexed up version of a nurse that they think I want to see. The disrespect and insult that came with that fairy just walking in the door makes me want to burn this fucking place the ground.

There's multiple reasons why I wouldn't do that but the urge remains.

I'M NOT SURE HOW MUCH TIME PASSES.

Dr. Stevenson tries to enter again to tell me that they haven't been able to get a hold of Anita as of yet and tries to come inspect me again but hearing that she hasn't been heard from, sends me into a rage. I leap off the bed and hold him to the wall with his feet off the floor by his throat. My natural vampire instincts take over as I hiss in his face as if it's his fault my little mate is still missing. I wish I could leave and look for her myself but I quickly found out that just getting out of bed drains my energy almost completely. It wasn't long before I collapsed and fought them on getting me back to the bed.

When they continued to ignore my wishes I had to make my point known. The same nurse from before had the nerve to come into my room against my wishes and proceeded to take off her scrubs trying to tempt me. I've been pushed for the last time and in seconds I had my hand around her throat and my fangs in her neck as I drained her of every drop of blood in her body. The door opened as I dropped her lifeless body to the ground. While her fairy blood gave me a boost, after the frantic hospital team removed her body I violently threw up every bit of her blood as my body rejected it.

No one can get within an arm's length of me now. Even my own parents finally stopped trying to enter my room after saying that I would pretend they weren't family if they kept defying my orders. My body is coiled tight now as I stare at the ceiling as worry washes over me.

She's fine.

She has to be fine.

I repeat this over and over enough times until I start to believe it. There's many reasons as to why she wouldn't answer her phone. I'm sure of it. She's fine.

The fact that I can't be on my feet more than a few minutes at a time without collapsing is pissing me off.

I try to relax and close my eyes and picture my little mate

healthy and alive. Her smile directed at me sends my nerve endings into a frenzy. I've never felt more alive than the few moments we've had to spend together.

I must have dozed off because I woke to the sound of the door to my room opening.

"I thought I said…" I start to shout but stop at the smell of citrus and vanilla.

"Sin…" She breathes out. Her hand is still on the door-knob as she closes the door softly.

My eyes snap to hers. She's really here.

"Anita…" I sigh, relieved she's really here. I let my eyes trail over her rumpled scrubs, messy bun, and face clear of makeup. She looks like she rushed to get here but is still as beautiful as ever. I swing my legs over the side of the bed, ready to get up and move my way over to her but stop dead in my tracks.

Her smile is happy but sullen and defeated at the same time. Her eyes, while relieved, are still filled with pain.

"What happened?" I ask.

"I should be asking you what happened. You're the one in a hospital bed." She tries to smile and joke but I'm not going to let her brush this off.

"Did someone say something to you before you walked into this room?" I push.

She flinches but recovers quickly. But not quick enough.

"Of course not, Your Majesty." Seeing my mate bow to me has bile rising in my throat. "You asked for me?" She asks.

"I'll answer your question if you'll answer mine honestly this time."

She freezes and looks at me with wide eyes before she lets a small smile appear on her face. "I already know you asked for me. They wouldn't have called me otherwise." She says. "Let's get you checked out so Dr. Stevenson can come finish the examination. You have people who are waiting to see you as well so let's not keep them waiting." She smiles and slowly makes her way to me while keeping her eyes on the chart I wasn't aware was in her hands and walks to the machines next to me to get ready to check my vitals.

I let her start her work as I keep my eyes trained on her, hoping that something on the surface will clue me in on what is going on inside her mind.

Her movements are quick and accurate. I can tell by just her demeanor that she loves her work. She seems to thrive in this line of work which has me wondering how long she's been a nurse. Unable to resist, I ask. "How long have you been a nurse?"

She looks at me briefly before her concentration goes back to her work.

"I've been out of nursing school for three years."

"But how long have you been a nurse?" I ask again.

She lets out a heavy breath before giving me her full attention. "I've been working in his hospital as a nurse for almost a year. Now, lay down flat so I can continue my exam."

I do as she says and she listens to my lungs before feeling along my ribs and stomach. Logically I know that she's being completely professional but my body can't help getting excited by her touch. I will my boner to not make an appearance.

"What did you do before you were a nurse here?" I ask, trying to distract myself from her dainty hands on my body.

"I worked here as soon as I got out of school. I also did some training to get other qualifications under my belt."

My bros furrow, "You just said..."

"Sinclair." She cuts me off and pins me in place with her eyes and the use of my full name. "I'm a human." She says it as if held all the answers to any of my future questions.

"I know."

She sighs before giving me that sad smile that twists my heart. "Your Majesty, I'm not sure how aware you are of us lower beings but because I am a human I had to work three times as hard as everyone else to even be considered to be able to work alongside higher up creatures. Even though I was more qualified for the job. That is the world we live in and I'm not complaining or expecting things to change. But please don't sit here and pretend like you don't know why it was hard for me as a human to get a mid level job." She says in a rush and I can hear her voice get more agitated as she goes on, passionate about her race's situation it seems.

She's right though. I'm not ignorant about her race's situation but in my mind because she's my mate half the time I don't see her as a normal human. She's the Northern Vampire King's True Mate, if people knew who she was to me then she would definitely get special treatment.

I also hate her addressing me as Your Majesty.

She takes a step away from me and looks down at the chart in her hands as she writes something down. "Well from what I can see you're very lucky that someone called you an ambulance when they did. While you were unconscious they were able to pump the poison out of your system."

"Poison?"

"Yes, Ricin. It looks like someone wanted to do some real damage to you, luckily being what you are saved your life. Vampires aren't easy to get rid of." She says with a small smile. "Since the poison is out of your system you'll be able to recover much faster. You'll still feel lethargic from moving around but your advanced healing should solve that for you very soon. Now, I'll get your doctor and there are people waiting to see you."

She goes to make her way to the door but I reach my hand out and stop her before she can. My skin in contact with hers sends volts of electricity through my veins. I hear her tense and gasp. I know she feels the same thing I'm feeling, maybe not as intense but she can feel the bond. I want to tell her everything but first I need to know what happened last night.

"Are you alright?" I ask.

"What do you mean?" She keeps her body facing away from me so I can't see her face but I can hear the tremor in her voice.

"I saw those two men carry you out of the bar last night. I tried to follow you but collapsed when I reached the street and saw that you weren't there." I say in a rush.

I see her take a deep breath before she turns to face me directly. "I'm fine, Your Majesty." She says with a smile that I can tell is a front to hide something.

"Please, don't call me that."

"Your Majesty?" She asks.

"Yes. Please, don't call me that. Not you." I say.

"Why?" Her brows furrow and she takes a step closer, searching my eyes for an answer.

"Do you feel anything when you look at me?" I ask instead.

She hesitates but answers, "Yes."

"What do you feel?"

She chews on her bottom lip and I have to strain to stay in place to not take that lip between my own teeth.

"Calm, but my heart races at the same time."

I smile and rub my thumb up and down the skin on her forearm. "Do you feel anything when I touch you?"

"Yes."

"What?"

"It feels like electricity..." She fades off as if not sure herself.

"I feel it too." I say and she snaps her eyes to mine, looking for a lie that won't be there. "Do you know what that means?"

"It couldn't be what I think it is." She says.

"Tell me." I tug on her arm until she is slowly coming closer to me.

"I can't be, Sin." She mumbles while looking down but

still allows me to tug her closer until she's standing between my legs so I can wrap my arms around her waist to keep her there.

"Why not, Anita?"

"I'm human."

"I don't care." I say firmly. I may have had doubts before but not anymore. Seeing her being handled by those men put a fear in me I've never known before, being poisoned myself put so many things in perspective for me. I want her to see it in my eyes and hear it in my voice that I'm choosing her despite what anyone may say.

"You should." She turns her head to look out the window.

I grab her chin between my thumb and forefinger to pull her face back to me so she's looking into my eyes when I say this.

"You're my True Mate, Anita Carras. Not a potential mate, but my True Mate. You being a human isn't going to change how I feel about you and the fact that I want to be with you."

I see her freeze as I speak but she doesn't say anything for a while. I probably shouldn't be saying this knowing she has a boyfriend but I honestly don't give two fucks. I try not to let the silence drag me down as a rejection because I know she needs a few minutes to process this but my wilder side is getting impatient for an answer.

"You don't have to answer right n-."

She cuts me off with her lips on mine, her arms around my neck, fingers laced in my hair, and body pressed against mine. I smile into her kiss before I flip us over and prepare to devour her whole.

Chapter 19
Sinclair

I cover her body with mine. I slip my right hand into her hair and my left grazing the outside of her thigh wishing the scrubs she's wearing weren't blocking me from her creamy skin.

"Sin-" She gasps.

"That's right, baby. Say my name again." I trail my nose along her neck, breathing in the sweet scent of her blood. My mouth salivates at the thought of tasting her on my tongue in every way possible.

"We're in the hospital." She breathes out while placing her hands on my chest but not pushing me away. Just letting her hands rest there.

"Yes, we are." I run my tongue along the column of her neck and I can feel the heat coming off of her skin. The slight taste of sweat on her skin hits my taste buds and only has me running my tongue over her again and again.

"Someone's going to catch us..."

"Then they're going to get a hell of a show, because I'm not letting you go." I say and cover her mouth with my own. I swallow her moan that has me pressing more of my body into her. Covering her completely.

Her hands on my chest grip my hospital gown tight and start to pull me in and I'm more than willing to oblige and show her just how much I want her. She gasps at the feeling of my rock hard cock pressing against her warm core through my boxer briefs.

I run my tongue along the seam of her lips and she opens her mouth immediately for me and I dive in and trace every inch of her mouth, exploring all of her. My hand grips her hair in a firm fist and tug lightly and I'm rewarded with the sexiest breathy moan I've ever heard that makes my dick twitch. My other hand trails the outside of her thigh lightly over her scrub pants, wishing that it was on her skin instead.

When my fingers reach the waistband of her pants I let my finger tips tug on the hem lightly and run across the skin there just above her underwear. I want nothing more than to strip her down and take her right here. There are so many things I want to do with her body, to savor the moment but right now my urges are taking control of my body.

"Ahh...Sin..." Her hands travel down without me realizing and I feel her dainty hands on the hard lines of my stomach that makes the muscles flex under her touch. The feeling of her touching me like this makes me feel like I'm being electrocuted with the bond pulsing under the surface, pushing me to complete our mating right here and now.

"Anita...I want to taste every inch of your skin." I smash my lips back to hers and let my hand slip into the front of her pants and her panties without much protest from her, too dazed with lust and desire.

I keep my movements slow in case she wants me to stop and to build up the anticipation of what she knows coming next. While I want nothing more than to take her and bury my cock so deep into her pussy that we become one person like our souls coming together as they should, I don't want the first time I have sex with my True Mate to be in an uncomfortable hospital bed.

I let my fingers trail down past the path of the small patch of hair so I can feel her slit and I run them over the length lightly.

"Mmmm...so wet for me already and I've barely even touched you." I smirk at the red hue coating her cheeks and traveling down to her breasts. "Does the risk of someone coming in and seeing me playing with your body turn you on? Dirty girl." I whisper in her ear before taking her ear lobe in my mouth and pressing on her bundle of nerves and moving in slow circles.

"Mmmmm!" She tries to quiet her moans but really any creature in a fifty foot radius can probably hear her moans of pleasure.

"Better be quiet, Love. Someone may hear me bringing you pleasure." I tut at her quietly with a chuckle and move my thumb to her clit and let my middle finger get coated in her juices before putting pressure on her tight little pussy. "I'm going to bring you that high you're wanting and you are going to come on my fingers. Can you do that for me?" I ask while nibbling on her jaw line.

She lets her eyes flutter open and I lean back to meet her gaze. She searches my eyes and I can see the moment she makes her decision to give into her desires. I smile at her and let my other hand slide down and wrap around her neck firmly but not hinder her breathing, just showing her who's in control.

"Yes."

"Good girl."

With that I plunge my finger into her pussy and she arches into me. I piston my finger and in and out of her dripping pussy while my thumb circles around her clit. While I would rather be able to take my time with her, I also don't want anyone to see my little mate overcome with pleasure. Anita in ecstasy is only for me to see.

I apply more pressure to her neck, "Do you think of me when you pleasure yourself?" I ask and she moans out behind her tightly closed lips. "Do you imagine I'm the one touching your needy pussy just like I am right now?" Her hips start to move to chase her orgasm and that has me adding another finger then another before curling them, hitting that spot inside that has her body shaking and her teething sinking into her bottom lip to keep herself quiet. I pick up my pace as I start to feel a little light headed but I'm determined to get my little mate off. "Come." I command then slam my lips to hers to swallow her cries of pleasure as she rides out her orgasm, using my fingers to prolong the aftershocks.

I tangle my tongue with hers until I feel her body sag when the final waves of her orgasm fade away.

"Such a good girl." I coo at her as I pull my hand from her panties. I keep my eyes locked on hers as I raise my hand to my mouth and suck the juices off my fingers. "You taste delicious, love. I can't wait to taste it as you come on my tongue."

"Sin!" She squeaks and throws her hands over her face and I see that beautiful blush take over her creamy white skin again.

I love seeing her turn red for me. I wonder what other ways I can turn that skin red...

"What about you?" She reaches forward for the band of my underwear but I catch her wrist before she can pull them down.

"Don't worry about me, little mate. This was for you. I'll be okay." I say and raise her wrist to my lips and plant a soft kiss on the vein there. It pulses for me like a siren call to have a taste.

Soon.

Soon I'll have her in every way I want, consequences be damned.

Chapter 20
Anita

I CAN'T BELIEVE WE JUST DID THAT IN A HOSPITAL room, in the hospital that I work at, with all of his friends and family right outside the door.

I want to curl up into a ball and die from the embarrassment alone.

"I love it when you turn red." His voice husks in my ear from behind me. I cleaned myself up as best as I could in the joining bathroom and came out with the intent to leave and let everyone in the room that's been waiting to see Sinclair but stopped when the thought that they heard everything crossed my mind.

"Don't tease me. We shouldn't have done that." I say.

He spins me around and pulls me against his hard chest. "Why is that?"

"We're in public Sin..."

"And?" He raises a brow.

"That should stay in bedrooms where it belongs." I say.

He studies me for a moment before a smirk grows on his face. "I'm going to have so much fun corrupting the conservative in you."

"On a different subject," I ignore his comment and pretend like my cheeks aren't flaming red like he seems to love so much. "What happened last night?"

"What do you mean?" He tucks a loose hair behind my ear that fell from my ponytail.

"You're in the hospital for being poisoned! How the hell did that happen?"

"You're a little spit fire when you want to be aren't you?" He asks with a chuckle but I am not amused. "Okay, okay." He raises his hands in defense and backs up until he reaches the bed and takes a seat and leans back to hold his weight up with his hands. "I remember taking a drink not long before I saw you being carried out of the bar. When I tried to follow, that's when I got dizzy. I was able to call Maverick and talk briefly before everything went black." He stares at the ceiling as he tells his story and his brows pull closer together as he goes.

"Do you know who did this?" I whisper.

"Yes." Is all he says and I can tell from his tone that he's done talking about this for now. It doesn't stop me from wanting to know who did this to him and make them pay for what they've done.

When he confirmed that we are True Mates so many things that I've been feeling make so much more sense now. I have been drowning in a guilt that I shouldn't have felt in the first place because he's the one person I'm supposed to spend my life with. How will this work though? Me? Queen? There's too much going on right now for me to think about, so I will just revisit that information later when I get back to Diana's house. She's going to lose her shit.

"You never told me what happened after you left last night Anita." He says and when I look back at him, he's pinning me in my place with his dark eyes like a silent command to tell him the truth right this second.

"Noth-"

"Do not lie to me, Anita." His eyes and voice are stern. Seeing him radiate such authority has my body crumbling and wanting to please him. I can see the king in front of me now, not the man that just brought me the most mind blowing orgasm with only his fingers.

I take a deep breath, "Nothing happened, really."

He studies me with narrowed eyes, "but something almost did." He states.

I look away from him and out the window. I don't want to think about what happened anymore. I had a boyfriend yesterday and now I've had another man touch me less than twenty four hours later. What kind of woman does that make me? True Mate or not.

I don't hear him move but I feel his hand on my chin pulling my face until our eyes meet and I see a range of emotions flashing in his red eyes. He doesn't say anything for a while like he's reading the story of what happened in my eyes and I don't try to hide the pain I feel over what almost happened from him. I don't feel the need to be strong in front of him because I can feel in my soul that he will always be strong for me when I can't.

"I'll kill them." He finally says with rage blazing in his eyes.

"They aren't worth it."

"But you are."

My heart flutters in my chest as his words and my body leans into his. I want to melt into his embrace and never leave this safe and comforting feeling I get when I'm around him. I lean my cheek on his chest as he wraps me in his arms and rocks us slightly side to side with his chin resting on the top of my head. There aren't any words needed right now.

The sound of a knock on the door has us pulling apart. I look to the door before turning my gaze to Sinclair but he's already looking at me.

"You have people that have been waiting to see you so I'll let you have time with them." I say although that's the last thing I want to do right now and go to pull away but he only grips me tighter.

"I'm not letting you out of my sight."

"Sincl-"

"No." He cuts me off and grabs my face in both of his hands. "If I let you out of my sight I will tear down everything and everyone in my way to get you back in my arms." He strokes my cheeks with his thumbs. "I need you to stay with me for a while, little mate."

I smile and nod my head and let him lead me back to the bed as he sits and I stand next to him.

"Come in." He calls out with such authority I feel a gush of wetness release into my already soaked panties. I see him sniff the air then snap his head to face me with a hungry look in his eyes.

As the door opens I spin away from the sinful vampire and pick up his medical chart and read over the results again for the tenth time since being in this room with him as a distraction.

"How are we doing in here?" I recognize Dr. Stevenson's voice as he closes the door behind him and makes his way toward the bed. I turn my head and see his eyes shifting up and down my body then to Sinclair. I'm not sure what he's looking for.

"She's satisfied." Sinclair responds and I nearly choke on air. I whip my head around with wide eyes and freeze.

"She is a great nurse. If she says you're out of danger then you must be." Dr. Stevenson smiles at me, completely missing what the naughty vampire was really saying. Thank Lord.

"She is." Sinclair agrees and gives me a sweet smile that melts off his face as he directs his eyes back to the doctor in the room.

"Well," he starts as he makes his way to me and takes the chart from my hands and places his hand on my shoulder that's farther away from his body. "There are some people waiting to see you so I'll send them in and we'll be out of your way." I look up and see Dr. Stevenson smiling down at me and giving my shoulder a slight squeeze as if he's doing me a favor by almost embracing me and trying to get me out of this room and away from Sinclair.

Said vampire looks ready to bust a vein.

"Nurse Carras is actually going to be staying behind with me until I leave this hospital." Sinclair says firmly, no room for objection. "Mother, I'm ready for visitors." Sinclair says in his normal talking voice but the door opens again and a beautiful older woman enters the room with three others with her. "Thank you, Dr. Stevenson. If I need anything else from you I will be sure to let you know." He ends the one sided conversation and shifts his focus to the other creatures in the room.

The older couple in the room I can tell are Sinclair's parents even if I didn't hear the words they spoke outside the room to me. They each are clearly vampires with their lighter skin and deep red eyes. The woman has the same fiery hair as Sinclair while his father has auburn hair and the same build as his son.

The man next to them seems to be around Sinclair's age. He's tall and very muscular with tattoos down both of his arms, his light brown hair is longer on the top and messy like he's run his hands through it. His orange eyes give away that he's a dragon as well.

The last one to enter the room is a small woman with dark brown hair, small pointed ears, and moss green eyes. The nymph has a shy smile on her face as she glances at me.

Sinclair grips my hand firmly that draws attention to the action that only causes my anxiety to grow but I do feel a sense of calm washing over me as he rubs his thumb over my knuckles. I can see a variety of expressions on each of their faces. Disgust, curiosity, excitement, and indifference.

"Could you excuse us? We'd like a moment with our son in private. I already told you as much before I allowed you to enter the room." The former queen says, and I can feel the power and authority still in her voice.

She did make it clear that I was only entering Sinclair's room because she allowed it for no other reason than to indulge her stubborn son but didn't hide her distaste at her son's choice in flings.

"Oh, of c-"

"No." Sinclair cuts me off and pulls me closer to his body. His voice is deep and angry. His hand abandons mine to wrap around and grip my waist. He tucks me close into his side, protectively. "She is staying by my side."

I'm not sure but it sounded like he meant more than just in this room and that makes my heart flutter even though we just acknowledged the fact that we're True Mates. I look at him, I'm sure showcases my admiration and he looks down at me with the tenderest affection I've ever seen that makes me melt.

"We'll discuss this another time." His father cuts in and diffuses the tension that was building in the room. He steps forward and claps Sinclair on the shoulder before giving me a brief look. "We'll talk more when you're home. We're just happy that you're alright, son."

Sinclair nods and watches as his father ushers his mother out of the room. As soon as the door clicks closed I'm scooped up into unfamiliar large muscled arms. "I'm so happy to finally meet you!"

I look up at the bulky man with a smile. His enthusiasm is contagious.

"Leave her alone, Ricky."

"Sure, sure, Clairy."

"Clairy?" I ask.

"Don't even think about it." Sinclair says with a straight face as the other man laughs. "Maverick is an idiot."

"I'm hurt after all I did to save your ass."

Sinclair's face sobers, "I do appreciate everything."

"Of course, we're brothers."

I smile at their exchange and look at the younger woman in the room. She gives me a genuine smile back that eases my mind. "I'm Mia. I'm King Archer's assistant."

"Mia."

"Mr. Archer."

"Mia."

"Sinclair."

"Mia."

"Sin." She sighs out and Sinclair smiles triumphantly. He seems to like being called by his nickname more than anything else.

"It's a pleasure to meet you Mia." I say and stick my hand out for her to shake.

"As am I, My Queen." She takes my hand gently and bows her head slightly.

My breath catches in my throat as I look at Sinclair, who has his eyes closed but his face tilted toward the ceiling.

I almost forgot what being mates with the Northern Vampire King means. Me, as the human queen.

Chapter 21
Robyn

"What the fuck did you do?" He yells as he barges in with his little friend and slams the door behind them.

"Kevin, if you ever come into my home like that again, slamming doors, I will kill you. Now, calm the fuck down, everything is fine." I wave my hand dismissively.

I don't care if this human is my True Mate, I'm going to be queen. Finding out this human is supposed to be my mate for life made me want to vomit. He could never compare to Sinclair in any way. I decided to use the bond to my advantage though when I found out his little girlfriend has been trying to gain Sinclair's attention.

"Have you not seen the news?" He huffs then marches to where the remote lays on the coffee table before turning it on and putting it on the local news station.

"A short leaked video was submitted to our office that shows our king, Sinclair Archer, in the hospital from a poisoning according to our source. While this seems like an attempt on his life we have yet to get word from the royal family on the matter and what is going to be done to track down the person responsible. There are also reports that King

Archer would not let anyone, including the doctors, into his room until one specific nurse he was asking for by name arrived. Our source tells us that one casualty has already taken place. This is not their first time meeting and seems to have some sort of relationship. The type of relationship is still unknown as the nurse is reported to be a human. We will be trying to get a statement from his highness as soon as possible but for the time being we will be checking in on this story and reporting when new leads come in. Thank you this is Channel-"

I snatch the remote from Kevin and turn the TV off. My breath is ragged as I struggle to rein in my rage. How could this have happened?

"Now, what the fuck did you do?" Kevin's little lackey repeats.

"I followed the plan."

"Then why the hell is my woman in that hospital room with that leech doing who knows what?" Kevin grits out.

"Why didn't you follow through on your end of the plan?" I ask instead.

"Little bitch had more fight in her that I thought she would in that state so she took us by surprise. I'll handle Anita, you worry about that vampire." He sneers.

"I'm this close to killing you, tread carefully." I say still barely holding the lid on my growing rage. "Sin darted outside before I could catch him that night. By the time I went to check outside the ambulance was already there and I couldn't get to him."

"Now they're together. We need to fix this." Josh mumbles. Always the pathetic little shadow pining after his best friend's girl.

"And this time," I start and look them both in the eyes, "we aren't going half way. There won't be any loose ends."

Chapter 22
Anita

It's been a long, stressful but wonderful few weeks all at the same time. Sinclair's finally been completely cleared of the poison in his system and discharged.

The entire time Sinclair has been a patient he has not let me out of his sight. He still doesn't want anyone close to him, even Dr. Stevenson. I've performed all of his check ups and exams then given the results to the Doctor on duty when the time came.

The looks I get from the other members of the staff are starting to make me anxious. I wish Sinclair would treat me like any other worker here but at the same time I like the special attention I get from him. I don't want to know what they're saying about this entire situation. I've been sleeping in the room with Sinclair and the only people that have seen me have come to his room. I even had to get Diana to bring me some clothes because with Sinclair's behavior I can't work but he somehow has me getting paid for my time in this room with him twenty-four seven.

She wasn't thrilled at first but after I told her the whole story she was over the moon. She even offered to go get my things from my apartment so I wouldn't have to face Kevin. I'm just not ready to see him yet after that night. She won't tell me what happened while she was there but the shit eating grin on her face tells me it was eventful. At least all of my things are back at her place now.

The dynamic between Sinclair and Diana was hilarious after the whole coffee fiasco she told me about. He kept his face emotionless the whole time while she cracked on him relentlessly the whole thirty minutes she was here.

I can't say that I didn't enjoy my time that week either. Being able to really get to know him on a personal level has made the possibility of falling for him a not so distant reality. I know that mates tend to fall fairly quickly but I didn't know it'd feel like this for me.

Sleeping wrapped up in his arms is the safest I've felt in a long time. He looks at me like an equal, not a vampire king and a human nurse. The look in his eyes like I'm the most important person in his life. Like I truly matter.

I've tried to be rational and take things slow with him. I know that jumping into a relationship is a mistake when I only ended my previous one last week. I may need to kick Kevin in the nuts this time to make sure he understands that we're completely over. Despite all of that, I want nothing more than to spend as much time with Sinclair as I can. I want to be wrapped in his arms, for him to see into my soul with those dark red eyes, to bring my body to life with his sensual and dominant touch. I just want all of Sinclair Archer.

Even if that comes with a crown.

I'm not sure how everyone will take us as a couple or me as an individual that's going to help rule Minaoz but I don't want to keep running and fighting fate. Sinclair and I are True Mates for a reason and I want to give us a fair chance, leaving no regrets in my mind.

I thought that once Sinclair was released from the hospital that life would somewhat go back to normal.

I was wrong.

Sinclair has stayed in constant contact with me the past few weeks. He has come to see me at the hospital with my favorite coffee and pastry in hand. I have received fresh flowers for every shift I work and delivered to Diana's loft that I'm staying in for now. Every time they're delivered I have to endure her embarrassing commentary.

He has been showering me with affection and attention whenever he can and I don't know what to do. I've never been treated like I was someone's everything before. I feel like I may burst with happiness.

When we first started going out in public it was mainly very small low-key places or he would rent out entire restaurants for just the two of us because of the media circling us like sharks in the water for a story. We still don't know who leaked the story about us to the media but it's made going out together difficult. Sometimes we spend our time in Sinclair's penthouse. We never run out of things to talk about and even when the conversation starts to thin out he just switches to doing all the talking with his body. I have no objections or complaints.

After a couple of weeks, threats from the royal family, and I suspect money, we were able to go out as a couple without being swallowed up by cameras.

We've had a lot of mixed reactions about a vampire and a human being in a romantic relationship, let alone the king of Minaoz.

My mother let her opinion be known. While she worries for me and what will happen, she's always been a full supporter of my happiness so as long as I'm happy she is too.

"Are you sure this is what you want?" My mom, Sheryl, asks, sitting across from me at our favorite little bakery.

"I'm happy with him, Mom."

She sighs but doesn't say anything for a minute just staring down at her pastry.

"What about Kevin?"

"Mom. I told you about what he tried to do, didn't I?" The frustration is clear in my voice though I don't want to snap at her.

"I know, I know. He has never been my favorite person. I didn't mean for you to take him back but have you had any other trouble from him?"

"Thankfully no I haven't." Kevin has been unusually quiet lately and I'm not sure how I feel about it. "I'm taking it as a blessing."

"A vampire..." She mumbles while looking out the window to the busy street as most of the other humans and creatures are flowing up and down the sidewalk on their lunch breaks.

"Is the fact that he's a vampire the only problem you have with Sin?" I ask.

"It's part of it." She admits. "I never told you much about your father but I don't want history to repeat itself with you."

"What do you mean?" I tilt my head. It's true she never mentioned much about my father over the years and after so long without him in the picture I didn't care to ask anymore but now I'm curious.

"Did I ever tell you that your father and I were True Mates?" She says so nonchalantly as if those words don't knock my world off its axis.

"True Mates? Then Dad is a-"

"He isn't human and that man isn't your Dad. He may be your father biologically but he has never been a real father."

Seeing the fire in her eyes has me saving that information for a later conversation. My father isn't human. That means

I'm only half human, but what else am I? Am I too young for an identity crisis because I feel one coming on.

"What race is he?" I whisper, trying not to further set her off because by the look on her face she's moments away from blowing a fuse at the mention of the man.

"It doesn't matter what he is." She huffs then stares me straight in the eyes. "What matters is that just because someone is True Mates doesn't mean that they should be together and I just want you to be careful especially after everything that's happened."

Not long after that we say goodbye and go our separate ways but the thought lingers in my mind about who and what my father is and then what I am.

Chapter 23
Anita

I STEP OUT OF THE ELEVATOR AND WALK UP TO THE door of Sinclair's penthouse. I raise my hand to knock but the door opens before I can and an arm wraps around my waist and I'm pulled inside.

He uses my body to close the door as he eliminates the space between us, molding his body to mine. His mouth crashes to mine and I can't stop the moan that he pulls from me. I feel his smirk and he presses further into me as if he's trying to consume me.

"Hello, love." Sinclair rasps when he pulls away from me but keeps his body molded to mine. I can get used to this.

"Hey." I breathe out, still trying to get my breathing under control.

His dark eyes watch me closely. Taking in the after effects of my body's reactions to him. His smile tells me that he's loving every moment of it. Sinclair grabs my hand and leads me to the living room.

"Have a seat, I'll get us some wine." He kisses the back of my hand before he disappears.

I've been to his loft a few times over the last few weeks but it feels different this time. We've got to know each other and I can tell that he's restraining himself for me, to take things slowly and at my pace even when I can tell he doesn't want to. I can't imagine a king like him would have to wait or restrain himself often, if at all.

"Here you go." He hands me a glass of sweet red wine and takes a seat next to me with a glass of his own blood red wine. His free hand rests on my thigh, innocent enough, but my skin buzzes with electricity and it goes straight to my core. "How was your day?" He asks and starts rubbing his thumb back and forth over my skin.

"I-It was good." I raise my shaky hand holding my wine up to take a sip, hoping for some liquid courage. I know he's smirking at my reaction to only his hand touching me without me having to look. He knows what he does to my body. His innocent act is fooling no one. "I met with my mom."

"And how is she doing?"

"She's good but you won't believe what she told me today."

"What?"

"My mom has a True Mate and that creature is my father!"

His eyes grow large momentarily before going back to normal as a pensive expression overtakes his face. "That's... unexpected." He admits.

"I'm torn between wanting to know more and not wanting to be disappointed." I admit.

He sighs and pulls me into his arms and I melt into his comforting embrace. This is just what I needed today.

"I can't imagine it's easy for her to talk about. While it's frowned upon to abandon your mate, it's not unheard of. I'm sure she'll tell you when she's ready." He kisses the side of my head as he holds me in his arms.

"I know. I guess it makes more sense that we're mated now." I laugh.

Sinclair laughs with me as he shakes his head.

"I don't think that your species has anything to do with us being True Mates and everything to do with our personalities."

"What do you mean?" I pull back just enough to meet his eyes.

"I mean that I can be cold, cruel, and short tempered. I have killed people for what you'd probably see as something I could ignore but being king holds me to a certain standard and I have to demand respect." His voice is firm and face serious as he makes sure I understand what he's saying.

I know that he's the king and that comes with behaving a certain way but I've only seen the sweet and kind side of Sinclair. I won't lie and say I'm not worried about the day I see the darker side of the vampire king. Seeing him stern like this is causing excitement to buzz through my body though. Straight to my core.

"That being said, when I'm with you I feel calm." Sinclair's eyes soften as he pulls me closer. "Anita, you're the only person that I could never and would never hurt. You're the only person that can pull me back from the rage and blood lust. You're the only one I want by my side in this long life I have."

The air leaves my lungs as his declaration settles in my heart. He may be the vampire king but he's still my Sin. He'll always be the man that quickly is taking hold of my heart and I couldn't be happier that he is. After Kevin, I wasn't sure I would be able to open up to a man again but Sinclair came into my life and left me no option but to happily surrender to him.

"I want to stay by your side for as long as I can, Sin." My breathy as I whisper the words.

"Forever, then." He smiles. "And now I have you all to myself, my little mate." He says taking my mind off everything as he leans in starts leaving a trail of kisses down my neck, nibbling on the skin as he goes.

I can't help but melt into him as my body surrenders to his touch, every time. I try to get my thoughts together. We haven't gone all the way yet and I know he wants to. I don't want to rush into anything and I want to be sure he really does want me for me, not what the bond makes our body's feel more than ever now after what I learned from Mom.

I know that some creatures have left their True Mates for a better suited partner. That's what happened to Mom and I don't want what happened to her to happen to me. She was so devastated that she almost lost me before she even knew she was pregnant with me. Her True Mate must have been higher up. The ones that hold the most resentment for humans are usually the creatures in the top tiers and are more likely to abandon their mates.

"Hey, where'd your mind go just now?"

I'm pulled from my thoughts by Sinclair turning my face so our eyes can connect and I can see his brows furrowed and a worried look in his eyes.

"I'm sorry. I was lost in my thoughts for a minute." I smile and place my hand over his that's still holding my cheek.

I don't think Sinclair would do to me what my father did to my mother but I also didn't think Kevin would try to force a threesome on me after drugging me so you can never tell what someone will do. No matter how long you've known them. I want to believe that he would only ever treat me right. I want to believe his feelings are genuine. Until he proves me otherwise I'm going to trust him.

"It's alright. Do you want to talk about it?" He asks and rubs my cheek softly with his thumb and my troubled thoughts disappear immediately. When I'm with him I'm the happiest I've been in a long time.

"It's nothing important. Just my human mind going to places it shouldn't." I joke.

His eyes go dark and serious. "Anita. Don't talk down on yourself for being human, like that makes you lesser in any way than me or anyone. You are an intelligent, gorgeous and caring woman. Now, what's wrong?"

I'm stunned into silence. I didn't mean to come off as if I was talking down on myself but as I play the words back in my head that's exactly what I did. It's so engraved into our society that it's not even a thought to be seen and understood to be at the bottom of the social ladder. That humans are expected to be inferior in every way.

"It really is nothing." I say trying to sooth him. "I just tend to be a worry wart." I smile.

"I still would like to know so I can try to ease your mind." He pushes softly.

He seems like he actually wants to know what's on my mind, not just saying the words because that's what's expected. It could be that, the feel of his skin on mine, or the serious and searching look in his eyes as they hold mine that have me telling him.

"I just want to be sure this is real before we get any more intimate." I rush out and I can feel my cheeks warming.

"What makes you think this isn't real?" He asks with one raised brow. "Did you not hear what I said before? I only want you."

"You're the Vampire King, Sinclair." I say ignoring his words. "I'm a human nurse. I can't be a queen and rule over creatures that despise me and my kind. Very few will approve of you being with me but I doubt anyone would let a human be queen. What if they make you choose a more suitable mate? What if someone tries to overthrow you because of me? What if they try to attack us or what if-"

"Anita!" He raises his voice and cuts off my rant that I

didn't mean to start. He pulls my tense body into his and I melt into him and relax my muscles and let him comfort me. "Calm down, love."

"I don't want to make your life harder and I feel like you being with me will only cause trouble for you."

"You're worth it." He kisses my temple and I try not to swoon at his words but fail. "I don't care what anyone says or what could come for us. You are the only one that can bring me happiness. I know that now that I've spent these last few weeks with you. No one is above their king so no one is going to make me do anything. I don't care that you're human and I'm not going to be letting you go now that I have you."

The conviction in his words has my heart swelling with love for this man. This strong vampire that leads this Northern territory. The fearless and respected king. I'm falling faster for him than I thought possible and I fear that I'm past the point that I would crumble if I ever had to lose him now.

"How can I not fall for you when you talk like that?" I ask, not caring if it's too soon. If I'm crazy because I just got out of a relationship recently. This is the man that holds my heart now and there's no point in denying that I've fallen in love with my True Mate. I see his eyes go wide and my heart starts to drop. "I-"

I'm cut off by him practically tackling me into the couch and covering my mouth with his. He doesn't wait for me to open my mouth but demands access and strokes every inch of my mouth. My eyes roll back in my head as I feel his hands grip my waist under my shirt and the skin contact just sends electric shocks straight to my clit and I can't help but rock my hips, trying to gain some friction. He's sucking the air right out of my lungs and all I can do is fist my hands in the front of his shirt and pull him in closer, as close as possible.

"You have no idea how happy that makes me." His breathing is fast and heavy like my own. "I think I fell as soon as these gorgeous hazel eyes locked with mine in my club." He whispers and places a delicate kiss on each of my eye lids. We smile at each other like two love sick fools and I've never been happier. He turns his head towards the door and gets up. I must have looked confused. "I ordered some food and I can hear the person delivering it getting out of the elevator. I'll be right back, love." He kisses my head and makes his way to the front door right as I hear the bell ring.

I lay back and close my eyes and let this warm feeling consume me. I have the love and affection of the Northern Vampire King, Sinclair Archer. I hold in my squeal of excitement barely. I feel like a teenager again.

I sit up as I hear Sinclair come back to the couch with our food in his hands already divided up and served on proper plates. He got one of my favorites, shrimp scampi. He turns the TV on and the news is talking about us again.

"I'll kill the person who sold us out if I find them." He mumbles before taking a bite of his own food.

"We're together, that's all that matters." I say.

"I know, love. I just wish I could've shown you off to the world the way I wanted to."

I lean into him and smile at his words. He isn't worried about what they're saying about him or what this could do to his position as a CEO and the king of Minaoz. He just wanted to introduce me to the world with a grand gesture and he didn't get to.

Yeah, I definitely love this man.

Chapter 24
Sinclair

I HAVE ALWAYS LOVED LIVING MY BACHELOR LIFE and spending my nights inside different women. Now I'm lying here in my bed with my little mate wrapped up in my arms. All we did last night was make out, watch some movies and fall asleep. Though I do want to be balls deep in that woman, what I feel for her goes beyond lust and I want her to know that. I know that she's had a rough time coming to terms with everything and the fact that her douchebag ex is still blowing her phone up even after she switched numbers. I'm about ready to kill the little fucker.

If I thought I could get away with it without my gentle little mate getting angry for killing the man, I would. I may still do it anyway. Better to ask for forgiveness than permission and all that.

Anita still won't give me the full story on what happened that night when I saw her at the bar before I got poisoned and just from the fact that she won't tell me tells everything I need to know. It was bad and that makes me want to kill him even more.

I'm trying not to let my past dictate my future. I like the

way we can relax and be in each other's company without sex. My balls are getting a little blue though. I don't want my past behavior and how I was with women to make Anita turn away from me. I've never been keen on commitment ever since Freya.

Just thinking of that bitch get's my blood boiling.

"Your heart's beating so fast."

I jump a little at her soft voice, thinking she was still asleep but I look down at her and see that my hand on her waist is squeezing the flesh there.

"I'm so sorry, I didn't mean to wake you, love." I rub the skin to sooth her and place a kiss on the top of her head.

"It's alright but are you ok?" She asks and her big eyes look up at me with sincerity and innocence that eases some of the tension I didn't realize I was holding.

"I'm fine just letting some past thoughts in that I shouldn't."

"Should I be worried?" She asks and bites her lip. Her insecurities openly displayed.

"No. I just thought of someone that makes me angry." I'm happy to see a little of that insecurity fade from her eyes at my words, but not completely.

"Do you want to talk about it? You did listen to my rant last night." She smiles and places one of her delicate hands on my stomach and my muscles jump at the contact. While it was an innocent act my body is already reacting to her. I'll have a semi in no time.

"Freya Summers." And there goes my erection. "She's a lower class Sprite/Human hybrid. She was bullied and taunted a lot when we were in school because of what she was. That never deterred me though, I always thought she was beautiful and sweet." I say emotionlessly. I can't remember the last time I really talked about her. Even after all these years though I don't give two shits about her anymore the betrayal still stings.

"You loved her." My little mate states.

I nod unwillingly. "I was a young fool in love." I shake my head at my own blindness. "My father was training me to be a strong king that puts his emotions aside and does what needs to be done no matter if others see it as right or wrong. We know what's best for Minaoz, he always said. I was a teenager and let puppy love blind me."

"It's ok to fall in love, Sin." She grabs my hand and gives it a gentle squeeze.

"Yes, but loving the wrong ones always comes with consequences." I sigh. "We dated for a while and I was head over heels, even thinking of proposing." My heart aches as Anita flinches at the words that I wasn't going to wait for her. I don't want to hurt her but I also want to be honest. "I never cared about having a mate or waiting for my True Mate. At the time I was blinded to everything but her."

I feel her tense slightly at my words.

"It all changed when I came home early from a meeting I was sitting in for Dad on. I went to his office to fill him in on everything that happened like I always do when I go to these things in his place. But what I saw when I opened the door changed a part of me forever. There my girlfriend was, naked trying to undress my father as he tried to push her hands off as gently as possible." I look down at Anita when she gasps and see a few emotions flash across her face. Shock, pity, and mainly anger. "Anyone who actually knows my father knows that he hates being touched unless it's by my mother. So when she tried to spin her situation around when I entered the room trying to say that my father was trying to take advantage of her I knew she was lying. My heart shattered. The woman I wanted to spend my life with was only with me to use me as a stepping stone to get a higher position in our society by trying to seduce my father. After that I promised I'd never let another woman close enough to me to hurt me that way ever again. Until you."

Though Anita's eyes are teary and a sad smile is on her face I can see that love shining in those watery eyes. I know she's different. I know she's genuine with her feelings for me. That makes me feel like even more of a fool for denying my bond with her.

"I'm so sorry you had to go through that." She rubs soothing circles on my skin and I feel my body relax to her touch.

"I've had a hard time letting any woman in after that which is why I never wanted to commit to anyone before. You're the only woman I'll ever want to spend the rest of my life with." I tell her honestly.

"Forever." She smiles and cups my cheeks before initiating a sweet kiss.

"I love you." I whisper into her lips.

"I love you too." She whispers back and we stay like that. Wrapped in our little bubble of love and happiness. I'm not ready for it to burst but the outside world will close in on us sooner rather than later.

"Sin." Mia peeks her head into my office.

"Yes?" I look at her for a moment before continuing on the paperwork I've been catching up on since I've gotten out of the hospital.

"Do you have a moment?" She asks.

"Yeah, come in. I'm almost done." I say and finish up on the last file I've had for today. "What's up?"

"I just wanted to see how you're doing. We haven't had much time to talk since you've been out of the hospital."

"I'm good. I'm happy." I smile at her and she beams back at me.

"I'm *so* happy for you. You found your True Mate." She squeals. "How are things going with her?"

"Anita's the most genuine and amazing woman I've ever met."

"You're in love with her." She states. "I can tell by that goofy smile on your face as you talk about her."

"I really am in love with her. Who would've thought, huh?"

We both laugh at that.

"Any harassment for her being human?" She asks softly.

"Not so far." I let out a heavy breath. I've been waiting for the call from the council, royal court, and my own family about my human mate but so far it's been radio silence. I think that unnerves me more. "Not many would want to cross their king. If they try I'll just have to remind them why I am considered a ruthless king." I say but I just have a feeling that something is coming. I'm sure I'll hear from the other kings at some point as well. "I don't care that she's a human. She will be my queen and if anyone has anything to say about it they can move to a new territory." I say.

"You're different." She says.

"What do you mean?"

"In a good way. I like this newer Sinclair Archer. You've always been a good man but I think with her by your side you'll be a great man and even greater king." She smiles fondly and I can't help but return it. Mia has been my assistant since a year after I started my reign and she's seen all my ups and down and demons. She saw my darkness and helped me anyway.

"Is that all the files we have for today?" I ask.

"Yes." She says and checks the tablet nodding as she double checks everything.

"You can take off for the day, Mia. I'm going to be leaving myself as soon as I put these files back." I say as I start saving all the documents I have on my laptop and closing everything down.

"If you're sure. Have a good night, Sin." She smiles and waves as she leaves, closing the door behind her.

I pick up my cell phone and dial Maverick's number as I'm collecting all the paper copies of these reports to file away. It doesn't take him long to answer.

"Hello, this is Mr. Wilder."

I snort, "do you not check your caller ID before you answer the phone?"

"I usually do but I have my hands full, literally. So I answered the call hands free." He huffs. I can hear the rustling of paper in the background. He's probably getting ready to leave his office too.

"You want to go for a drink?" I ask, closing the filing cabinet in my office once all of the reports are in their proper place.

"What's wrong?" He asks.

"Nothing, just want some time with my best friend." I shrug though he can't see me.

"We'll pretend I believe you. Where are we going?" He asks. He knows me too well. I don't usually call him specifically just to drink unless I have something on my mind, and these days I have a lot on my mind.

"My place."

"Anita working tonight?" He asks.

"Yeah, she's on a night shift." I grab my belongings and shut off the lights and lock the door on my way out of my office and head to the elevator.

"Alright. I'll be there in about thirty."

"Okay. I'm getting in the elevator, see you then." I end the call and make my way down then to my car. I try to keep my thoughts neutral as I drive home.

When I unlock my door and enter the loft it's quiet because Anita already left for work a couple hours ago. I hate that they have her working such long shifts. I wish she'd let me take care of her, but she loves her work and it's also one of the things I love about her. I set my things down on the entry table before making my way to the liquor cabinet to grab a bottle of mine and Maverick's favorite scotch. I pour myself two fingers worth before throwing it back and pouring three fingers of scotch in each glass now as the front door opens and closes.

"Already starting without me I see." My best friend closes the distance between us and takes his glass in his hands. He studies me with his orange eyes before he clinks our glasses together and we shoot the liquor down and he grabs the bottle and pours us each a more generous amount in our glasses to sip on now. "So what's going on?" He asks, not at all fooled with me saying I want to just casually drink.

"Just have a lot going on." I sigh.

"With what exactly?"

"Anita, the fact that she's human, the royal court, the council, my family, the one who poisoned me is still loose, her ex being a nuisance..." I trail off trying to see if I left anything out.

"Damn, anything else." He screws his face up and scoffs.

"I hope not."

"So walk me through it. Let's start with the court, council, and your family."

"Nothing happened yet but I'm waiting for them to contact me. I'm waiting for them to demand I end my relationship with Anita because she's human. The council may try to take shares out of my companies, the court may try to overthrow my hold on the throne, and I know my family doesn't approve without even trying to get to know her. It's all a giant headache." I rub the bridge of my nose with my thumb and forefinger.

"Sin." I bring my eyes to meet his. "You can't worry about things that haven't happened yet, and they may never happen. You don't know anything for sure yet so let all that go for now. Worry about the things within your control." He says.

I know he's right but I can't help but want to prepare for everything to protect my little mate with everything I have from anything that comes our way. I won't lose her now.

"Besides you hold the most power so ultimately they can't do that much of anything to you anyway."

"Doesn't mean they can't make my life extremely more difficult."

"Then you just make it more difficult for them." He shrugs like it's simple. In a way it is but I wish it wasn't necessary.

"And you and I both have people looking for the fucks that poisoned you so it's only a matter of time before they're found and dealt with. As for her ex...I say we just kill the bastard and his little friend." He growls.

Can't argue with him there. I've wanted to kill the fucker long before he almost abused my mate.

"His days are numbered for sure, I just have to do this as quietly as possible." He nods in agreement.

"Now, how are things with your beautiful mate?" He leans forward and wiggles his eyebrows at me.

I roll my eyes at his attempt to rile me up. Luckily for him I know he would never betray me in that way or he'd have my fist in his face by now for being flirty toward her.

"Things are great, actually." I say with a smile.

"Then why is she on your list?" He asks, confused.

"I love her." I say.

"That's a good thing though."

"It is. I just worry about the past repeating itself, both of my actions and others." I say.

"You can't let Freya have any more hold over your happiness. You've let that bitch and what she did dictate how close you let people to you for years. Don't let her take any more time away from you. She was never worth it anyway."

"I know that and I know that I only want Anita but I just don't want to fuck this up."

"Then don't. It's that simple." I shake my head with a small smile at him. It seems so simple when he says it like that but when he meets his mate he'll know that it isn't. "I feel like there's more to it than that though."

Always the perceptive one.

I sigh and nod my head. "We're immortal, Mav, and she isn't." I say and fist my glass tighter. "I'm trying to figure out if there's a way that I can turn her." I admit.

"Is that what she wants?"

"I don't know. I didn't want to bring the idea to her until I was sure I could do it. What if it is what she wants and I can't find a way to change her, I would've gotten her hopes up for nothing."

"I see what you mean. We'll figure something out." He says, always the optimist. "What will you do if you can't turn her into a Vampire?" He asks.

"Nothing. I will stay with her and love her for the length of her life regardless. I just don't want to have to live without her." I admit and let my vulnerability show.

"You really do love her." He states.

"More than my life."

The smile he has on his face is a sad one as he stares into his glass. My heart aches for my best friend. Maverick has always been a hopeless romantic. He refuses to be with a woman that is not his mate. While years ago I may have teased him on his virginity, especially once we passed one-hundred, I admire him. He is staying faithful to his mate even before he's met her.

I did the complete opposite and I wish I could have shared all my firsts with Anita. I just have to make sure all my firsts from now on are hers.

"How do you like living together?" Maverick's voice pulls me from my thoughts and I can tell his trying to change the subject from the one pulling his mood down.

"She hasn't *officially* moved in but when we aren't working we're here together as much as we can." I can't stop the smile that spreads on my face.

Having a woman in my home has always been a hard no for me. I didn't want anyone in my private space. That's the main reason I don't live in the palace. I wanted privacy. But having Anita here feels so right that I can't imagine being here without her now. The bond we have as mates is so strong I wonder how I ever fought it off.

"Why don't you make it official?"

"I just didn't want to rush her." I shrug.

"Let her decide that."

I let his words settle in my mind and smile. I do want her here with me, calling this her home. Now I just have to ask my little mate.

Chapter 25
Sinclair

AFTER TALKING THINGS OUT WITH MAVERICK I'VE tried to be more optimistic about my chances of keeping Anita by my side for the rest of our lives. We talked about the places to start first in our search for a way to turn my little mate if the time comes and that's what she wants. I told him about what she told me regarding her mother and her True Mate. I think he must have been higher up on the social ladder to think of rejecting a human mate. I don't know exactly what that means for her being turned but it could make it all easier if I could find out who her father is.

"Sin?" I hear my little mate call out as the front door closes. I look down at my watch and see she's a little early.

"Hey, love. I'm in the kitchen and I'm almost done with dinner. You got home earlier than I thought. I can pour you some wine while you wait though. I'll get it while you get more comfortable." I say then turn and freeze.

I take in the redness in her eyes and the moisture that's building there, the red tint that's building up on one side of her face. My blood boils.

"Did someone fucking hit you?" I growl as I stomp my way over to her quickly but slowly reach for her face. She flinches away from my touch and that makes my heart twist. "Anita?" She just shakes her head at me and more tears build in her eyes until they start to spill over her cheeks. "Love, what's wrong? Let me see your cheek." I command softly but firmly, letting her know that I will take a look whether she likes it or not.

With that she doesn't move and lets me take her chin between my thumb and forefinger and tilt her face away from me so I can examine the skin that's reddening. Sure enough a faint handprint is slowly appearing on her white skin. "Who fucking hit you?" I grit out, trying to keep my growing rage under control in front of her.

"It doesn't matter." She sniffles. "I think I'm going to stay with Diana for a few nights."

My heart drops to my stomach, "Why are you leaving?"

"I just need some time."

"What do you mean? You have to tell me what's going on." I try not to let my frantic state show as my panic of losing her starts to build inside me.

She lets out a sigh and heads to the kitchen with me on her heels. I watch her reach in the cabinet and pull down a large wine glass before pouring herself a hefty glass. I wait as I let her take a couple sips then she meets me eyes with a tortured look in her eyes that breaks my heart.

"I ran into Ms. Belmont during my shift today." She starts and I wait for her to continue.

"Did Xari say something to you?" I ask when she doesn't continue. "Is she the one that hit you?" I grit out.

She scowls down into her glass as if it's the one that hurt her. "She was upset that I stole her mate from her and I'm delusional to think that my place at your side isn't more than an easy fuck. I could never rule over creatures of superior rank." She says and slowly shifts from explaining briefly what Xari said to talking as if she believes what she's saying.

"You don't believe that do you?" I ask.

"No. I don't know. I want to believe that isn't what's happening."

"That's because that isn't what's happening, Anita. I thought I show you enough everyday for you to know how I feel about you." I say, hurt by her lack of faith in my affection for her.

"No, Sin, please. I know you love me and you know that I love you. I know that when I get in my head it's frustrating but I can't help feeling insecure. I know that I'm not good enough to be your mate..." She trails off.

At her ending words I close the distance between us, take the glass from her hand and set it on the counter behind her, and wrap her in my arms. "I love you more than I've loved anyone, Anita. No one is going to take you away from me. I don't care what they think or say. And I'm the one that's not good enough for such a kind and loving woman. You make me want to be a better man every day." I say pulling tighter against my body and kissing the top of her head, hoping that she can feel me trying to pour my love into her to chase away all of her doubts.

"Everyone is going to be against us aren't they?" Her small voice asks.

I sigh and give her one last squeeze before easing my hold on her so I can lean back to look into her eyes. "Some may be against us, and some may support our relationship, but what matters to me is that we're happy and in love. That you'll always stand by my side like I will stand by yours. That's all I care about." I say and sway us side to side slowly.

She smiles up at me and more tears start to spill from her eyes. I reach my hand up to wipe them as they fall.

"No more tears, love."

"These are happy tears." She sniffles. "I don't know what I'd do if I ever lost you Sin. You're quickly becoming someone I can never be without." She leans her forehead against my chest as she takes a series of deep breaths, trying to get her emotions under control.

"Anita." I say, taking her face in my hands so that I have her focus for what I'm going to say. "I'm not going to say that I've never been with other women. I'm not going to say that I've never been intimate with my potential mates. I will promise you though with all of my soul that I've only ever loved you and you're the only one I want. I haven't seen or spoken to another woman that way since the moment you stepped into my hospital room. You're it for me, Anita."

"You're it for me too, Sin." She smiles and leans into my hand holding her face.

"Now," I say, pinning her in place with my eyes. "Tell me who hit you."

She tenses for a moment before she sighs. I know it isn't that she doesn't want to tell me. It's more of what she knows I'm likely to do when I hear the name. She's right. I'm going to fucking kill them.

"It was Ms. Belmont." She whispers with her big hazel eyes, red from tears, locked on mine.

I had a feeling already that it was her but hearing it confirmed from my little mates mouth has me raging. I'm careful to let Anita go gently so that when I clench my fists she's not feeling the force of my anger.

We both jump at the sound of my phone ringing. While I don't want to ruin whatever was left of the moment we were having, I also needed the distraction. I give her an apologetic smile before I look down and answer the call.

"Hello, mother." I bite back a smile at Anita's wide eyes at my words.

"Son, you haven't been to the palace in a while." She huffs out.

"I'm a very busy man."

"Yes, well, I need you to be here for dinner tomorrow night."

"I'll see what I have going on."

"You will be here, Sinclair Garrett Archer. We have important people coming to dinner and as our son and king of Minaoz you need to be there." She demands.

"Then I guess we'll be seeing each other for dinner tomorrow." I say and look to my little mate to see her face pale and fear build in her eyes. I pull into my chest and run my hand up and down her back trying to sooth her.

"You can leave your pet at home." My mother sneers.

Just like that my anger comes back full force.

"Speak about her like that again and you'll never see or speak to me again, mother. Do not test me." I grit out.

There's a pause on the line as she takes in my words, probably trying to sense if there's truth in them. She knowns I don't fucking bluff.

"Fine." She huffs. "Tomorrow night, Sinclair. Don't be late, six o'clock." And the line goes dead.

I slide my phone back into my pocket and wrap both of my arms around my little mate. Her body against mine instantly calms me.

"She hates me." She mumbles into my chest.

"When she gets to know you, she'll love you." I say confidently.

She doesn't respond but we stay in our little bubble for a few more minutes before the fire alarm goes off. We both jump and I curse before running to the kitchen. Frantically turning off the stove I forgot was on and placing our ruined dinner in the sink. I turn to the sweet sound of giggles behind me.

"I guess we're ordering in." She continues to laugh and I can only smile at her.

This is the kind of life I can get used to.

Chapter 26
Anita

I STAND IN THE MIRROR TRYING TO SMOOTH OUT THE nonexistent wrinkles in my knee length mint green dress. I can't stop fidgeting.

I look into my eyes and see simple fear there. I'm about to walk into the den of the monsters like a sacrifice. I know that Sinclair will stand strong by my side but that doesn't soothe my worries that this is going to be a disaster.

At least my face wasn't bruised. I don't want to seem any more weak and incapable than I already do.

I should just stay home.

"Don't even think about it."

I look behind me through the mirror at the sound of his deep gruff voice. I see his intense dark red eyes boring hole into mine.

"What do you mean?" I tilt my head at him.

"You aren't staying here and making me endure this dinner on my own. I may kill some of them there without your touch to calm me down." He closes the distance between us and takes my waist in his hands and pulls me back into his firm chest.

"I just don't want to cause you more problems than I already am." I mumble as I turn and bury my face in his chest.

I feel his chest heave under my cheek as he sighs. His large hands take a hold of my face and tilt my face up to see him looking down at me.

"Anita." Sinclair runs his thumb under my left eye gently. "I never see you as a problem or inconvenience in my life. I want you by my side and for the sake of others safety if they can't keep their mouths shut, you being there will probably save their lives...maybe." He smiles at me like he didn't just say he'll be murdering later on during dinner. I believe he'll do exactly that too.

"My big bad vampire king." I sass, smiling up at him. I know his reputation as being a fearless and at times ruthless king but I don't know that side of him.

He smirks down at me and takes my hand in his, bringing it to his mouth to kiss my knuckles.

Sinclair's comforting words soothes a lot of my anxiety over this dinner tonight, but not all of it. I can't shake the pit that's forming in my stomach. Besides the fact that I'll be facing his parents again, after they didn't hide their distaste for our relationship, there's also supposed to be guests joining us and I have no idea what to expect.

The former king and queen are intimidating for good reason. Stories of their iron fist rule over Minaoz is known by everyone. They kept the lines of the hierarchy clear and it was a rare few that could escape the level they were born into. None of those were ever humans.

I'm ready to have this dinner done and over with and it hasn't even started.

"Don't worry too much, love." Sinclair pulls me out of my racing thoughts as he tugs me into his arms. "While I'm breathing, I won't let harm come to you." He promises.

And I believe him.

"I trust you, Sin." I smile and push up onto my toes as he leans down to seal his lips over mine. "I can't help but worry though."

"I know, but we'll make it through this dinner then I get to have you all to myself again." His brows wiggle up and down as he grins at me.

I giggle at his way of breaking the tension that was building up inside me. He always finds a way to ease my mind and tonight I need it more than ever.

I take a step back out of his arms to see him dressed smart but casually in a charcoal button down shirt with the sleeves rolled up to his elbows. His dark blue jeans are hung loosely on his hips as his shirt tails flow over his waistband instead of tucking it in like he would for work. My eyes trail back up his body to see his hair isn't styled but still looks neat but relaxed.

My eyes meet his amused ones and my cheeks warm as he clearly just watched me check him out from head to toe openly. I'm not embarrassed for eyeing my mate but his intense stare always as a blush coating my cheeks.

I keep my eyes locked on him as his fingertips trail from my cheeks, down the column of my neck, over my shoulders, and down my arms to my hands that he gently takes in his. He pulls me forward while raising my arms and placing them around his neck. His hands then trails my sides before taking a hold of my waist in a firm grip. He yanks me forward until my front is flush with his.

My breath hitches as he takes in my scent from the soft spot of my neck where my pulse is jumping wildly.

"I want to taste you." He murmurs in my skin then places a soft kiss there.

I know that drinking blood from your mate is extremely intimate for vampires. I've thought of Sinclair tasting my blood more than once and each time it makes me ache with want. I thought I'd be scared to have such a predator holding my life in my hands, but not Sinclair. I trust him and I want this with him.

"Please."

I feel his smirk before the tips of his fangs graze over my skin. A shiver wracks through my body and goosebumps cover my skin. Then his fangs sink into my skin and my eyes shoot open at the sharp pain that comes with it. My mouth opens in a silent scream before the euphoria floods my system and my eyes roll back, moaning at the feeling.

My toes curl in my heels and I grip tighter onto Sinclair's neck holding him where he is as pleasure shoots straight to my pussy.

I've heard and even treated some humans that chose to be live blood donors to the vampires of the city as their occupation. I could never understand why someone would want to be a walking blood bag but if this is how they feel every time they surrender to these powerful beasts then I know why now.

I can feel the blood being pulled from my body. Sinclair's body vibrates under my palms as a purr-like growl emits from his throat. The vibrations seem to go straight to my pussy as it throbs for more attention. I never expected giving blood to feel this erotic.

I don't know how much time passes before he pulls his fangs from me and licks the wound closed then places an open mouthed kiss there.

"God, you taste so fucking good, just like I knew you would." Sinclair moans out before he crashes his lips to mine.

His tongue swirls with mine violently and I taste some of my blood but surprisingly it tastes sweet and I moan at the taste. My hips rock against nothing trying to find friction anywhere I can. Sinclair's grip on my hips tightens as he pulls me impossibly closer against his. His erection is straining in his jeans and my mouth waters at the thought of having a taste of my mate.

Without a second thought I pull my lips from his and drop to my knees desperately trying to release his cock from its confines.

"You don't need to do that, love." He says but his voice is husky from the desire he's feeling and I want nothing more than to bring him pleasure right now with a determination that I've never had before.

"I want to." I look up at him through my lashes as my hands continue to work on his jeans. He lets out a deep growl as he looks down at me and threads one of his hands through my hair before getting a gentle but firm grip.

I look back toward his hips as I finally get his cock out and it springs free with force to slap against his stomach. My eyes widen at the size and I wrap my hand around his base giving it a few slow strokes.

Sinclair groans and I look up to see his head thrown back. Without wasting any more time I place my lips around the crown of his dick and push myself forward, taking as much of him in my mouth as I can before he hits the back of my throat.

I moan around him as his pre-cum coats my tongue and that only spurs me to double my efforts and I'm working my mouth up and down his shaft.

"I'm not going to last long with you working me like that, love." He groans out and tightens his grip on my hair then starts to apply pressure to my hair, working my head that way he likes while he starts to move his hips at the same time, chasing his high.

I move one of my hands to his thigh and the other down between my legs. I slip my fingers into my panties and start to rub my clit in quick circles wanting to get off when he does.

"Fuck, you look so fucking sexy playing with yourself while you choke on my cock." He groans and picks up his speed, causing me to choke on his dick. "That's right, baby.

Rub your little clit. I want you to come on your fingers while I come down your throat."

His words have my orgasm coming quickly and it doesn't take long before I'm moaning loudly around his cock as my orgasm pours over me in waves. It's only seconds later that his hips stutter before he holds his cock deep in my throat as he comes with a growl.

He helps me to my feet and dominates my mouth.

"I really want to taste you now but we'd be late so I'll just have to have you for dessert when we get home." He whispers against my mouth.

Fuck. I forgot about the dinner for a minute and now all I'm going to be thinking about is later tonight having Sinclair between my legs while he has his dessert as promised.

Chapter 27
Sinclair

PULLING UP TO THE PALACE, I PLACE THE CAR IN park and look over to my little mate practically vibrating with nerves again even after the stress relief we had before we left. I can't blame her for being nervous, if the situation were reversed I'm sure I would be too but she's facing everything head on like a true queen even with her fears and I couldn't be more proud.

"Are you ready, love?" I reach over, taking her hand in mine and try to soothe her by rubbing circles on the back of her hand.

She takes a deep breath before looking at me with a soft smile.

"I'm as ready as I'll ever be."

I walk around the car and open her door before taking her hand and leading her up to the palace doors trying to send her strength because I know it's going to be hard for her.

The guards' faces are emotionless as they bow and open the doors for us to enter. My hair stands on end as I sense the number of people that are actually here and rage burns in my veins as I smell who's actually here.

How fucking dare she.

I keep my demeanor calm not to scare my little mate, but under the surface I'm a storm of emotions.

Anita grips my hand tighter as we round the corner. She sucks in a breath as she takes in the people that are seated around the long table with all of their eyes on us.

I lock eyes with my father first and he has a look of defeat on his face as well as indifference. I know that he doesn't care for my mother's theatrics and drama but she's always been his weak spot so he doesn't openly go against her either.

My little mate's hand starts to tremble in my hand and I give her a comforting squeeze though I know that it isn't going to be very effective right now. I can almost hear the words running around in her mind right now. She feels inferior and that was my mother's goal all along. To make her feel like she doesn't belong.

I scan over our guests before meeting my mother's smug face. She invited all of my potential mates and their families here at the same time.

I see Robyn sitting between her parents with her expression flickering between a lusty confidence and anger. I already know how her obsession with being my mate has caused her to act in the past but I'm surprised she had the nerve to show up today.

I see Norah looking as proper as ever between her parents. She looks over at me with a sad smile and looks about as uncomfortable being her as I am. She looks at my mate and sends her a warm smile.

Lastly, my eyes move to Xari. She's sitting there with the same face as my mother looking smug and confident. Xari's eyes flit to my little mate, and a look of disgust covers her face as she sneers. A low growl comes from my throat and she pulls her eyes back to me with a fiery expression. I've never wanted to hurt a woman before, but I'm tempted now.

I pull Anita towards our seats with a little resistance from her before she follows me in stride. The closer we get I realize there's only one chair sitting at the head of the table between my mother and Xari. Xari has her head held high on my right side where Anita should be sitting. The spot for my queen.

"Only one chair?" I lock eyes with everyone in the room briefly before staying on my mother, knowing that she's the one behind this little stunt.

"I told you there wasn't room for your pet and for you to come alone, Sinclair." Mother waves me off like I'm the one being ridiculous.

"Call my mate a pet once more and I'll completely forget the fact that you're my mother and treat you like a threat to the future queen." My voice is firm and cold, showing my mother that I'm not to be pushed because I will follow through with my threat.

My little mate's steps falter for a moment but I keep my hold on her firm as we come to stand in front of the lone chair. Without batting an eye I take the seat and sit down while keeping my eyes locked with my mother. Before Anita can take a step back I pull her down to sit in my lap. I see her flush out of the corner of my eyes as I wrap my arms around her waist keeping her in place. She tries to resist probably thinking that this isn't how she should be sitting in front of the former king and queen, but I am king now and if I want to have my mate sit in my lap while we eat then I fucking will.

I ignore the various emotions at our display and smirk as their idiotic stunt failed. I don't know why they thought the small fact of not having enough seats would have made me turn my mate away. I should actually thank them. I already have so many thoughts shifting in my head that I can tease my little mate during this dinner to keep myself from killing anyone tonight.

Perhaps I will enjoy myself after all.

I nod to the servants to start bringing out the food. I ignore all the eyes on us as I let my right hand leave my little mate's waist and trail along the skin of her exposed thigh right before the bottom of her dress.

Anita lets out a shaky breath while keeping her eyes straight ahead with her head held high. Seeing her look so regal has my cock harding in my pants. By the way her chest moves more rapidly I know she can feel it pressing against her ass.

I let my left hand rub soothingly on her stomach as my other hand trails up higher on her legs. Her thighs tremble slightly but she keeps her legs open for me.

Good girl.

I keep my focus on her as the plates get set in front of everyone here at the table. My mother may be brave enough to test me for now but those that work for me know who's in charge here. Very soon everyone else will be reminded of the fact as well.

I keep my fingers grazing her creamy skin higher and higher until I feel the moisture of her lower lips.

A low growl comes from my throat and I look up to see a small smirk and mischievous gleam in my little mate's eyes. She's not wearing any underwear and I want nothing more than to lay her across this table and have her for dinner instead of dessert.

Little minx.

I smirk as I run my finger up her slit and circle her already swollen clit. Anita's breath hitches but keeps her face impassive. It's impressive really but I want to see how long she can hold her composure.

Acting like we're alone in this room is hot as fuck and I don't give a damn about the others that are here. Her hand reaches down and her nails dig into my pant leg. I lean into the curve of her neck to hide my smirk.

"I can't wait for dessert." I whisper in her ear then suck her lobe into my mouth as I pull my hands from her now dripping pussy.

The faces around the table are a mix of disgust and rage. I smirk as Anita keeps her head high while her breathing comes back to normal. I don't give a fuck what they think. If I want to touch my queen, I sure as fuck will.

Chapter 28
Anita

I DON'T THINK I'VE EVER FELT SUCH CONFLICTING emotions as I do right now.

As soon as we entered the palace and saw all of the people we'd be having dinner with I knew they were trying to intimidate me, and I'm ashamed to say it worked. I feel like the canyon that shows just how far apart our two worlds grew to the size of galaxies. They made it clear that I would never belong.

Then Sinclair being Sinclair, blew that notion out of the water. A swarm of butterflies takes refuge in my stomach as he rubs his thumbs over my hips keeping me firmly in his lap. He runs his nose along the column of my neck and goosebumps cover my skin.

I'm not sure how I was able to keep my blush from showing on my face when I think about Sinclair's hand that was just rubbing me beneath my dress. I thought not wearing panties would tease him but that plan backfired on me. If I'd known the full extent of the company that we'd be in tonight I would have never tried to be so bold.

It's hard to regret that decision when Sinclair looks at me

with such love and pride in his eyes though. I have to admit that I'm also a little proud of myself for keeping my head up and face straight as he rubbed my clit in front of these people under the table. I'm sure they could smell my arousal but being with Sinclair gives me confidence. A large part of me doesn't care what they think about it.

No one speaks for a while and I keep my eyes straight ahead until the food is served. I lean back into Sinclair's chest trying to find comfort in his embrace. He tightens his arms around me.

"Hold your head up, love. No one is above you." He whispers in my ear. His words are exactly what I needed to hear and for the first time since entering the room I raise my eyes to look at everyone in the room head on instead of just into empty space.

His mother is staring daggers at us and if looks could kill I'd be six feet under by now. Her distaste for me is more than obvious and it seems to be for no other reason than my race. I could tell from the moment I met her that she had a superiority complex. I can't really blame her because most upper class creatures do. Her being the former queen still gives her a sense of authority.

I move my gaze away from her murderous one and see his father is wearing a little smirk while his eyes go back and forth between Sinclair and I. He seems okay with us for the most part. I can tell that Dryden Archer just wants to see his son happy. His personality took me off guard for the former king when I met him at the hospital. It's like his years on the throne took so much life out of him. At least he seems to let his son make his own decisions unlike his wife.

I decide to blatantly ignore Sinclair's potential mates. I don't want to see them again.

I know Xari the most from the hospital and what I do know of her is awful. She's like most of the higher class species believing in the older ways. The hierarchy is a hard thing to break but when the creatures in power hold prejudice against humans or any of the lower lever species there will never be change. Seeing her here and sitting in Sinclair's lap makes me so thankful that he is so open minded with me being his mate.

I haven't forgotten her confrontation when she slapped me at my work. Trying to put me in my place.

Robyn is on my shit list too. I'm pretty confident she's the one that poisoned Sinclair. He said that he knew who was responsible and he has plans in place to take care of whoever it is but he hasn't said anything to me about it. I'm trying not to get all in his business but if it was Robyn he wouldn't be sitting here so calmly with his attacker right?

I've never met Sinclair's werewolf potential mate, Norah Virac. He talks very highly of her and the friendship he has with her. He told me a little about her situation and how she's struggling to get on a peaceful common ground with her own True Mate. I hope I can meet her under different circumstances.

"Son, this isn't appropriate for the dinner table." His mother's voice cuts through the silence and I turn to look at her just as Sinclair runs his fangs along the vein in my neck. I have to resist letting my eyes roll back in my head remembering how it felt as he fed from me.

Sinclair ignores her as he reaches for the single plate in front of us. He pushes the food around the plate before turning his head toward the doors the servants were coming out of.

"Haley, is Vergil in the kitchen?" He asks the little maid standing on the right side of the door.

"Yes, Your Majesty." Haley responds while keeping her head down.

"Haley." Sinclair bores holes in her head with a stern expression and I worry for the girl and why he's looking at her like that. I hear a snort and see his mother glare at the girl and smirk.

Haley raises her head and smiles at him. "Sin."

I smile but the rest of the room is either shocked or enraged at her use of Sinclair's nickname so informally.

"How dare yo-"

"Haley, can you tell Vergil I want to talk to him real quick, please?" Sinclair asks with a smile and I melt even more into him. That's the man I love.

"Of course, Sin." She bows with a smile before disappearing behind the door.

I turn to look at the man I love and he's already smiling at me. He leans in and gives me a soft kiss.

"Sinclair!" His mother yells. "You let a maid speak to you in such a way?"

"Haley is a friend and I let all my friends call me that." He says without taking his eyes off me.

Before she can say anything else the kitchen doors open and a large human man comes walking out dressed in all white and a chef's hat on his head. He looks to be in his forties with slight wrinkles around his kind brown eyes. He has a stern look on his face as he looks around the room before a wide smile grows on his face as he sees Sinclair with me on his lap.

"Sin, how are you doing, boy?" Vergil asks once he's next to us and reaches out his hand that Sinclair takes immediately to shake. Vergil's eyes move from Sinclair to me and back again with a twinkle in his eyes.

"I'm doing well, Vergil. There seems to be a problem with the food though."

"Oh?" Vergil's brow raises as he eyes everyone's plates that all look exquisite. "And what would that be?"

"My little mate doesn't have a plate."

My eyes widen as I realize what he's doing. They purposely excluded me when they told the kitchen to prepare food. I almost forgot that I can't eat anything even from Sinclair's plate unless I want to have blood. I shiver at the thought.

"Oh! Well I can whip something up real quick for her." He turns his kind eyes to me. "What would you like to eat tonight?"

"Oh, anything is fine, really." I don't want him to have to go out of his way. I'd be happy with a sandwich honestly.

"Anything is fine, Verg. I just don't want my little mate to starve." I elbow Sinclair gently. Saying I was going to starve was a little dramatic but my heart swells at him making sure I'm taken care of regardless.

"I know just the thing." He bows slightly before making his way back to the kitchen.

"Ridiculous." I hear someone scoff.

"Problem, Xari?" Sinclair growls.

"Why are you indulging this human?" I assume the woman is Mrs. Belmont. "We all know her kind can never rule."

Anger flares in me at the comment but nothing to the degree of Sinclair's.

"I am not *indulging* my True Mate, Xena. She will be your queen so I suggest you show some respect to your future queen and your king. No one is above exile." He spits at the dragon. "Or execution."

"Sinclair Archer! You will not speak to our guests this way!" The former queen shouts.

"I will speak to whomever I want as I wish, mother. I have apparently let too many things go and some people in this room have forgotten just what kind of king I am." He growls back at her.

I shiver at the deep tone and strength of his voice. I've heard stories about the ruthless King of Minaoz but the Sinclair I know doesn't match with the man now. While everyone in the room shifts uncomfortably in their chairs I find myself shifting in my seat for a different reason.

Sinclair's hand takes my chin and turns my face toward him as his nostrils flare. A sexy smirk forms on his face as I'm sure he can smell my arousal at his little display of power and it causes a deep blush to color my cheeks.

I jump when a plate is suddenly set down in front of Sinclair and I and that's when I realize I was so lost in his presence that I didn't even hear Haley come back with my food.

I turn to the table to see a plate of grilled salmon and vegetables. I've always wanted to try it but it was not something I could ever really afford to buy.

I go to reach for a fork to take a bite but Sinclair beats me to it, cutting into the fish and bringing a bite up to my lips. I blush as I open my mouth and let him feed me. The others at the table make small talk while looking at us from the corner of their eyes but I don't care. The fish is amazing and melts in my mouth.

"This is amazing." I whisper.

I hear Sinclair chuckles as he gets another bite and feeds me. "I'm glad you like it, love."

"I can feed myself, Sin." I say, trying to reach for the fork only for him to keep it out of reach.

"Let me take care of you."

Sinclair continues to feed me until my food is gone before he starts on his own food.

"You should have seen the disgusting woman. The human had no sense of self respect." I hear Xari say.

"I know exactly what you mean. Whoring themselves out to the first wealthy man that shows them attention. It's pathetic." Robyn adds.

"Those types of women should stay at the bottom where they belong." Sinclair's mother sneers.

"Those women are in their position because of people like

you." I whisper forgetting that in a room of creatures they can hear me clearly.

"What did you say, human?"

I stare at Xari as the anger that's been building through the evening comes to boil. I've let their comments brush off me and let their blatant disrespect for me as a person go. But I need to say my piece on this.

"Are you saying this woman is a prostitute? Having sex with men for their money or status?" I ask.

"Yes." Robyn adds in confidently.

"So she's just like you both then?"

Chapter 29
Sinclair

DEADLY SILENCE FILLS THE DINING ROOM AND ALL eyes are on my little mate.

Anita keeps her head held high and her gaze strong as she keeps her eyes flickering between Robyn and Xari. Pride swells in my chest at her standing up for herself.

"Who do you think you are?" Robyn seethes. "You are no one, just an insignificant human trying to latch yourself to our king."

"You think that you can talk to me like that? You seem to have forgotten your place just because you seem to have the king's favor this week." Xari adds.

It seems like they're the ones that have forgotten their place. I go to show them just that when my little mate surprises us all.

"I know that I'm a human. I am painfully aware. I know that our system of justice is flawed and the hierarchy is broken. While you all sit at the top of the totem pole you seem to have forgotten the ones at the bottom that help you stay there." Anita speaks in a calm emotionless tone. "You ask who I am?" She looks at Robyn. "I'm Anita Carras. I'm a human nurse working at Minaoz Central Hospital in the emergency room. I've worked there for years and had to work my way up from the bottom as a cleaner because our system says that as a human I will never be able to move up in the world. I refused to let that happen and made sure they had no choice but to hire me as I was so severely over qualified when the time came."

She looks around at the others before zeroing in on Xari, her eyes narrowing. "Who are you to think that you can speak to anyone anyway you see fit?" Xari's eyes flare but Anita's stance is strong. "You have no idea what it's like to live with every possible odds stacked against you. You don't know how it feels to go without food or shelter or work for long periods of time due to the other racist species. You throw your weight around with violence and intimidation to get what you want even when you don't deserve it."

Anita straightens her back as she sets her sights on my mother and I can feel the power starting to radiate from my little mate.

"You think that your blatant disrespect for others you deem lower than you makes you the most powerful person in the room? If our situations were reversed at least I know that I can still thrive at the bottom while you would have died a miserable death unable to provide yourself with the basic necessities."

Perhaps letting Anita handle their disrespect is better than any violence from me. I can't imagine the hit to their egos that a human is putting them in their places. It's much more entertaining and less messy.

My fiery little mate looks back at me with a worried look for the first time since she started her speech but I smile and try to convey my support through my eyes. She relaxes into me before she looks back at the shell shocked and angry faces of the women she's targeting.

"You want to defame a woman for doing what she needs to do to keep food on her table and roof over her head while you seek the affection of *my* mate just for everything that comes along with him. It's disgusting. I may be human but I'm not weak. If you continue to push me into a corner you will find out what I'm capable of."

By the end of her speech my cock is throbbing. She's sexy as hell standing there like a true queen.

"You're going to be an incredible queen." I say proudly then kiss her now rosy cheeks. She stands fearlessly in front of these women and puts them in their place but is as shy as ever when it comes to me.

"You can't be serious, Sinclair." My mother seethes.

"I'm deadly serious. She has shown more grace and class than anyone else in this room. You took shots at her in any way you could and she took it all in stride. I'm ashamed to call you family. This is the last occasion that I'll tolerate disrespect from anyone towards me and my mate."

"Sin..." My little mates pull on my hand to get my attention and when I see pride and happiness in her eyes my heart sores.

"Are you ready to go home, my queen?" Anita looks back at me with a sparkle in her eyes and nods.

We stand and I give my father a quiet nod before giving Norah a soft smile and make our way towards the doors.

"Sinclair! You cannot let her talk to me and our guests this way!" My mother shouts and charges after us.

"My mate can speak to others any way she seems fitting." I say without stopping as I push the doors open and pull my little mate through.

"I will never approve of this. That human will not be queen. I forbid it!" She screams.

I stop and look back at my mother. We have the same hair and similar features but that's where our similarities end. I'm not sure if she's always been this way or if she got bitter and pretentious over the years but I am embarrassed right now that this is my mother.

"You seem to think you hold any kind of power over me or Minaoz. You are no longer queen and you should be thankful that you are my mother or you would not even be in Minaoz anymore. You have disrespected me as king, as a man, and as a vampire more than once tonight and far too many times to the woman I love. I can never forgive you for that. If your status is more important than your son's happiness then you no longer have a son."

"Oh and one more thing." My little mate stops me and she looks past my mother into the room of stunned people and stops her eyes on Robyn. "Robyn was there the night Sin was poisoned. You should probably be more careful with who you let into your home."

With that I haul Anita out of that horrible atmosphere and we make our way to the car. I'd planned to confront Robyn when the time was right about what happened that night but I'd been so preoccupied with Anita that it slipped my mind.

Until now.

Chapter 30
Anita

As we walk through the door to the loft the anger still hasn't subsided within me and I stalk to the kitchen for a drink glass to pour myself some whiskey.

"Hitting the hard stuff tonight are we?" Sinclair asks from behind me before I feel his arms circle my waist and his chin rest upon the top of my head. "You read my mind, love." He kisses my temple before reaching forward for his own glass then turns me to face him. He tilts my chin up with his forefinger, searching my eyes. "I'm so sorry for the way tonight went, Anita."

"It's not your fault." I sigh and take a large sip of my whiskey and relish the burn as it goes down my throat. I'm not a big straight liquor drinker in general but after tonight a simple glass of wine wasn't going to cut it. "I'm sorry too."

"You have nothing to be sorry for." He states firmly. I can tell he's still upset by everything that happened too. I can't imagine how embarrassed I'd feel if my mother acted that way toward him.

I know he says I shouldn't be sorry and I know I did nothing wrong but I can't help but wish I could've done more, *been* more. I know that if I wasn't a human tonight would've gone differently and never in my life have I wished I was something other than myself until tonight.

"So what do we do now?" I ask, following behind him as he makes his way to the floor to ceiling windows that look over Minaoz. *Our* city.

"We continue the way we have been. We keep getting to know each other, fall deeper in love, then one day I'll make you my wife and my queen." He says with a goofy grin on his face. It makes my heart flutter seeing him so happy. "The sooner the better."

"Wife, huh?"

"Definitely."

"And if I say no?" I smile and take a step back.

He follows my movements like the predator he is. A smirk grows on his face as he advances on me slowly. "I don't think I'll have to worry about that."

"Oh? And why's that, my king?" I ask and smile as I see the tremor that goes through his body when I call him that. His red eyes darken with desire. I'll have to remember that for later.

"Because, my queen, I know you'll say yes." His smirk widens as he sees my body mimic his previous reaction. Shaking with anticipation and wet with need. Any time I hear him call me his wife or queen sends my body into overdrive. "I bet if I touched that sweet pussy right now it'd be dripping wet for me." He says with a smirk then in blurred movements he's in front of me in an instant taking my face in his hands and kissing me with deep abandon that has my eyes rolling back. Sinclair swallows my moans before moving to kiss along my jaw as he backs me up against the nearest wall then nibbles on my ear. "Just like I thought...soaked." He whispers in my ear as his hand comes up to rub in between my legs, reminding me of how he touched me at dinner.

His hands make their way up my body taking my dress with them until he pulls the fabric over my head and tosses it to the side. I copy his movements and help him remove his shirt and then his jeans follow. We stand now with him in his underwear and me in only my lacy bra and desire burns in our eyes as we drink each other in. With his inhuman speed it takes only seconds before I'm being gently tossed on the bed and his body covering mine completely.

"Time for my dessert." He whispers and I giggle, "I've been thinking about this pussy since I realized you didn't have any underwear on at dinner. Naughty girl."

I can feel his hands everywhere as he takes his time reacquainting himself with my body. I know that he's been restraining himself when it comes to being intimate with me for multiple reasons. I know that vampires are much stronger than humans and though he's never said anything I know he's worried that he's going to hurt me by accident. Feeling how gentle he is with me right now, how sweet and loving, I know that he'd never hurt me.

The other reason we haven't gone all the way yet is because I can tell he's waiting for me to make the first move or make it known that it's what I want. With everything that happened with Kevin and how that night after the bar almost ended with me being raped I know he wants me to be sure this is what I want. With the way he's sinfully biting my neck right now I know that I've never wanted anything as much as I want him inside me right now.

"Sin..." I moan out as his hand makes contact with my core over the thin layer of my panties. My voice has his eyes meeting mine but not slowing his movements. "Make love to me." I whisper and hold his gaze through the embarrassment of having to ask but I want him to know I'm serious and want to take our relationship to the next level.

Chapter 31
Sinclair

I stare into Anita's eyes, looking for any trace of hesitation or unease but I don't see any.

"Are you sure, love?" I ask just to be sure.

"I've never been more sure." Her voice is soft but firm.

A smile builds on my face as I try to keep my body from trembling as I look over her gorgeous body because of the anticipation and all the things I want to do with her, to her. I let my hands rest on each of her ankles and rub my thumbs over the soft skin there before working my hands up and over her skin at a painfully slow pace. Her soft moans only spur me on and make me want to take my time to savor every moment of our first time together.

When my hands go up and over her knees toward her waist I let my lips meet the skin on her inner knee and kiss the flesh there. She shutters and her breath hitches. I smile against her soft skin as I look up at her and see her eyes squeezed shut and her brows pulled together.

I raise up and crawl up her body until I'm hovering over her, no longer touching her body anywhere. Her eyes slowly flutter open and I see confusion in her eyes as she meets mine.

"Anita, I don't want you to force yourself to do this. You don't seem like you want to do-"

"No! I do!"

I pull back slightly and snicker as she goes beat red at her outburst. She quickly covers her face with her hands but I peel them away and pin them on either side of her head.

"Love..." I stop as I see tears building in her eyes. I sigh as I let her hands go and catch the tears with my thumb before they can run down her face. "What's wrong?" I ask softly.

"I'm sorry. I'm just so nervous and I don't know why. Now I'm ruining everything." She pouts.

I just smile and lean in to kiss her pouty mouth. "Breathe." I command and continue to hold her face with one of my hands while the other rests on her hip, rubbing soothing circles there. I give her a few moments to calm herself down. "You have nothing to be nervous about. I love you and I'm going to show you how much on every inch of your delicious body." I smirk at the deep red color growing on her skin. My favorite color.

"I love you, too. I just haven't had the best experiences and I don't want to disappoint you." She confesses in a soft voice with a sad smile.

Getting reminded that her sex life was lack luster and that the last time she was almost intimate was against her will has me seeing red. It makes me more determined than ever to have her forget every other man who's touched or tried to touch her until she can only remember my body against hers. I can't help the guilt coursing through my body at her insecurities because of my past with women. Tonight I'm going to make her see that she's the only woman I see, want, and will ever need.

"Let's change that then." I don't give her any other warning before my hand runs over her slit collecting some of her juices before I'm rubbing her clit in firm circles. She moans out and back arches almost immediately.

She's so sensitive to my touch.

This is going to be so much fun.

I continue playing with her clit with increasing pace as I slide my face into her neck, nibbling on the flesh there as I make my way down to her cleavage. I can smell her sweet blood and feel it pumping through her veins. My fangs ache to sink into her sweet flesh and have my fill of her.

I run my hand down her spin then flick the clasp of her bra before tossing it somewhere in the room. I take a moment to examine her breast and my mouth waters at the hard dark pink nipples there and take one in my mouth.

"Ahh, Sin…"

"That's right baby, say my name." I switch to her other breast, pulling her nipple between my teeth and biting it before soothing the slight pain with my tongue and continuing over and over while giving each of her breasts equal attention.

I run my knuckles over her slit before I push in one finger. I start pumping in and out as she squeezes her tight pussy around my finger before slowly loosening up and before long I add a second then third finger. I alternate between twisting my wrist and curling my fingers, hitting that spot inside that has her arching off the bed and grinding down on my fingers. I keep her right on the edge for a few minutes until she completely surrenders to her need to come and nothing else.

"Please. Sin, please." She begs.

"What do you want, love?"

"Please, let me come. I'm so close."

"I know you are." I whisper in her ear but don't stop my relentless menstruations on her body. "Are you going to scream out my name?" She nods her head aggressively. I bet she'd agree to anything I asked of her if only her coming was the end result. "Hmmm, such a good girl." I purr in her ear before licking the shell of it and pulling her lobe into my mouth for a moment. "Come." I breathe into her ear. Anita immediately convulses as her orgasm rockets through her body. I don't stop moving as she rides out her high and when the aftershocks finally settle and her body relaxes. I sit back on my legs and place my fingers covered in her juices in my mouth.

I moan at the sweet taste of her and meet her eyes as the flames of desire burn bright at the sight of me enjoying her taste.

"So sweet." I say before getting off the bed and pulling my briefs down and kicking them away. My cock springs free and slaps against my stomach. Anita's eyes are trained on me and the look in her eyes is surprise and hunger. I grasp myself and stroke myself as I let my eyes feast on her spent form. Her legs are still parted with her center still glistening that has my mouth watering for a taste. Her chest is heaving which causes her breasts to bounce slightly up and down and her sultry eyes are trained on my dick that has it jumping at the attention and ready to perform.

"Sinclair." She pulls my attention back to her face and she beckons me closer with her finger and I don't waste a second getting in between her legs.

I hover over her with my hands on either side of her head and rub my tip over her slit.

"Condom?" She asks in a small voice.

I smile, "Mates can't get pregnant until they complete the mating. So until I place my mark on you, you have nothing to worry about." I assure her.

"And you've worn one with your past partners?"

"Always, but I want to feel you, Anita." I keep my eyes on her so she can see my honesty. She nods.

I grip myself and guide myself to her opening and slowly start sliding inside.

"Ugh, baby, you're so fucking tight." I grunt out and fight to go slowly so she can adjust but I want nothing more than to slam into her completely. "You feel so damn good." I moan out.

"Oh, God." She moans and opens her legs up more for me and I slide in a couple more inches. "You're so big." Anita reaches her hands up to my neck and pulls me down to her lips. I pull out slightly and push back in a little further. We both moan into each other's mouth as the feeling.

Once I'm fully seated I stay still, waiting for her before I start moving.

"Sin, please move. Make love to me." She claws at my back.

You don't have to tell me twice.

I sit back and place my hands on her hips as I slowly pull out and watching her stretched pussy housing my dick has me groaning before I slam back into her hard but still being cautious of her human body.

"Ahh, yeah, right there!" She arches and I tighten my grip on her waist before I piston my hips into her hard and fast. I can feel her tightening around my cock as her orgasm approaches.

"That's it, baby. Squeeze that tight little pussy and come all over my cock." I pick up my speed and it only takes a few more pumps before her orgasm has her spasming underneath me. She has me in a vice grip making it harder to move but I don't slow down as she rides out her orgasms and I chase my own release. "Fuck, I'm gonna come." I grunt.

"Fuck, fuck, fuck!" She chants. "Sin!" Her scream echoes off the walls as her third orgasms ripples through her with me following, emptying my load inside her warm channel.

I rest my forehead on hers as we catch our breath.

"What's this? I've been meaning to ask." She rasps while running her fingers over my day-walker mark on my shoulder.

"That, my love, is the mark of a day-walker." I kiss the vein still pulsing in her neck.

"Day-walker?"

"This mark," I cover her hand that was still on my shoulder, "is what allows me to walk outside when the sun is out."

"I never even really thought about it." Her head tilts to the side as the wheels turn in her mind. I'm surprised she never asked before now.

After a few moments she just smiles up at me and tries to pull away. I tighten my grip on her hips keeping her still.

"I'm nowhere near done with you yet." I tell her as my cock starts hardening again while it's still resting inside her. Her eyes widen and that only has my smirk growing. "Hope you weren't hoping to sleep tonight." I say before I flip her on her stomach, slowly push back into her and start moving in and out of her again. "Because I don't plan on separating my body from yours anytime soon."

Chapter 32
Anita

I'VE NEVER BEEN HAPPIER IN MY LIFE THAN I AM with Sinclair. He's everything I've ever wanted in a man and he treats me like I'm the most precious thing in his life. I've had my reservations about getting into a relationship with him because of his past and his position as king but he's proven to me that he'll always put us first and I couldn't ask for more.

I haven't seen Kevin or Josh since that night but I have had multiple messages a week from Kevin. They all range from pleading, sweet, angry, demeaning, and threatening. I haven't told Sinclair about them because I don't need him to fight my battles for me. I know how to handle Kevin. For now I'm going to let him cool off and realize that I'm not coming back to him. I'll never settle for someone less than I deserve again. I shouldn't be surprised that Sinclair and I fit together so well considering we're True Mates.

I say goodbye to Wendy and Katie and make my way to the Hospital parking lot. I'm so exhausted after working thirteen hours on my feet, this is the third day in a row that they've given me the graveyard shift. I can't wait to get home and cuddle up to Sinclair and relax. I smile at the thought.

"You know I don't like being ignored, Anita."

I whirl around and come face to face with an unimpressed Kevin leaning against the wall in the parking garage.

"Kevin. What are you doing here?" I ask, tightening my hold on my bag and close my fist around my keys.

"I can't visit my girlfriend at work?" He smiles innocently which is the last thing he is.

"We aren't together anymore Kevin and we haven't been in a while."

"I don't remember agreeing to that." His features harden.

"I don't need your permission to end our relationship, especially after what you tried to do. If I have to make it painfully clear I will. I'm done, Kevin. I don't want to see you anymore." I say and make my way quickly to the car Sinclair let me take to work.

"A guy like that would never take a girl like you seriously!" He shouts after me. "If you think he isn't fucking every woman he can behind your back then you're a fool! You'll come crawling back to me sooner or later!"

I ignore him as I close the distance to the vehicle and climb inside, locking the doors immediately. I take a deep breath and look up but Kevin's gone like he was never there to begin with. I shake my head and once my heart is calm I start the car and make my way to Sinclair's loft that I've been spending all of my free time in. At this point I'm practically moved in. We haven't talked about moving in together yet and it may seem fast on the outside but I want nothing more than to spend every available second I can with him and based on his words and actions I know he feels the same.

I stop on the way home to get us some lunch since I'm off early and want to surprise him since he's working from home today.

I step off the elevator on his floor and use my key to unlock the door.

"Sin. You'll never believe who showed up at my work spewing all kinds of bull-"

I stop mid sentence and my heart drops into my stomach and bile rises in my throat. My hands shake and my eyes water as I watch Sinclair with his hands on another woman that has her tongue down his throat.

I can't look away as I watch the physical representation of my heart shattering into microscopic pieces that I'll never be able to put back together again. I'm not sure how much time passes as the seconds feel like hours before they break apart abruptly at the sound of the food in my hands slipping from my grasp and crashing to the floor.

Those red eyes immediately latch onto mine but instead of seeing love and lust all I see is panic and guilt which has more tears running down my cheeks.

"Anita..." He says softly and takes a step toward me but I shake my head and take two rushed steps back and feel the handle to the front door in my back. I quickly grab it and bolt out the door. "Anita! Wait, please!" I hear him call after me but I push myself faster ignoring the desperation in his voice.

It was all a lie.

It's all a lie.

I only turn around as the doors of the elevator are closing and I look up as the doors shut and catch an anxiously wild look in Sinclair's eyes that almost has me second guessing myself but I push the thought back. He could have pushed her away, he could have never let her in his home that I was supposed to be the only woman to be in, he could have reached me easily as I was leaving with him being a vampire.

None of those things happened.

It was all an allusion.

I fooled myself into believing that I could live this fantasy life where I find true love with the king and despite me being a human our love overcomes it all because we're True Mates and we're meant to be together. Are we even True Mates or was he just wanting to expand his record to include a naive human woman?

I get off in the lobby and run straight to the doors and out to the street. I'm sure I look like a hot mess with my eyes red and tears streaming down my face. I wonder how many other women have left Sinclair's loft in the same state.

Once I'm a few blocks away I pull my phone from my bag and dial Diana's number. I need her now more than ever to talk me out of walking back to him for answers when I can't even look at him right now. I hear the first ring as a body presses against my back and a hand covers my mouth, muffling my panicked screams. I thrash trying to get free then I feel a prick in my neck and the world around me starts to sway. My arms fall limp and my limbs don't respond to me wanting to keep fighting to get free.

Then everything goes black.

Chapter 33
Sinclair

I STEP OUT OF MY BEDROOM AND INTO THE LIVING room just before noon for the first time in years. I'm used to working long hours and rarely spending any time in the loft. I worked double time and rescheduled whatever I could to work from home so I can have lunch with Anita since she's getting off her shift around lunch time. I can't get enough of her. Whatever reservations I had in the beginning are completely gone now.

Walking toward the kitchen I stop short when I see who's standing in my entryway.

"Hey, baby."

"How in the hell did you get in my house? How did you even find out where I live?"

Robyn smirks as she struts toward me with an exaggerated sway in her hips that I'm sure is supposed to be sexy but isn't in the least. "Happy to see me?" She asks, completely ignoring the fact that she's breaking and entering.

"How in the fuck did you get into my house, Robyn?" I grit out.

"Your mother gave me a key since we're engaged silly." She beams at me.

What in the actual fuck is going on?

"What the fuck are you talking about?" My voice raises. How could my mother do this to me after she just embarrassed the shit out of me with that shit show of a dinner she orchestrated, and of all people Robyn is who she picked? "We've never been together and I'm in love with Anita." I say and look toward my watch. I need to get her out of here as soon as possible, Anita will be home soon. "You need to give me that key and leave." I hold my hand out.

"Why?" She pouts but comes closer holding the key out to give to me. "We're so good together, baby."

"All we ever did was fuck, Robyn. You know that." I grunt, ready to be done with this whole situation. I'm going to have a long talk with my mother after this or finally display my power as king if she wants to keep testing my patience.

She closes the distance and stumbles right into my arms. My hands instinctively grab onto her waist to steady her and her arms circle my neck. "Rob-" She cuts me off by shoving her tongue into my mouth and tightening her hold on me with a strength I didn't know she had. I try to pry her off but she's latched onto me like a leech. I'm resisting the urge to throw her off the balcony at this point.

A thud pulls us apart and I look toward the door and feel the color drain from my face. There with tears in her eyes and our lunch scattered at her feet is my little mate looking at me with so much hurt and betrayal in her eyes that I feel the wind get knocked out of me.

"Anita." I breathe out and step toward her. I need to explain. I need to defend myself. She needs to know that it wasn't what it looked like, that I didn't want this, that I only want her.

I don't get the chance as she turns and bolts out the door. I rush after her but I'm stopped by a hand on my arm.

"Let that little human go, baby." Robyn purrs and it grates my nerves.

I'm done.

"Get the fuck out of my house and the fuck out of my life. If I see you again around me or Anita I will kill you myself." I sneer before ripping the keys to my house out of her hand. I turn and chase after my mate.

I run as fast as my feet will carry me but I'm too late. I barely catch the sight of her tear stained face and broken eyes stare into mine before the elevator door closes. My rage boils over as I march back into my loft and grab Robyn by her throat. Her struggling does nothing to help her as I push my way through the emergency stairs taking them as fast as I can down the flights, hoping that I can still catch my little mate. She needs to give me the benefit of the doubt if she loves me like she says.

I burst into the lobby, looking around but I don't see her anywhere. The elevator is on the ground floor. She's gone. My heart sinks into my stomach and dreaded fills me. I move out to the sidewalk and toss Robyn on her ass. She doesn't waste a second running as fast as she can. She can run for now but she'll be seeing me soon for the last time before I end her life.

I search the crowd for her even though I know Anita's long gone. I try to find her scent but it's so mixed along with everyone else on the street that I can't distinguish it from all the others. I follow it as best as I can and the longer I follow it the more panic sets in. I pull my phone from my pocket and try to call but it goes straight to voicemail.

She couldn't have blocked my number already, right?

"Anita, Love, please call me back. I need to explain, please. You know I only want you. I love you." I leave a message and pray she calls me back.

I find her scent the strongest a few blocks away from my building. She must have stopped here, but it ended abruptly. My brows furrow and I take a deeper breath trying to figure out why she seems to have vanished. I catch the smell of something that both burns my nose and boils my blood.

Midazolam.

Someone sedated Anita.

My little mate was taken from me.

Whether she wants to see me again or not, I'm going to get her back. No matter the cost.

Nothing will save the ones who took my queen.

I PACE MY LIVING ROOM AS I WAIT FOR MAVERICK TO get here. I called him as soon as I realized Anita was taken. He has a better nose than mine at least and I could use him as back up if it comes to it. Having a dragon in your corner is always a good thing.

"What happened?" Maverick bursts through the door and bee lines for me. Straight to the point.

I take the time to explain to him in detail what happened from the moment I got home to Robyn being here, her little stunt that caused Anita to believe I'm a cheating bastard, and her running away from me as fast as she could which led to her kidnapping.

"I always hated that bitch." He grits out. "What do you want to do now?"

"Kill anyone that's touched my mate." I sneer while staring out over my city.

Where are you, love?

"Okay so how are we going to find her?" He changes his question.

"We're going to need a few highly trusted friends on our side. Some wolves to help sniff them out, I have a few guards that I trust, and if you have anyone in mind. We can use all the help we can get to have the future queen return home safe and sound where she belongs." I say. "We'll need to divide up and follow multiple leads. I want someone on Robyn and her friend, Anita's bastard of an ex and his fucked up friend, along with Xari and my mother."

We start making the calls and start setting a time to have everyone meet and form a game plan to move forward.

"We'll find her, Sin." Maverick claps his hand on my shoulder, trying to comfort me.

"We better."

Chapter 34
Anita

THROBBING IN MY HEAD WAKES ME UP BUT WHEN I open my eyes I don't see anything but darkness. I tilt my head to the side and I feel something on my face.

A blind fold.

My heart stutters and panic seeps into my veins. Where am I? Is anyone looking for me? I can't remember what happened.

The last thing I remember is getting home to the loft with lunch for Sinclair and I but we didn't get to eat. I walked in on Robyn making out with my mate. The heartache slams into me for a second time. That's why I ran. I couldn't stand the sight of him so I got away as fast as I could.

I called Diana when I got a few blocks away. Wait. I tried to call Diana but someone came from behind me and I think they injected me with something?

I don't know how long I've been here but my arms are sore from being bound behind my back to this chair I'm in. I try to move my arms and legs, testing the restraints but they're tight as fuck. I move my body trying to scoot the chair but it won't budge. Tears fill my eyes before they pour down my cheeks.

Why am I here?

What did I do that someone would want to take me?

I'm scared to scream. I don't know if I'm in the middle of the city right under everyone's noses or if I'm in the middle of nowhere and screaming will only bring my kidnappers to the room. I don't know what they plan to do with me but I doubt it's anything good.

I try to hold the tears back. I don't want to show them any weakness, anymore than I already am. I already feel weak and helpless. If I was a different species I could probably save myself, but I'm not. I'm human and I've never resented that fact so much until now.

There's only one reason someone would want to take me.

King Sinclair Archer.

Someone that probably doesn't want me as the king's mate decided to take me out of the equation.

I don't want to blame him but the ugly emotions are building up. I imagine how my life would be if he had kept his distance like he did in the beginning. I would probably be at work right now, helping people. I'd probably still be with Kevin until he did something that ultimately woke me up like that night at the bar then I'd live my life for myself. I'd be happy and live my life. The best life a human could.

The moment he decided to seek me out and draw attention to me is when the target was drawn on my back. That's when people started to go out of their way to find out more about me and my life. That's when I started to live under a microscope.

If he was just going to continue being a fuck boy then he should have let me live in ignorance. I finally left Kevin and ended up with a lying cheating bastard anyway.

What pisses me off the most is how much my heart is still yearning for him.

I'm pulled out of my thoughts with the sound of the door

being unlocked and opened. My heart jumps in my chest and fear seeps from my pores as the creak of the door is the only sound surrounding me. The anticipation is torture as I hear multiple sets of footsteps and the sound of something being drug in with them.

"Please, let me go." I beg quietly, trying my luck even though I know in my soul that nothing I say is going to get me free. "You don't have to do this. I won't tell anyone."

The only response I get is a low chuckle that sends a shiver of dread down my spine.

The air is sucked from my lungs as ice cold water is blasted in my face, freezing me down to the bone in moments. I choke on the water being thrust into my face and my nose burns as the water gets into my airway. My body shivers violently as I'm soaked in seconds. My teeth chatter so hard I'm afraid I'll break my teeth. With whatever air I have left I let out a scream before water is poured down my throat and I choke trying not to drown.

When it finally stops I can tell my face is covered in tears and snot from my nose. My eyes burn even behind the cloth and I wouldn't be surprised if they were bloodshot. Pain and sobs wrack my body.

"Please, stop." I hunch over as sobs shake my body.

I wish I was stronger.

I hear the same sound of something, the water hose, being dragged along the floor before the door slams shut and the lock is engaged.

I cry until my body is too exhausted to stay awake and unconsciousness takes over.

THE NEXT TIME I WAKE UP I'M STILL IN DARKNESS behind the blindfold. I don't know how much time has passed but I'm still so exhausted it only feels like minutes have passed.

Time passes slowly and I have no way to tell how long I've been in this room. No food. No water. My body is weak as the time passes and I can barely feel my limbs from being stuck in the same position for who knows how long.

It could've been days already.

It feels like a lifetime.

The only indication that time is passing at all is that periodically someone comes into the room with the same hose of freezing water and hoses me down. I learned fast that I have to try to hold my breath for as long as possible to prevent myself from drowning because with each time they come in here they focus more and more on my face.

My head is hanging limply when I hear the door open again and my body tenses preparing for the cold water. I wait and wait but don't feel the water.

I hear a crack and a piercing scream is torn from my throat.

I feel the fiery pain blaze on the skin of my thigh. I can't control my breathing because it's coming in and out too fast for me to catch my breath.

Crack.

My other thigh gets cut by the whip and I choke on my scream. My body vibrates in agony. I can't even get my mind to focus on anything other than the pain to make my body function properly.

The blows start coming fast as they slash through my skin at the deafening sound of the whip cracking through the air has me flinching in the otherwise silent room.

They circle around me, hitting every available place they can that isn't blocked by the chair I'm sitting in. My body is on fire and I'm praying for the icy hose instead of this. I can feel my clothes falling loosely off my body from being shredded by the whip. I feel a slight breeze coming from the person moving around the room and goosebumps cover my now practically naked skin.

I feel warmth run down my skin and I know that I'm probably bleeding. My entire body is throbbing in a numb kind of pain now. My mind is dizzy and I don't know how long I'll be able to stay awake.

I cry silently and think of only one thing.

One person.

Sinclair.

I don't care anymore. I don't care what happened. I just want him to come and save me from this. He's the only one that can get me out of here now.

I can tell by the force behind the strikes of the whip that the person in control isn't human. The force that it's digging and tearing at my skin is definitely a creature and with the strength behind it. I wouldn't be surprised if they are doing this for personal reasons. Why else would they go through this for a human? I just don't know who would want to do this to me, especially to this extent.

TIME PASSES ENDLESSLY AND I CAN ONLY COUNT THE times they come into the room as days. Hoping that they give me enough time in between visits to recover because it seems like they only want to torture me endlessly but not kill me. Yet, at least.

I can only hold on to the hope that Diana got my call and eventually she realized something's wrong and is looking for me. Maybe she even filed a report with the police.

I wonder if she told Sinclair. I don't know if he's been

looking for me on his own or if he is back in his loft with Robyn or maybe another woman by now. I don't want to believe that he'd do that. I want to believe that he truly meant it when he said he loved me and he'll find me.

I hold on to the dream that they'll bust through the door any minute now and this will all just be a nightmare one day that I'll put behind me after some time. If they come soon I might be able to get back to my life somewhat like I was before. I don't know how much of the Anita they know will be left if I have to endure much more of this.

If I get out of here at all.

Chapter 35
Sinclair

A week. My little mate has been missing for a week without a trace.

I've been stuck in a frenzied state looking for her. I have used every connection I have as king, I've sent all my trusted men to follow any leads we have, I have Maverick and his team trying to find clues, I even have Alpha Aiden from the Black Moon pack in the mountains down here helping me find my queen.

When Diana called me in hysterics that she answered a call from Anita but didn't get a response and couldn't get a hold of her after the fact it only cemented the fact that she's really gone.

When I told her what happened she cursed me with every word she could think of and I let her. I tell Diana that I'm going to get her back even if I have to destroy my city to do so.

I don't care about anything other than getting my little mate back in my arms. Guilt and agony wrack my body at how the last time I saw her went.

All because of that manipulative fucking bitch.

Robyn.

She shoved her tongue down my throat knowing that Anita would be walking in our home at any moment. She set me up to drive a wedge between Anita and I. I feel horrible that this could've been avoided if I'd been quicker in my reaction to Robyn. The bitch has gone off the grid for now and that just makes me more suspicious that she's behind this. Smart on her part but it only has me more murderous and it only gets worse the longer my future queen is away from me. She has to be working with others because she was with me when Anita was taken. I'm going to hunt down every last person involved and end their lives in the most brutal way I can think of.

My stomach churns. I've never felt the level of panic and anxiety I feel now. I need to know that she's alive, that she's alright.

I've made enemies over the years as king. Some were unavoidable dealing with corrupt scumbags but others were not my fault. When you're in a position of power you will always have someone trying to cut you down and take everything you have out of greed.

I hate nothing more than knowing that the only reason Anita was taken is because of me and who she is to me. The helplessness I feel grows by the hour that I can't find her. How am I supposed to look her in the eye when I find her when I couldn't protect her. If we find her.

No.

I will find her.

"I think we should try this area next."

I shake from my dark thoughts at my father's voice. We're leaning over a map of Minaoz in my home office. It didn't take him long to hear the news and came to offer his help in any way he could.

"Yea. okay." I mumble.

"Sin." He sighs and grabs my shoulder. "You can't lose

hope yet. She needs you to be strong and burn down the city if you have to to find her. Be the king I know you are. Be the man I know you are." He gives me a squeeze before releasing me.

My father is a man of few words but the ones he chooses to say are almost always impactful enough and he's pulled me out of the depths just enough to get back to work for my little mate.

"I just hope that when I find her I can explain everything and earn her trust back." I sigh.

"Love isn't easy, son. You're lucky you have your True Mate. Living with a potential has extra challenges." He grunts, no doubt thinking of my difficult mother. "Your mother may have her flaws but she was a firm queen and what I needed to rule this kingdom. Not everyone even finds their True Mate, I think everything will work out."

I understand what he's trying to say but it doesn't excuse Mother's behavior.

I wish Anita would have given me the benefit of the doubt and let me plead my case with her. I thought I showed her how much she meant to me. I know that I could've pushed Robyn away faster but I was surprised and I froze. I know that it hurt her regardless of the circumstance. I want nothing more than to hold her in my arms and tell her how much I love her and only her.

I focus on finding her now and begging for a second chance once she's home.

My father nods to me before leaving the room. I make my way to my desk and sit behind my laptop. I have been searching for Kevin, Anita's ex, as well but he seems to have disappeared in the same way Robyn has. Either they're both dead in a ditch somewhere or they have something to do with my little mate's kidnapping. I don't think I'd be lucky enough that they would both just kill over. It would also be disappointing because at this point I want to be the one that makes the life leave their eyes.

My thought process is that if I find either of them then I'll have a lead on Anita. That's what I'm hoping for unless someone can pick up on her scent.

I've been keeping tabs on Xari as well, but she seems to be living her life as normal. I'm keeping a tail on her until Anita is found regardless.

I hear a knock on the door before I see Mavericks' sad smile.

"Ms. Carras is here, Sin."

I take a deep breath and nod for him to let her in.

The wind is knocked out of me when an older version of Anita walks into my office. The same shade of brown in her hair, identical hazel green eyes.

"Ms. Carras, hello please come in."

"Sheryl is fine. I know that you are my daughter's True Mate."

"Okay, Sheryl. Please have a seat."

"Where is Anita?"

I freeze momentarily at her question. She sees my reaction before I can cover it up and panic bleeds into her features. I look down and the words I prepared to explain to her the situation leave me.

"I don't know." I sigh and fall into my chair and let my head fall into my hands.

"Where is my daughter!" She shouts, standing from her chair and pointing at me like I'm the cause. In a way I guess I am.

"We got into an argument and she stormed out. By the time I caught up with her she was gone."

"She wouldn't just disappear and not tell me."

I pause and raise my eyes to meet those similar ones that break my heart. "She was taken." I whisper.

Her hand flies to her mouth as a choked sob comes from her mouth. She shakes her head rapidly. "No."

"I'm doing everything I can to find her." I rushed out. "I have everyone I can looking for her and I promise I will find her." I say.

"Why did you fight?" She looks slightly calmer now as she holds my gaze.

I pause not knowing how to say this other and being completely transparent.

"I walked into the living room to find one of my potential mates here. When I asked her to leave she fell into my arms literally and kissed me. Right as Anita came through the door. I froze." I run my hands through my hair. "I know I shouldn't have taken so long to react but I was just caught by surprise and now she's gone because of me."

She's silent as I let the pain take over. I flinch when I feel Sheryl's hand on my shoulder. I look up to see her teary eyes and I fill my own fill but I don't let them spill over.

"You love my daughter." She states, no question at all.

"I do, more than anything."

She gives me a sad smile. "You'll find her, Mr. Archer. My Anita is strong and she'll survive whatever they throw at her until you can bring her home. I trust you, don't let me down."

"Please, call me Sin." I give a watery smile before I stand and pull her into a hug.

The motherly feeling I get from my little mate's mom's embrace almost floors me. I didn't realize how much affection I was missing from my own mother until now. I didn't realize how much I needed this until now.

We stay like that for a moment before she gives me one more smile before she takes her leave.

I'm going to find Anita, no matter what it takes.

MAVERICK AND I HAVE CONTACTED EVERYONE WE can to help in our search for the future queen. Sheryl has been at the loft more often than not trying to make sure we all eat and keep up to date on her daughter's case along with Diana. I wish I had more good news to give them though.

I've had Colt keep an eye out for Robyn, Krista, Kevin, Josh, or Xari and spread the word discreetly to his friends that are bouncers at other clubs in Minaoz. Hopefully they emerge soon.

Norah has done as much as she can and keeps in contact with Alpha Aiden and helps him on the werewolf side of things.

I begrudgingly contacted Max Stevenson, Anita's boss and let him know what was going on and for him to keep an eye out for anything suspicious.

My father has done what he can with his own contacts with city central from his time as king. My mother has helped tremendously by just keeping her mouth shut because if she said anything about my mate right now I won't be held responsible for ending her life.

So far we can only set the feelers out and hope we catch on to a lead that gives away some information about Anita's location.

I pray that she's okay for now and can hold on until I get there.

Hold on, love. I'll find you. I promise.

Chapter 36
Anita

I'M WOKEN UP BY A STINGING PAIN IN MY CHEEK that shocks me awake. Once my mind catches up with me I recognize the sensation of being slapped after my time here. I'm still blindfolded and bound in the same place I've been since I've been here.

"Good, you're awake."

My brows pinch together as I squeeze my eyes shut. I know that voice but I can't place it right now. Someone I know is doing this to me?

"Let's just get this over with." I hear a voice whisper, trying to speak soft enough that I wouldn't hear but because I've been without my sight for an extended amount of time my other senses have heightened enough that I heard him clearly. That voice stirs anger, betrayal, heartbreak, and disgust within me.

Kevin.

"Shut up, Human." The female growls.

I hear the sounds of her heels clicking against the concrete floor coming closer to where I am. She stops when she's close to me and I feel the blind fold ripped from my head and tape is pressed over my mouth. I blink my eyes trying to focus my sight for the first time in I don't even know how long. When the blurred vision leaves my eyes I take in the room around me first. Cold concrete floors like I imagined under my feet, plain concrete walls that are covered in a layer of moisture. It must be hot outside which means summer is officially here now. I've been here for a few weeks at least.

I let my eyes trail over to the single steel door then to the man standing just to the side of it. My gaze hardens when I look over Kevin, not really surprised to see his scum of a best friend at his side. Kevin holds my gaze but Josh looks away avoiding my eyes on him. If I could kill them with my eyes they'd be six feet under and I'd never lose an ounce of sleep over their deaths. I've never been an angry or violent person but I can't stop the ways I'd murder these two men from revolving around in my head. Kevin smirks at me maliciously and I'm vibrating with rage from where I sit. I want to spit the venomous words I have on the tip of my tongue and he's lucky that there's tape over my mouth so that I can't.

"I don't see what everyone's obsession is with this weak human." She says, sneering down at me. I don't give her an ounce of my attention as I keep burning holes into Kevin's head since he decided to avoid my eyes now. I hear the sound of her hand hitting my skin before I feel the familiar sting in my cheek. "Look at me when I speak to you, you worthless bitch!" She spits in my face.

I don't look at her and that only infuriates her more as her breathing gets more ragged before she digs her manicured nails into the skin of my face as she forces my face to face her's. I match her glare and I can tell my defiance is pushing her closer to the edge. Good. Being the kind and quiet Anita isn't going to do me any favors here. I don't like this much hate pulsing through my veins but at the same time it's an adrenaline rush like no other.

"Robyn, this isn't what we agreed on." Kevin suddenly says as I feel drops of blood start to drip down my face from her nails starting to pierce my skin but I don't show her my pain on my face.

"I make the rules here human." Robyn grits out as she keeps her vicious gaze on me.

Robyn. I discreetly look her over and it all falls into place. She's the woman that was with Sinclair the night he was drugged and she was the one kissing him when I walked into his loft. She planned all of this, everything, down to the smallest detail.

"Can you not damage my wife's face though at least?" Kevin asks.

His wife? What in the fuck is he talking about? I look to him like he's lost his mind and he only smirks back. He thinks I'd marry him? After all of this? I can't help myself. I start to laugh.

"What the fuck are you laughing at you little whore?" Kevin growls out, losing patience with me it seems. I can't even catch my breath to answer him.

When I catch my breath I look back at them. Robyn looks disgusted, Kevin is shaking in anger, and Josh looks completely sullen and uncomfortable being here. Good, he should. Then my eyes fall onto the other woman in the room that I haven't noticed. She's very small in stature with delicate features. I let my eyes roam over here and because of my job I know she's a sprite. Must be the psycho nymph's friend.

Robyn looks over to her friend and smirks.

"Do you think this human black mailed my Sin, Krista?" Robyn asks her friend.

Her Sin?

Hell no.

"She'd have to, it's not like she's anything to look at." The other woman laughs.

"Why would a human think she's worthy to be our king's mate? Everyone knows they deserve to stay in the gutter where they belong. Below us."

"Sin must've stayed drunk constantly to be able to look at her ugly face. I bet someone's forcing him to be with her as a political move. That's the only thing that makes sense."

"You're right. That's probably it. She could never be queen anyway. No one would allow a lowly human to rule over superior species."

"There's nothing enticing or queenly about her."

They continue going back and forth taking shots at any aspect about me trying to tear me down and sadly it's working. I've never been the most confident woman in my own skin. I know that they're doing this on purpose whether what they're saying is true or not but I can't help but let it fester in my mind when those same thoughts have come to my own mind over the last few weeks.

I haven't thought I'd be a leader to stand by Sinclair's side as his equal to help him govern the Northern territory. He always expressed his confidence in me and his love for me but if you don't see that potential in yourself then it doesn't matter what anyone else says.

"I mean she's a *nurse*."

"What could she do for Minaoz or Sin besides take his temperature?" They laugh and I roll my eyes at their stupidity.

"You know I heard something and I wonder if it's true. Kevin?"

My eyes follow hers to see him leaning against the door with a small smile on his face when he locks his gaze on me.

"Yes?" He says.

"Is it true that Anita has daddy issues because her own

father wanted nothing to do with her or her whore of a mother?" Robyn giggles.

What the hell?

"Yes, it is." He says.

The betrayal comes back full force no matter how much I loathe him now. I was with Kevin for years and confided in him about my feelings about the fact that my father didn't want anything to do with my mother and I after her found out I was growing in my mother's stomach. I told him so many of my insecurities and now he's throwing that all back in my face. That insecurity brought a dark spot to my heart that I confided in him. This is what happens when you trust the wrong people, and only one other person knows about that besides Diana.

"I didn't know if Sin was just making a joke." Robyn laughs.

My heart fractures more. I shake my head and fight to keep my tears from falling. Sinclair wouldn't do that to me. I know that Robyn's behind all of this. She probably barged into his apartment and threw herself at him and Kevin had to have told her about my father. They're working together. I push the thoughts of Sinclair's possible betrayal out of my mind. I need to hold onto the fact that he's still mine and he's coming for me or I'll never survive this place even if my body makes it out while it's still breathing. I will have died here.

"Don't worry, baby. I'll make you forget about that vampire." Kevin says and I didn't realize he had closed the space between us and now is running his fingers over my cheek. I try to pull away from him but I can only move my head away slightly.

"Maybe you should have Josh help you." Robyn laughs as her and the other woman move to the side of the room and sit on some chairs they have placed there.

Have Josh help him with what? My eyes widen as what

they're saying sinks in and I start to fight against my restraints. I won't let them take my body like this. I refuse to let them finish what they started that night they drugged me.

"That's a great idea."

I finally let a choked sob out as I feel their hands on my skin and they don't stop until I lose all the hope I have left.

Chapter 37
Anita

I don't care how much time has passed. I don't care about the fact that I probably won't get out of this disgusting room. I don't even really care what they continue to do to me anymore.

The only thoughts that have been going around in my mind is what I could've possibly done to deserve any of this. What signs did I miss?

Kevin has always been a little controlling but I had no idea he had the capability to kidnap and rape someone. The thought of him has rage and nausea bubbling within me. I can't believe I ever loved him.

No matter how many things I let run through my brain I know that the only thing I did was meet and fall in love with my True Mate.

Sinclair Archer.

Our vampire king of the Northern territory, Minaoz. The petty thoughts about him kissing Robyn don't matter anymore. If he really did cheat on me I can't find it in myself to care about it. I want nothing more than to hear him say my name, feel his hands on my skin and his under my fingertips, his lips on mine, and his eyes looking at me in that way that I love like I'm the only thing of importance in his life one last time.

I wonder if he's still looking for me or if he's picked one of his other potential mates by now. I'd like to think he's stopping at nothing to find me, but these cruel people here have a way of warping your mind. You can only hear something so many times before you start to believe it.

More than anything I guess I just want him to be happy. I know he's going to continue to grow into the kind of man and king I know he can be. He has the ability to really make a difference in our broken system where those at the bottom are used as doormats and stepping stones to get to the top. I wanted to watch him make that difference. I wanted to help him do it.

I try not to think about what our life could've been like together. That doesn't stop the thoughts from circling in my mind, though. I day dream of what our wedding would have been like, my coronation, the day I'd find out I was pregnant with our first child and the heir to Minaoz, how I would tell him he was going to be a father, and how he'd show me how happy he was. I think about what it would've been like if I could be turned into a vampire and live forever by his side and never have to grow old and leave him and our children in this world.

I've long since ran out of tears but that doesn't stop the need to cry over the future I've lost. Even if I make it out of here alive I'm not sure I'll ever be the version of Anita that everyone remembers.

My regret from all of this is that Sinclair never got to hear me tell him how unconditionally I love him one last time. That I forgive him and I know that what happened that day wasn't his fault. I don't care that he's a vampire. I don't care that he's the king. All I care about is the way he treats me and makes me feel. I love Sinclair Archer, and I hope I get to tell him again.

Chapter 38
Sinclair

I'VE BEEN PACING BACK AND FORTH IN MY OFFICE for what feels like an eternity while pulling at my hair. It's been weeks now that she's been gone and I become more harsh and violent as the hours pass by. We should've found a clue to where she is by now but it's like she's vanished.

I've locked myself in my office for two days now and if anyone came to bother me with anything other than my little mate's whereabouts then I'd kill them with no remorse. I'm tired of not seeing results. One vampire learned that lesson the hard way and served as an example to everyone else. He came into my office with nothing to report on top of the fact that he didn't think we should keep searching for Anita. I moved too quickly for him to react as I plunged my hand into his chest and ripped his heart straight out. A couple of seconds passed as he saw his heart outside of his body before he collapsed. Even Maverick has kept his distance and focused his time with his elite team searching for Anita.

Guilt is trying to drown me along with the various other emotions now controlling me.

I wasted so much time that I could've spent with her. I

pissed away all that time because she was human and now I'd burn this whole kingdom I denied her for to the ground to find her. I'm not sure when my world started to revolve around her but now I can't properly function without her here with me. I want to see her sweet shy smile and hear her breathy laugh again. I want to smell her intoxicating citrus and vanilla scent.

I could've had so much more time with her. It's easy to look back now and wish for more. I wish I could've loved her harder, for longer, more selflessly, purer. Now I may never get to tell her how hard I've fallen for her. I'm ready to defy anyone who's against our relationship and show her off for the world to see. I just need to find her first. The more time that passes the more anxious I become that I may never find her. I'm not sure that I can live in this world without her. I have to hold out hope that I'm going to find her and when I do I'm going to make everyone involved in her disappearance wish for death.

Heaven help them if I find my little queen damaged in any way.

"Sin..."

I whip around to face Maverick just as he's closing the door behind him. From the sullen look on his face I know that he doesn't have any new news for me. I can't help the disappointment running through me as another lead was a dead end.

"Why are you here?" I ask coldly and walk to the shelves behind my desk to pour myself three fingers of Scotch.

"I'm here because I'm worried about my best friend. You can't keep wallowing in here and biting off everyone's head that's around you. You need to get yourself together, man."

I scoff but don't answer. I keep my back to him but I hear his heavy sigh. I know he means well but I don't know how to handle the emotions running through me. I've never cared about another person like I care for Anita. I didn't want to give a woman the power to hurt me, that's the main reason I never dated seriously before after what happened with Freya. Anita's different though. My little mate quickly became everything I never knew I needed and now I'm lost without her. I want to be out there searching for her myself but I don't want to draw more attention to the situation in the media and I'm sure I'd hurt more than one innocent life on my war path to my little mate.

"When's the last time you fed?" He asks.

"You know how vampires are when they meet their mates."

"It's been weeks, Sinclair! Are you trying to starve yourself?"

"My smart little mate donated blood for me to keep on the off chance she had to work extra long hours at the hospital so I could still feed." I say as I grab the third of blood left in the blood bag and pour it into my drink. I swish the liquid around to mix the blood with my alcohol. Though her blood is enough to intoxicate me on its own usually. "I've been drinking it sparingly."

"How much do you have left?"

I hold up my glass with what I'm sure is a miserable look on my face. His face falls as he realizes that what I just poured into my glass is all I have left of my little mate's sweet blood. I don't know how long it will take for the blood lust to take effect if we don't find her soon.

"I need her." I whisper. For the first time in days I let my vulnerability show.

"I know you do." He whispers back. Maverick's the only person in this world besides my little mate that has ever seen any of my weaknesses. When he closes the distance between us and crushes me in a hug I have to choke back the tears that want to fall for my missing love.

We stay like that for only a few minutes before I harden my emotions and take a deep breath and clear my mind. I need to come up with a new plan.

"Have the werewolves had any more luck with following her scent or the other scents from the place she was taken?" I ask as I turn around to take a generous sip of my drink.

"Aiden and his crew have tracked them to the outskirts of the city but are having trouble finding a clear path to follow from there. He's sent word for his top tracker to make her way here to help with the search. She should be here today. We can only hope that she can find whatever the other's are missing."

I nod, happy to hear that we may finally have more on her scent.

"And you and your team?" I ask.

"We-"

"Sir!"

We both turn ready to attack at the sudden intrusion but settle slowly at Callum in the doorway.

"What is it, Callum?"

"We have a lead!"

"What lead?" I stalk toward him with my heart pounding in my chest.

"The little sprite just turned up at Black Door. We got a call from Colt since you haven't been answering anyone's calls that weren't a select few. His friend saw her show up at the club and is keeping her there until we can arrive."

I send Maverick a sinister smile which he returns. He may not be as quick to violence as I've been known to be but given the circumstances he's raring to go.

"Let's go."

I'll see you soon, my queen.

Chapter 39
Sinclair

I give Colt a call once we're in the car and instruct him to go and retrieve Krista for me and bring her to the warehouse. I'm not taking any chances with her seeing me and bolting. Colt has proved his loyalty to me and I trust him with the truth of the situation I've found myself in. Him being Norah's mate is just icing on top. When he heard of Krista's possible involvement in my mate being taken from me, he was more than happy to deliver the sprite to me on a silver platter.

My hands clench the steering wheel as I speed through downtown and pull into my warehouse. I purchased this building a few months ago but haven't decided what to do with it just yet so the empty building is the perfect place to have this little...conversation.

One way or another I'm ending this tonight. I'm going to find out where Anita is and bring her home to where she belongs.

I've long since reached the end of my patience and my sanity is waning with the lack of proper blood in my system and the calming presence of my little mate at my side. I don't have to wait more than ten minutes before Colt comes through the door with a struggling Krista in his hand. The size difference is comical as he's probably at least five times her size and is able to carry her in with one hand as if he's holding an animal but the scruff.

He tosses her to the ground a few feet in front of me. She falls to her knees and immediately starts to cuss him out for handling her the way he did but stops short when she raises her head and her eyes meet mine. I see the clear fear in her eyes and hear the speed of her pulse racing at the sight of me giving away her guilt in the situation. Krista has been around me a number of times while she followed Robyn around and never showed an ounce of fear in my presence before now.

"Where is my mate?" I ask.

"I-I don't-"

I close the distance between us instantly, closing my hand around her wrist twisting mine causing her bone to snap. She lets out a piercing scream but I cut off the annoying sounds with my hand around her throat. I lift her so that we're eye level now and my eyes bore into hers.

"Where. Is. My. Mate." I spit out, tightening my hold on her for a few seconds before releasing enough for her to get just enough air in her lungs to answer.

"She's at an abandoned building on the outskirts of town in the human's sector. Please don't kill me." She squeals like the vermin she is. It took seconds for her to tell me where Anita was. Disgusting.

"Who was all involved?" I ask as I throw her to the ground.

She whimpers in pain as she cradles her broken wrist to her chest and tears stream down her face getting no remorse from anyone else in the room.

"I didn't even do anything to her personally but say some mean things."

"Who else is involved!" I yell as my patience snaps and take a threatening step toward her that has her spilling her guts again.

"Robyn, Kevin, Josh, and Xari."

I imagined as much but Xari was a bit of a surprise. It's not that I don't think she's capable but she's good at covering her tracks as I've been watching her closely. I crack my neck. I've been wanting an excuse to snap her neck after she slapped my mate and now I can do whatever I want to her.

"You are a spineless disgrace." I spit and kick her to the side.

She continues to beg and plead through her sobs. I don't care about her tears and no amount of pleading will spare her life for taking what's mine away from me. I look into Maverick's cold eyes before meeting Colt's emotionless face. I go to take a step forward to end her life myself but surprise over takes me when Maverick partially shifts and sets her ablaze with his fire. I study him for a moment taking in the murderous look in his eyes. He's always hated her for trying to cling to him and chase all women away from him. Dragon's are different when they meet their mates. They only have one, they don't have as many potential mates as other species. Maverick has always been a hopeless romantic and desperate to find his mate. He's seen how I've suffered with her absence and did this for me. I can't help the satisfaction at seeing her burn but I worry about him taking her life this way and having it weigh on him later.

"Rick..."

"Don't. Let's go get our queen."

He abruptly turns and stalks out the door with Colt and I following behind him.

"Aiden. I need you to meet us on the west side of Minaoz at the location I'm going to send you and follow the scent of my mate if you find it there. We should only be ten minutes out." I say into the phone as I go to open my car door. We all jump in as I end the call and speed back through town to the woods. At the speed we're going we get there in no time and I stop just when the building comes into view.

As we step out I try to hear Anita's heartbeat but can't hear a thing. I try not to let the panic set in before I check every inch of this property I can. I see no other signs of a creature in this area at all. I suppose that was a good choice then for them to keep her here because no one is around to find anything suspicious. I ignore Maverick's words for me to wait for Aiden as back up and quickly make my way into the building.

I take a deep breath for her scent and move around the building until I catch a faint scent. My heart races as I pick up my speed following my mate's scent getting more potent as I move.

She's here.

As I come up to a large metal door that's locked with multiple locks and chains Maverick, Aiden, and the others catch up with me. I take each lock in my hands and rip them from the door like snapping a twig until there's nothing keeping from entering the room. I burst in and my stomach churns and rage floods my veins.

There in the middle of the room is my little mate. She's bound to a chair with coarse ropes while blind folded and tape over her mouth. My anger flares more when my eyes take in the fact that her clothes have been ripped from her body and the scraps of fabric are still hanging from where the ropes have kept them in place. A cross between a hiss and growl comes from my mouth as I whip my head to the other men who drop their eyes to the floor and back out of the room. I silently meet Mavericks eyes and convey what I want from him with my eyes, he nods as he leaves the room to search for anyone else in this building.

I close the distance to Anita and crouch down beside her. I take a deep breath and remove her binds. Her breath hitches and she flinches when she feels the ropes move against her skin.

"Love." I whisper and take the tape from her mouth as gently as I can.

"That's not going to work again. I know Sinclair isn't really here." She says coldly though her body is trembling. Fear is rolling off of her. They used me against her here? My nostrils flare as I try to keep a lid on my rage.

"It's really me, little mate." I say as I take in her delicate skin that's now marked from whatever she's endured while here. I reach up and untie her blind fold.

She has her eyes squeezed shut when it falls. She's still trembling and I stay crouched down in front of her now. I wait though I want nothing more than to secure her tightly in my arms and take her away from here. I haven't ever seen Anita so vulnerable before though. I need to proceed with caution.

After what feels like an eternity she lets her eyes flutter open. She first looks down at her body to see that the ropes are gone and she slowly raises her head to meet my eyes. She stares for a moment and blinks repeatedly before the tears start to build there.

"Y-you're really here? You came for me?" Anita's lips tremble as the tears start to rain down her cheek and I can't wait anymore and pull into my arms. I almost tear up with the feeling of her in my arms safe again. She tries to bury herself into me and sobs into my chest while I hold her firmly and keep repeating that she's safe and with me.

"I'd always come for you, love." I whisper and place a long kiss on her hair.

I remove my jacket after a few minutes of us soaking up each other's embrace. I drape it over her body and lift her into my arms. It's only moment's before she cries herself to sleep in my arms and only then do I let my rage come forward and show on my face.

Maverick and Aiden are waiting when we come around the corner. From the looks on their faces I know that Anita was the only one in the building.

"Aiden. Were you able to pick up any other scents?" I ask.

"Yes. I have some of my people following it now."

I nod and look at my best friend.

"Call Dr. Stevenson and let him know that we're on our way and to be ready for when we arrive. No delays. Call her friend, Diana, and have her meet us there and bring Anita some clothes."

He nods before he walks off with his phone to his ear.

I look down at my little mate against my chest and I can't describe the feeling of having her back. I'm complete now and fuck anyone who has a problem with my future queen and wife.

Chapter 40
Josh

I ROUND THE CORNER TO THE CLUB, BLACK DOOR, where I'm meeting with Krista. I need a fucking beer after these few weeks of hell that Kevin's dragged me into. I'm not the best guy but even I am having a hard time stomaching what those two are doing to Anita.

I'm all for some fun and games but I didn't sign up to torture and rape an innocent woman. I was high as a kite the first time we had her in that little cell but after that I kept my distance and didn't participate. It's too much for even me to handle and I want no part of it.

I stop short when I see Krista being carried out by a large ogre and tossed into the trunk of his car before he speeds away with her.

What the fuck?

Panic shoots through me as I turn and sprint back to my truck and call Kevin.

"What do you want? I'm busy." He seethes through the phone.

I roll my eyes.

"You two need to leave. Someone just picked Krista up

and it's only a matter of time before that stupid bitch spills her guts about everything we've done." I rush out and drive away from the bar and head to the opposite end of town from the warehouse where we have Anita.

I knew this was going to explode eventually, I just hope I can get far enough away before we all get dragged down in the flames.

"Fuck!" He screams then ends the call.

What a cluster fuck.

I dial the next number and wait for her to pick up.

"What do you want?" Her voice growls through the phone.

"Xari. Krista just got taken by one of the vampire's men so it's only a matter of time before she tells them everything. I want what you promised me." I pant out as I race toward the dragon's house.

"I didn't get what I wanted out of this if that cunt tells them everything and if Anita is still alive when they find her Sin will never let her out of his sight again."

"I need out of the damn territory Xari! This was all your master plan, now keep your word!" I scream as I tear into her driveway.

"I'm not giving you shit." She says and ends the call.

I scream and punch the steering wheel. I open my door to get out when I hear the beeping and crouch down to see under my truck. There strapped to the undercarriage is a bomb. With a countdown clock ticking down.

4.

3.

2.

1.

Chapter 41
Anita

The sound of a familiar beeping stirs me from my sleep. I struggle to open my eyes. My mind is groggy and my entire body feels heavy and hard to move.

I furrow my brows and blink hard before my eyes finally flutter open and I immediately close them back tight as a bright light assaults my sight. I blink my eyes open again slowly this time and let them adjust to the light. I scan the room to see I'm in a hospital room.

I'm at work.

Did I have an accident at work and they let me rest here? That seems very out of character for me and my coworkers.

I try to lift my hand but I'm stopped before I can reach my face. I look down and see the IV attached to the needle inserted into my inner elbow. The confusion flows through my brain. I examine everything closer and see that I'm in a hospital gown.

I'm a patient?

What happened?

I start to panic as I can't remember how I got here.

"You're awake."

I snap my eyes to the sound of my mate and the memories come flooding back.

Seeing him in his loft with Robyn, me running away filled with heartbreak, getting drugged, and all of the torment and abuse those four did to me while I lost all hope that I'd never see anything other than those four walls, then Sinclair coming in as my savior, but everything after that is blank.

"Sin?" I whisper with a scratchy voice. He comes to my side in an instant with a cup of water in his hand. He helps me take a drink to soothe my throat. "What-"

"I'm so glad you're ok and I'm so sorry, love. This is all my fault."

My heart aches at the tormented look on his face as he trembles from the emotion of seeing me alive and in front of him. I don't know how I know all of this, but I just do. He's my mate and I know he didn't do this. I don't want him to feel guilt over this when I know who is truly responsible.

"This isn't your fault." I say.

He shakes his head before I can even finish getting my words out. "If you weren't my mate you wouldn't have been taken and they wouldn't have hurt you." His voice is both angry and trembling. I can only imagine how he felt while I was gone.

"How long was I gone?" I ask.

"A month... I've never felt so helpless in my life. I tried everything to find you sooner but it was like you vanished." He mumbles.

My heart breaks for him. A month. It didn't feel like it had been that long for me but at the same time it felt like it lasted for years. I'm just relieved it's over and I'm back home in Sinclair's arms. The more time I spent in that warehouse with those disgusting people the more I knew that Sinclair had no hand in any of this and the moment I walked in on Robyn kissing him was staged to make me run from him so that they could easily grab me to fulfill their plan.

If I learned anything from all of this is that I'm no longer a regular human. I need to be more aware of my surroundings and I wouldn't mind learning to defend myself so that I'm not a victim ever again. The other thing is that I need this man by my side and me by his. If I have Sinclair in my corner and my heart filled with his love then there isn't anything I can't do and everything will be okay. I can overcome anything with my vampire king with me.

"I love you."

The words are soft and tender but it takes the air straight from my lungs as I widen my eyes at his soft deep red ones holding mine captive. Though I know in my heart that he did love me and he's told me as much but I thought I'd never hear those words again. Tears spring into my eyes as I reach for his hand, he closes the distance and wraps my small hand in his larger ones.

"I love you, Sinclair Archer." I smile at him. "Forever."

"Forever, my queen." He places a soft kiss on my knuckles while never taking his eyes from mine.

We stay like that in a trance. He gently runs his fingers over my skin, almost as if he's afraid to stop touching me and I'd disappear if he stops but also tracing the marks that now mar my skin. Evidence of my abuse. His soothing whispers in my hair as he repositioned us carefully so as not to disrupt my IV and placed himself behind me with my back now leaning back against his chest. He whispers soft and sweet words into my hair as he caresses me. I close my eyes as his deep husky voice soothes me with words of comfort and affirmations. He tenderly holds me in his arms and I melt into his body never wanting to be apart from him again, even an inch. He whispers promises of justice against the ones responsible for this and normally I would be against violence but for the first time I have murderous thoughts and want them to pay for what they've done to me and I won't lose an ounce of sleep over it.

"I don't want to be apart from you again, love. Move in with me?" He mumbles into the column of my neck that he's been running his nose up and down inhaling my scent.

I smile and raise my hand to run my fingers through his hair.

"I'd love to." I answer with no hesitation. We've lost too much time already, I don't want to waste another moment in this life I have with him.

I can feel his smile against my skin that causes goosebumps to appear on my skin.

"Sin." I take a deep breath wanting to get this off my chest and out in the open so we can leave it to rest and move forward without it hanging around unaddressed. He raises his head to meet my eyes, leaning to the side so he can see my face more clearly and there's worry clear in his eyes. "I know that Robyn set you up so that I would see her kissing you. I just want you to know that I don't blame you."

Pain shoots through his gaze. "I saw the heartbreak and betrayal on your face. It was like my heart was being ripped from my chest seeing that pain in your eyes and knowing it was my fault. I shouldn't have froze, I should've pushed her away quicker. For that I'll always be sorry."

I shake my head.

"It's not your fault. I want us to move on from this whole thing stronger than ever. Can we do that?"

"Anything for my little mate, my queen." He places a soft but lingering kiss on my lips before resting his forehead on mine.

We stay quiet for a few moments before I feel him take a deep breath.

"Do you want to tell me what happened?" He asks softly.

He didn't need to say more than that, I know exactly what he means. His words bring a reel of memories of my time with Robyn, Kevin, Josh, and Krista. I hear the heart monitor start to beep erratically echoing my heart's frantic pace in my chest. Sinclair holds me tighter and shushes me trying to calm my frantic anxiety at the mention of my time away.

"I'm not ready." I whisper.

"It's okay, love. I'm here for you whenever you are."

"Where are the nurses and doctors?" I changed the subject.

"I told them not to enter until I told them they could after they stabilized you. I didn't think you'd want to wake up with a lot of people in here. You've been asleep for three days. I was selfish and wanted you all to myself much to your red headed friends displeasure. The only one that's been in and out is your mom. I sent her home to sleep or she'd still be here."

I giggle. Diana is a firecracker for sure. I'm surprised she listened to his orders even with him being the king of Minaoz. My heart breaks for my mom. I can't imagine what she went through when I was gone. I'm all she has.

"You have no idea how happy I am to have you in my arms again." Sinclair says while tightening his hold on me. "I know you were wary about being with me given my reputation." I start to shake my head to disagree but he wont let me. "Let me say this, please." I swallow, stay quiet and listen. "I was hurt by a woman when I was a teenager, as I've told you. After that I didn't want to give a woman the power to hurt me again and I figured that getting my pleasure then letting them go was the best option for me. Then you came into my club." He smiles and rubs his thumb across my cheek. "I knew I was a goner as soon as I smelled your sweet scent but when I looked into your eyes and heard your soft voice, my heart belonged to you."

I have no words to say to this sweet man that's all mine

now so I do the only thing I can to show him how I feel instead of words. I pull him down to my lips and pour all of my feelings into it and Sinclair greedily consumes them all.

Chapter 42
Sinclair

ANITA WAS DISCHARGED FROM THE HOSPITAL ONLY A couple of days later and I've been working from home so that I can stay with her. She's taking a leave of absence from work until she's fully recovered and ready to return and I made sure the hospital knows that they aren't to contact her until she does first. She needs time to herself now, she needs to heal.

While that first day when she first woke up Anita seemed so composed and serene, it didn't last long. As soon as the nurses and doctors came into the room to check her vitals her panic came back full force and they had to sedate her to calm her down. I almost ripped their heads off for drugging my mate and Maverick had to hold me back and make me see the reason that this is only going to help her recovery and they weren't hurting her. That's the other reason I'm working from home. I can't stand to be away from her due to my own trauma and fear that I'll come home and she'll be gone again.

It seems like my presence is the only one that puts my little mate at ease besides her mother and Diana. Her friend and mom come by the loft as often as she can around her work schedule and gives us our space.

There are moments when I see my old little mate but for the most part Anita is now insecure, scared, and....broken. No. She's not broken, but she thinks she is and it's torture to see.

I've dedicated my time to her completely and only get some work done while she sleeps. I stay by her side when she needs me there and give her as much space as I can when I need to. I hold her when she wakes up from her nightmares of what those scum did to her. I'm her shoulder to cry on when she can no longer hold the emotions inside, trying to spare me from seeing her in pain because I know she knows how it tortures me to see her so vulnerable and feeling so small. I've tried to make all of her favorite meals to help get her some weight that she lost back. When she feels so down that she can't move I help her bathe and keep my touches innocent. I worry that I'll scare her if I try to be intimate with her. Right now I don't need that, I just want her to be comfortable again.

This has been our routine for the past few days. I've tried to make my little mate as comfortable as possible. I've catered to all her needs and it's never made me happier to feel like I'm being useful to her after the past month without her where I felt so helpless being unable to find her. At the end of each night I count everything I've been doing as progress when she lets me lay beside her in our bed so that she can come to me for comfort if she needs it. I still haven't pushed the physical comfort because I want her to come to me when she's ready but I'm always here for when she needs me.

A PIERCING SCREAM JOLTS ME FROM MY SLEEP AND I instinctively go on the defensive and reach for my little mate but don't feel her in the bed next to me and I go into panic mode.

I jump from the bed and search for Anita and zero in on her huddled in the corner of the room, curled into herself, trembling while holding her knees to her chest.

I make my way to her but stop short when she holds her hand out to stop me from approaching. My heart cracks at the rejection but try not to let it show on my face. When she looks up at me and tears start to flow down her cheeks I know I wasn't successful.

"Wait. Please." Her voice wavers as she trembles while holding my gaze and her breaths turn to gasps as she tries to get a handle on her emotions. My own body trembles from me physically restraining myself from going to my distraught mate. "I don't want you to force yourself to be near me."

I furrow my brows. Force myself to be near her? I'm having to force myself to *not* wrap her in my arms right now. "I want to have you near me always, love." I say, confused as to why she would think this.

"You don't even touch me anymore! You don't even know what they did to me and you don't touch me! So I know you won't want me at all when you know the truth!" She gets hysterical as panic and fear waft from her curled up form.

"That's not true, love. I just didn't want to push you to where you weren't comfortable while you're healing from what happened. Nothing would ever make me not want you." I say softly to her with my hands up. I hate treating her like a caged animal but I've never seen her like this and I don't know how to handle this situation but to tread carefully.

"What if I told you that they whipped, cut, and beat me to where my skin will never be as it was. The evidence of what they did to me is now stuck on my skin permanently. Scarred and ugly." She says through gritted teeth, letting her own anger at the abuse come forward in her tone. That I already knew and still doesn't fail to make my blood boil at those responsible. I can't wait to get my hands on those mother-fuckers.

"That doesn't matter, Anita. You are beautiful." I'm trying to convey my honesty. No matter if she was covered in so many scars that you couldn't see any unmarred skin she would still be the most beautiful woman in the world to me.

But she isn't listening to me.

"What if I told you that they touched me." Her voice loses some of its fire as the words are like a punch to my gut. Those mother fuc- "That they touched my skin while I could do nothing to stop them. That they shoved their fingers, tongue, and dicks inside of me and there was nothing I could do to prevent it. That there was nothing I could do to stop my body from responding to their disgusting touches even though I didn't want it! That my body came even though I was the furthest thing from pleasure! What then!" She screams at me with choked sobs.

I close our distance and crush her body into mine and hold her firmly even as she screams and fights my touch until she collapses with heart wrenching wails coming from her. My heart shatters, my rage climbs, I want blood. I want to end their worthless lives for what they've done to this kind woman, my woman, my mate, my queen.

She thought I didn't want her because of what they've done to her. It's the furthest thing from the truth and I feel as if I've failed her all over again. I can only squeeze her tightly and kiss her temple.

"Nothing in this world will ever tear us away from each other. I want to spend the rest of my days and nights with you. I want to stand at your side as you take your revenge on these disgusting beings that did this to you. I want to hold your hand as you bathe in their blood. I want to straighten your crown so that the world will see and respect you for the queen that you are. I love you and will love you forever, Anita Carras. And soon you'll be Anita Archer."

Chapter 43
Anita

Over the last few weeks I've slowly started getting back to the old me, or the closest I'll ever be to her again. Sinclair has been my rock though it all. After that night when I told him about what happened to me in that warehouse we've been closer than ever and even though all of that happened, I've never been happier.

"Hello, beautiful." I smile as Sinclair kisses my cheek as he comes into the room. He's finally gone back to work at the office, not for very many hours at a time still but he's trying to not hover though I know he wants nothing more than to keep by his side always.

"How was work?" I ask as I place my book down and watch him as he loosens his tie before pulling it from his neck and shrugging off his jacket.

"It was fine until I had an unexpected visit from my mother." He grumbles.

I can't stop the grimace that overtakes my face at the mention of his mother. She's still being subtle with her nasty attitude toward me and our relationship. I can't say I like her that much either. My own mother was ready to go after the former queen when I told her of how she was making back-handed comments about my kidnapping as if the entire situation is my fault and I'm only smearing their good name. Sinclair was about to forget the fact that she was his own mother too.

"How was that?" I ask, trying to be nonchalant as possible but his smirk tells me he sees through me.

"As you would expect I'm sure." He chuckles. "She's been hounding me about having an official queen at my side." He says as he removes his shirt and I can't help but gawk at my sexy mate showcasing his muscular body and day-walker tattoo on this shoulder. I want to run my tongue over his abs. "Is that drool on your chin, love?" He teases.

"Probably." I shrug with a smile.

He shakes his head and comes to give me a deep kiss that has me melting into his arms. Love swells in my heart for this man and I can feel his love for me pouring through our bond. I've started to slowly feel more and more as the days pass.

"When I told her that we'd hold the ceremony for you as soon as we decided on a date she lost her shit."

"So what did you do?" I ask and his smirk only grows.

"I cut her off."

I stare blankly at him, not sure I understand.

"Wh-what do you mean you cut her off?"

He laughs lightly as he holds me tighter. "I told her that if she couldn't back this mating with you then she was no longer a mother to me. She made her decision and I made mine."

No matter how I felt about Seraphina, she is still his mom. I hate that it's come to this and I hate that I'm relieved I don't have to deal with her anymore.

"Now. Are you ready to be my queen for the world to see?" He asks against my lips.

I pull back to search his eyes and the joyful gleam in them has my own soaring.

"More than anything, but don't you think it will cause problems having a human as a queen over all of the other creatures?" My insecurities still take up a hefty space in my mind.

"Fuck them." He shrugs like it's no big deal.

"Sin, this is important."

"All I care about is that my True Mate is by my side as my queen and my wife."

"Wife?" I ask. "Are they not the same?"

He shakes his head. "Only humans get married though in a sense it is similar to having a mated pairing." He says.

"So we are not mated yet so we aren't mates in the eyes of your people?"

"No. I will need to mark you here with my fangs." He runs his forefinger over the soft spot where my neck meets my shoulders. "While we make love, I bite you here and drink from you as we've done before but it matters with what intent you bite. When I bite you with the intent of marking you as my life long mate you'll also have to drink from me as well. Then we will be bonded for life. As for becoming my queen we will have to have an official coronation with all of the other royal families from the top species and we will be crowned king and queen as the ruling couple of Minaoz." He says with a smile while still tracing the skin on my neck leaving goosebumps in his wake.

"Will it hurt?"

"Quite the opposite actually." He smirks and I know what he means and a blush blooms in my cheeks. "Ah, my favorite color on you." He teases only causes my cheeks to tint darker.

I bite my lip and reach my hands out to run my fingers over his chest and down his stomach letting my nails drag against his skin. He groans in response and I can only smile up at him. I reach for his belt and slowly undo it while keeping eye contact with him. I remove his belt from the loops and drop it on the floor and move to undo the buttons of his slacks. As I make work of removing him of his clothes he stays still while the fire in his eyes burns brighter and brighter that I can feel the heat of it warming my skin as the anticipation rises.

I've been waiting for this moment. Sinclair has been so patient and catering to me these last few weeks since I've been home from the hospital but now I want nothing more than to have his body on mine again, to feel him fill me up completely.

"Anita..."

"I want you to mark me, Sin. I'm ready." I whisper while holding his gaze so he can see the certainty in my eyes.

"Are you sure?" He asks once more.

I nod. I'm ready.

He wastes no time colliding his lips with mine. He grips my silk night dress in his hands before he rips it from my body and gives a husky groan when he sees that I was bare underneath.

"Naughty girl." Sinclair smirks as he palms my breasts. "I bet you're wet for me already, aren't you?" He asks though I'm sure he can already smell that I'm soaking for him. I wrap my hand around his throbbing cock now that he's bare for me and he leans his head back with a moan.

I stroke him a few times as he massages my breasts and pinches my nipples before he hauls me up on the bed and dives down in between my legs with no warning. He sucks my clit into his mouth and I let out a loud moan and arch my back. My hips move to grind into his face for more. I need more.

"Sin." I moan.

"You always taste so fucking good." He dives his tongue into me, taking more of my flowing juices in his mouth as he spears me with his tongue. He brings his thumb to my clit and rubs my little bundle of nerves in fast circles making my climax approach quickly. "That's it baby, come on my tongue." His words send me over the edge and I come hard, my legs trapping his head between my legs and my hips buck against his tongue as I moan out his name.

"Sin!"

Sinclair kisses my clit softly as the aftershocks of my orgasm still have me trembling. He trails kisses up my body to my mouth where he kisses me deep, having me taste myself on his tongue.

"Are you ready, love?" He asks.

"More than ready." I smile and pull him down by his neck to continue our kiss.

He shifts and lines himself up with my entrance, rubbing the head of his cock up and down my slit coating himself in my juices, then slowly enters me. We both moan into each other's mouths at finally being connected again in this way. There's nothing compared to being with this man in this way.

"Oh, God." I moan.

"God has nothing to do with what I'm about to do to your body, little mate." He smirks before pulling out and slamming back into me.

He keeps up his fast and demanding pace holding on to my hips to steady me while his pistons his hips in and out of me relentlessly. I can't stop the continuous moans coming from my mouth at the feeling of him stretching and hitting me so deep.

"Ah, Sin…" I claw at his shoulders holding onto him as my back arches and push into him wanting him to give me more. I want it all. "More."

"I fucking love you." He grunts as he increases his speed and pressure to a bruising pace and I'm loving every second of it.

"I'm gonna come." I rush out as my orgasm starts to rush through me.

"Come on my cock, baby. Show me how much you love

me pounding into this sweet little pussy." He groans as I squeeze around his shaft as the waves of pleasure over take me and I scream my release. "Fuck, yes." He reaches between us and furiously rubs my clit making a second orgasm pull from me taking my breath away. "Ready, love?" He asks and all I can do is moan and barely nod my head as I continue to shake as the second orgasm is still crashing over me in waves.

He leans down, sinks his fangs into his wrist and places it on my mouth and sinks his teeth into my skin and I push myself further into him as he pumps himself even faster into me. I let his blood flow into my mouth and while I was worried about the taste before now I gulp his blood greedily now as it has the most addicting taste I've ever had.

Sinclair's hip stutters for a moment before he gives one last hard push into me and holds himself inside of me as he empties his essence deep within my womb with a growl.

He removes his wrist from my mouth and extracts his fangs from my neck. He gives me a long slow lick where he punctured my skin before he brings his mouth to mine and kisses me deeply, our blood mixing from both our mouths.

"Now you're mine forever." He smiles at me and brushes my sweaty hair from my forehead.

"I already was."

Chapter 44
Anita

Sinclair and I have stayed in our little bubble of love since we've become officially marked mates much to his mother's displeasure but even she can't burst the happiness we're surrounding ourselves with now that she's out of our lives. His father keeps us updated on things going on in the palace though for now.

He's started to walk me through what will be expected of my coronation as queen and it's a little overwhelming. Besides getting the castle decorated for an event that I have the last okay on, I also have to have multiple dresses fitted for the occasion because this is a week-long event that leads up to the moment that the crown is placed on my head and I will rule Minaoz besides my king.

I also have so much to learn about the politics and royal duties that I will be doing alongside Sinclair as well as tasks that will be my responsibility. I need to learn more about the other creatures, the central city, and our territory as a whole. All of the other vampire kings will be there and the thought makes me nervous. Though Sinclair has no doubt that everyone will love me just not as much as him.

Diana is over the moon that she'll be able to brag about her queenly best friend saying that I was always a queen. She's really excited to attend the coronation and all the new men she can tempt. Her parents are also in attendance and she's looking for any excuse she can to continue her rebellious ways. But I love her for it. She keeps me grounded.

We still haven't been able to find Robyn, Kevin, or Josh after everything settled down it seems like they've vanished. Xari has also made herself scarce since I've been back. While I'm not really worried about them coming back for me I still feel restless not knowing where they are. From the moment Sinclair said I'd be able to dish out the punishment for what they've done my hunger for vengeance has been simmering beneath the surface. A dark spot on my soul has taken root in my heart and I can't say that I hate that I've hardened my heart in a way that I will no longer let anyone walk over me like I'm beneath them. I'm beneath no one and having Sinclair by my side solidifies that fact. My mate is the only one who gets to see the old me now.

Sinclair's promised that they are still searching for them and they won't be able to hide forever and I trust him whole-heartedly. He said he wants to be the one to handle Xari as soon as I'm better. So his plan for her will be coming very soon and I can't wait to see it.

I'm standing at the full length windows in the living room that look over the city in our loft. I still can't believe that I get to live in this beautiful home with my handsome mate. So much has happened over these months and I couldn't be happier at what my life has become.

I feel strong arms wrap around my waist from behind and lips press against the base of my neck for a lingering kiss.

"What are you doing, love?" Sinclair whispers into my hair.

"Just looking over the city thinking of how much my life

has changed since the moment I stepped into your club." I say honestly.

"*Our* city." He corrects. "Both of our lives have changed. I was truly lost before you and now I can only hope I can become the man you deserve and the king this city needs."

"You already are. You don't give yourself enough credit." I turn in his arms and wrap my arms around his neck.

"I'm glad you think so." He smiles and places a sweet kiss on my lips.

I press my lips harder into his and he gladly deepens the kiss while hoisting me up and I wrap my legs around his waist and he presses me up against the glass. We drown in each other and I can't wait to spend the rest of my life with this man.

"I have some news." He pulls away from me after one more kiss. "Josh's body was found dead this morning. It was dumped in the river and it washed up but they say it was an explosion."

I feel the satisfaction that comes with his words and I almost wish I could have some sympathy, but I don't.

"Before I may have been a little sad, but now I'm glad that another one of them is gone." He nods. I remember him telling me about Krista a few weeks after I was home and I felt nothing when he told me how she died.

"Now I have a surprise for you."

I smile and take his arm, letting him lead me to the front door.

WE PULL UP TO A WAREHOUSE. MY BODY TENSES remembering being in a place like this tied to a chair.

"Shhh, love." Sinclair wraps me in his arms and rocks me

back and forth calming down. "This is a different place and I'll be with you the whole time. Do you trust me?"

"Of course." I say without hesitation, looking up into his eyes.

"Follow me."

He leads us inside and down a few hallways before he comes to a stop outside a door guarded by Colt and Maverick. Sinclair nods to them and they step aside as he opens the door and leads us inside.

I stop short and my eyes go wide at the sight in front of me.

Kevin and Xari both tied to separate chairs with taped mouths and wide fearful eyes. I look back to Sinclair and he's already watching me with a curious expression. He's waiting to see what I'll do. I look to the side and see a variation of tools and a smirk slips on my face.

I walk over and pick up the whip. I turn my eyes on Kevin and he's already tearing up and shaking his head. Sinclair chuckles at the pathetic man in the chair and smiles at me. As sadistic as it is, it turns me on.

"Payback is a bitch." Is all I say before I start releasing all my frustration and rage out on Kevin. I whip and whip until I can't hold the whip anymore.

Kevin is passed out in this chair and even the dragon next to him is shaking slightly as she watches the whole thing.

"Sin..."

Immediately his arms wrap around my waist holding me up against his chest.

"I'm done. I want it to end now." I whisper.

"Anything for you." He whispers back. "Rick, come take Anita to the car please." I don't fight it when he passes me off to his best friend because as the rage left my body I'm too exhausted to do much of anything right now.

As we make it to the exit we hear Xari's muffled scream

before it cuts off by the door closing us off from what's going on in the warehouse.

It's finally over. Only one left now.

A sense of peace washes over me and I'm ready to start this new chapter in my life.

Chapter 45
Sinclair

Once I see Anita round the corner I turn back to the bodies restrained in front of me.

Kevin's body is still slumped over since he lost consciousness from my little mate's anger. I would've done worse than the whip but this isn't about me. It's about Anita. She needed this closure to conquer her demons from her time in that warehouse similar to this one. She needed to take control over her life and now she has.

A whimper pulls my eyes away to Xari's shaking form. Her eyes are wide and glistening with tears that haven't fallen yet. I feel my lips curl over my teeth as I sneer at her now.

Xari has always arrogantly flaunted her power and status in our world and that attitude is what's led her here. She thought she was above punishment from me because she's one of my potential mates. She thought she was untouchable because she has always held favor with my mother. She's always believed that I held enough affection for her to let it slide that she was involved in my True Mate's kidnapping and torture.

The look on her face now shows that she finally knows the

truth.

I don't give a fuck about who she is, who her parents are, or what she is.

Anyone that touches Anita is living on borrowed time until I put them six feet in the ground.

"Xari, so good to see you." The malicious smile on my face has her shaking even more. "You know I've had a rough month recently but things have really been turning around. Do you know what I mean?" I ask, walking toward the table letting my hand run over the different tools I had laid out for Anita.

I look back and see Xari trying to free herself from the steel I have her bound with. "I guess you've had better days too." Chuckling darkly I turn back and pick up a hammer.

"You know Xari, I knew you were a cocky little bitch but I never thought you were stupid." I strut back to her, waving the hammer around to exaggerate my words. Her eyes follow my movements.

I stare at her with growing fury before I slam the hammer down onto her left hand, shattering the bones instantly. She shrieks behind the tape on her mouth, causing the idiot next to her to stir from his short nap.

"Because you'd have to be fucking stupid to think you could get away with kidnapping and torturing my mate, Xari!" My calm facade drops as I scream in her face as she breaks down in sobs trying to shake her head. "Do not lie to me! I know you're involved. I know you think you'd come out on top and that you're untouchable. But guess what? I don't fucking care what you were to me or who your parents are." I spit in the face of her wide terrified eyes. "You're going to die in the same place Krista did. You're going to die in this room tied to a chair just like my mate was while she was taken from me."

I slam the hammer down, breaking the bones in her right

hand as well.

Xari's screams finally bring the bitch boy next to her back into the room. He seems confused until he locks onto my burning red eyes.

"I've been waiting to officially meet you, Kevin." I smirk.

The fear rolling off both of them is ecstasy to me. I breathe it in and smile. I drop the hammer back on the table in exchange for a long butcher knife. Large, messy, and personal.

"For your last moments, Kevin, I don't have much to say. I just want to say thank you for being a piece of shit human. Knowing all that you've done to my little mate makes ending your life all the sweeter. Let me handle this dragon cunt first then I'll be right with you."

I smile and turn back to Xari that has her head hung low.

"We could have had a great work relationship and made a real difference in Minaoz if you didn't try to take something that wasn't yours to take. Me and the throne were never yours to claim. I could've possibly overlooked your previous disrespect for me and my mate if you had just stayed out of my way but you couldn't. You participated in the kidnapping and torture of my future queen and I can't let that slide."

She keeps her head down as I finish. I don't waste another moment before driving the knife straight into her skull. Her body slumps forward and Kevin starts thrashing in his seat like he'll be able to escape his fate. I turn to him and don't waste my breath on any more words for him and swing the knife to the side. The movement slices his throat wide open. I watch as he chokes on his blood, the life leaving his eyes as the weight leaves my shoulders.

It's over for now. Only one left and her death won't be as fast as these two. For now I'm going to enjoy my time with Anita as we start his new chapter in our lives.

I smile at the thought and down at the bodies before I leave the room and back to my little mate.

Chapter 46

. . .

THAT STUPID CUNT, KRISTA, RUINED EVERYTHING. If she would've just done as she was told that disgusting human would've never gotten away. Josh is lucky he got away before I could kill him. I would've done more than blow his ass up. It's only a matter of time before they start picking us off one by one.

I strut to the palace gates and eye the guard standing post.

I suck in a deep breath, "I'm here to see the king." I say with as much confidence I can.

The guard keeps his face expressionless as he stares at me but touches his ear piece and speaks so softly that I can't hear what he says. He waits a moment then opens the gate for me and I slip through, a little surprised that I was actually let inside. I wanted to come and speak with the king but I didn't think I'd be let in so easily.

A servant is waiting for me when I reach the large steps that lead to the front doors of the palace. The little human bows to me that has me smirking and raging all at once because she reminds me of the little whore that took everything from me.

I grit my teeth as I follow the lowly human servant through the grand entrance and to a set of magnificent wooden doors decorated in intriguing designs. She lightly knocks on the doors before she bows again and backs away from me and the doors. They swing open with two armed guards stepping forward toward me that has me stepping back quickly but not fast enough.

The guards seize both my arms and haul me into what I see is the throne room and there at the end of the aisle on the deep red throne is a man. The vampire king of Azigora. King Ronin Sidorov.

King Sidorov is a beast of a man. His body is tall and full of solid muscle. His face is set in a scowl and his deep red eyes are cold and harsh. His shoulder length light brown hair is tied back with only a couple of strands falling into his face. I chose to come here because I know that Sinclair and Ronin have never really gotten along.

"Why are you here, nymph?"

I resist the scowl wanting to overtake my face at his insulting tone as if my race is scum. I was meant to be queen.

"I'm here looking for help in getting my revenge." I grit out as I'm tossed to the King's feet.

"And why would you assume I would help you?" His monotone, bored.

"Against Minaoz," I pause seeing a flicker of something enter his eyes. "And the future queen." I spat.

"Little Archer is finally taking a queen is he?" He muses with a sinister smile on his lips. "Very intriguing." He cuts his eyes to me, a mischievous and dark look in his eyes. "What is your name, nymph?"

I smirk.

"Robyn Brown."

Acknowledgments

I'm so excited to get this book out in the world! *Sinful Bite* has been an idea of mine for a while now and I love how the story has evolved and changed from the time I started it.

I have to give a BIG shout out to my best friend for always letting me bounce ideas off her and try to filter through my clustered thoughts. She's always been such a big support in my writing career and I don't know how my stories would be without her input.

This is my first true romance novel and I hope everyone enjoys the characters and the world I created as much as I do. Like every story they hold a special place in my heart.

About the Author

K. N. Gallo is an emerging author in the romance genre with her debut novel, *Sinful Bite*. She's always had a love for the written word and feels as though she communicates better this way. All of her books will have romance ingrained throughout.

She spends most of her days in Texas with her family and working full time. When she has down time and isn't writing she's usually reading a good book or chasing her kids around.